SILV

STILL

OVER 100
GREAT NOVELS
OF
EROTIC DOMINATION

If you like one you will probably like the rest

NEW TITLES EVERY MONTH

If you want to be on our confidential mailing list for our Readers' Club Magazine (with extracts from past and forthcoming titles) write to:

SILVER MOON READER SERVICES

Shadowline Publishing Ltd
No 2 Granary House
Ropery Road
Gainsborough
DN21 2NS
United Kingdom

telephone: 01427 611697
Fax: 01427 611776

NEW AUTHORS WELCOME

Please send submissions to
Silver Moon Books
PO Box 5663
Nottingham
NG3 6PJ

Silver Moon is an imprint of Shadowline Publishing Ltd
First published 2007 Silver Moon Books
ISBN 9781-903687-86-4
© 2006 Geoffrey Allen

AFRICANUS
ARENA OF TORMENT

By

GEOFFREY ALLEN

CHAPTER ONE

Quintus Varus shifted slightly on his seat, making room
for a young naked slave girl holding a jug of wine. A sweet
smell of almond oil emanated from her skin as she bent
over the table. One glance at her erect nipples told him she
would willingly spread her legs if he so desired. Yet
strangely, he ignored the slim thigh rubbing suggestively
against him and pushed her rudely away. The young slave
took the hint and withdrew. In that mood there was no
telling how he might react. Quintus was not a man to cross
and more than one slave girl who had angered him had
been flogged raw, her back and buttocks tasting the whip
until she screamed for mercy.

His best friend Clodius eyed him censoriously. How
could any red blooded Roman refuse such a blatant
invitation as that? Why, the girl was practically begging
for his cock.

For several minutes the two men sat drinking lost in their
own thoughts, almost oblivious to the numerous naked and
semi naked young women who scurried back and forth.
From somewhere across the courtyard came the
monotonous creaking of timber like the mast of a ship
swaying in a heavy sea.

It was Clodius who broke the silence.

"What's troubling you, my friend? If it's a woman or
girl you need, you only have to say the word and I'll have
her fetched immediately. If you've a mind, I'd recommend
that young Gaul. She's half savage and not yet broken in
but gives a good ride."

"There's nothing more I'd like than to sink my weapon
into the slit of any one of your young slaves," Quintus
admitted, taking another hefty draught from his cup. "But

the truth is my mind is distracted."

Clodius' eyes rolled in despair. "Not that old chestnut again," he sighed. "I've told you, Quintus, spending money on training women to fight in the arena is money down the drain. It just won't wash. It's men who do the fighting. Women simply aren't built for it. Fucking and scrubbing floors, yes. Armed combat, no."

Quintus rolled the stem of his cup between his fingers; thinking.

"You're wrong Clodius. I've seen them in Rome at the Colosseum, women who…"

"Who perform novelty acts," Clodius interrupted. "Just wrestling and brawling, tearing each others eyes out, or boxing each others ears. If not that, then mating with bulls or stallions. It's all they're fit for."

There was a lot of truth in that. Women only provided a distraction between the main contests, naked flesh, breasts and buttocks bruised and beaten for the pleasure of the crowd, or performing outrageous sexual acts. Here in the provincial town of Marcellum the idea of female gladiatrices was absurd.

"I'm not thinking of Marcellum," Quintus said seriously. "I'm thinking of Rome. You know the position I'm in. If I don't come up with something soon I'm ruined."

That was true as Clodius well knew. His best friend was heavily in debt and his arch rival Polonius was now the main supplier of gladiators. It cost a fortune to train a gladiator and if he was quickly dispatched his owner could just as quickly face financial ruin.

"Your plan then is to train up a woman gladiatrix to fight in the Colosseum," Clodius suggested, reading his friend's mind. "All right, I agree, if that's good enough for Rome then go ahead. You have the means of training in your own school and instructors who can teach them well

6

enough. But where are you going to find the sort of woman you need?"

Good point. There were plenty of female slaves who could be bought and sold, but none that came anywhere near the standard required in the arena.

"I thought you might know of one or two," Quintus said hopefully. "After all, you are the biggest slave dealer in Marcellum."

Clodius signaled the young slave girl who came hurrying over. He needed time to think and thinking was thirsty work. The girl replenished the cups and he gave her rump a playful pat. How old was she he wondered, mid to late teens perhaps, but well formed with pert buttocks and rounded breasts if a little on the small side. He couldn't remember if he'd had her or not.

"I'm going to make you a present of her," he told Quintus. "She's yours after this tiresome matter is concluded. But in the meantime if you want to view some robust slave women you need look no further than the grinding house."

The two men arose and made their way to the sound of the groaning timber, which in fact was an apparatus used for grinding corn, another little side line of Clodius' providing the bakers of Marcellum with flour.

In the centre of the room a stout timber pole reached from floor to ceiling and at waist height long wooden poles were attached horizontally to the main shaft. The whole apparatus was turned by women slaves chained by their wrists to the horizontals. Quintus had never entered the grinding house and he now stood fascinated as the women went round and round in a huge circle, straining to turn the grinding stones unseen in the room below.

One glance at the women slaves told him why Clodius had brought him there. They were nothing like the slim girl slaves who waited at tables, or in their master's bed chamber. It needed strength to turn the wheels and Clodius had selected his slaves wisely. Urged on by a whip wielded by the corn master, the women flexed their powerful thighs and arms, grunting from sheer exertion as sweat ran from their glistening bodies in rivulets, running ceaselessly down their spines and between their buttocks, trickling over their breasts and into their thick unshaven sex mounds.

One of the slaves immediately caught Quintus' eye. A black slave with well shaped legs and firm protruding buttocks was chained to the outside of one of the horizontals, her whole body shining like polished ebony as she struggled against the pole. He could see her large pendulous breasts swinging to and fro as she bent over the shaft. The nipples, he noticed, were extraordinarily erect from a recent lashing. Her arms and legs were perfectly sculpted, the muscles already well honed from so much hard labour. He nodded in satisfaction. The woman was strong and already he was beginning to think he had found exactly what he was looking for.

In gladiatorial combat strength was not everything. It was speed and agility which counted that and the ability to think fast, to be able to guess what the opponent was going to do next and get in first. That would come with training. First he needed to gauge her stamina.

"The black slave. Who is she?" he asked, turning to Clodius.

"Her name is Africanus. I bought her from a slave market in Carthage. She works well but is more trouble than she's worth. I wouldn't advise you to choose…"

"Have her unchained," Quintus interjected. "I want to see how well she holds up against the whip."

Clodius shrugged and summoned the corn master. "Have the black slave released and taken to the whipping post."

The corn master bowed wondering what she had done

8

to deserve a flogging. But it wasn't his place to argue, and he went to the front of the pole and unfastened the manacles around her wrists.

She stood upright, groaning and straightening her back, rubbing her hips and flexing her shoulders. Seen upright she was much taller than Quintus at first imagined, at least six feet in height, maybe an inch or two above. Her legs were long, capable of carrying her quickly and for several seconds he marveled at the length of her thighs and tight, strong buttocks. Her large breasts would look good in moulded armour.

"Take her to the whipping post," the corn master ordered, and then for the first time Quintus saw her face.

Her eyes, wide and lustrous narrowed into angry slits. "Why am I being flogged?" she hissed at the corn master. "I haven't done anything."

Defiance, Quintus noticed, a good quality in a gladiatrix, but one that would have to be subdued before she swore total obedience to her new master.

"Not your place to argue," the corn master replied confidently.

But that was before a well aimed kick crushed his balls. Doubled with pain he fell to the floor rolling over and over both hands clasping his throbbing nuts.

The guards rushed forward and grabbed her arms pinioning them behind her.

"You'll get an extra ten strokes for that," Clodius informed her.

A wry smile creased Quintus' lips as they dragged her to the whipping post. The more he saw her the more he liked her. Breaking her spirit was going to be a challenge in itself.

"Up on your toes, slave," the guard barked, forcing her hard against the post.

Africanus stood on tiptoe and Quintus saw how the muscles in her beautifully shaped calves bulged and tightened. The softer under parts of her buttock cheeks lifted, and for a brief moment clenched into a deep sensuous crease.

While she stood on her toes, the guards quickly shackled her wrists. A length of chain was speedily fetched and fitted to the shackles. One of the guards taking no chances drew his gladius; the sword favoured by the conquering legions, and prodded the point into the small of her back.

"Move and I'll kill you," he whispered.

It was a bluff, she knew that, but a look of dull resignation spread across her voluptuous lips. Obeying his instructions, she reached upwards while the length of chain was passed through a ring at the top of the post. The two guards took hold of the chain and pulled hard lifting her clear off the floor. Quintus heard her grunt as her manacled wrists bore her whole body weight. He moved to the front of the post and feasted his eyes on her uplifted breasts. She stared back at him, no longer so defiant but with an expression of helplessness.

"The corn master may have the pleasure of flogging her," Clodius grinned as the man struggled to his feet. "Give her twenty strokes."

"Only twenty?" he protested. "She deserves at least forty."

"The decision is not yours to make. Twenty strokes of the cat o' three tails are enough."

Grumbling, the corn master gathered them in his hand, long thin lengths of tightly woven leather, knotted at intervals.

"I want to see her thoroughly humiliated," Quintus said, seating himself comfortably.

"Whatever," Clodius shrugged. "I'm sure the corn master

10

will oblige. But first we shall slake our thirsts."

At his bidding the young naked slave girl who had so blatantly offered herself to Quintus came hurrying into the grinding house. She set a tray of goblets and a flask of wine between the two men.

"Anything else, master?" she purred.

Clodius was about to dismiss her but suddenly changed his mind.

"Get on your knees," he ordered, parting his thighs.

The girl knelt between them; head bowed awaiting the next command.

"While the slave is being flogged you will suck my cock," he said flatly. "And when I come make sure it's deep in your throat."

"Yes master," she whispered, filling the cups and then lifting the hem of his tunic.

Expertly, she rolled it up over his thighs exposing his throbbing member. Her tiny hand grasped his shaft and guided it slowly into her open lips. Clodius emitted a faint purr of satisfaction when her hot soft mouth glided down the shaft.

"Let the punishment begin," he chuckled, and folded his hands lovingly over the back of the girl's bobbing head.

Quintus leaned forward in his seat watching intently as the corn master approached the hanging body of Africanus. A fine bead of sweat trickled down her temples as she braced herself for the first blow. But to her surprise the whip she expected to come whistling into her naked and defenceless buttocks was laid gently on her shoulder. Her body shivered when the three leather tails tumbled over her breasts. Slowly, the corn master withdrew the whip letting the tails pass over her now fully erect nipples, each length of plaited leather teasing the teats even harder. He let the whip trail down her back and then, grasping the

11

handle wormed it into her bottom crease, twisting it back and forth pushing it deeper inside her bottom hole. His free hand slapped her left flank and she swallowed hard.

"If you're going to flog me just do it," she almost pleaded, unable to bear the delaying torment he was inflicting.

"There's plenty of time," he taunted, taking the handle from her bottom and passing it under her nose. "See how sweetly your arse smells," he gloated. "I wonder if your cunt smells as good."

Clodius laughed at that but Quintus didn't share the joke, instead he kept his eyes on Africanus' face, constantly watching the changing range of emotions; anger, defiance, acute embarrassment, and a curious mixture of both hatred and arousal. Even though she knew the whip would soon descend on her naked flesh she seemed to find the prospect sexually thrilling which intrigued Quintus. It wasn't often a whipped female slave was sexually aroused. Ignoring the young slave girl busy sucking off her master, he watched ever more closely, only diverting his attention briefly to raise his cup.

"You two slaves," the corn master shouted, "open her legs."

A couple of slave girls ran over the tiled floor and quickly knelt at Africanus' feet. Taking her ankles they slowly parted her legs, drawing them further and further apart until each ankle was raised enough to rest on their shoulders. In the half light Quintus could just make out a tuft of glistening black curls bristling between her legs. He thought he saw a brighter slit of pink, but it might only have been a trick of the light.

The corn master placed the whip handle at the apex of her thighs and gently eased it over the pubic mound, teasing the sex lips and letting the handle penetrate her, but only a fraction, enough to send her pulse racing but at the same time denying the complete fulfillment her body was beginning to crave.

Quintus saw her voluptuous lips part and a dream-like expression come into her eyes. Then suddenly they opened wide and he heard a sharp intake of breath as the handle was rammed deep into her sex.

"You've got a cunt like a cow," the corn master jeered, revolving the handle inside her.

For the first time since she had been shackled to the pole Quintus permitted himself a wry grin. He couldn't help but grudgingly admire the way the corn master tormented his victim, almost bringing her to the point of orgasm and then stopping short leaving her in agonies of frustration. Her splendid thighs quivered at every insertion. Sweat was breaking out all over her dark, silky skin. Her breasts heaved when her clitoris was touched and she cried out to be whipped rather than suffer the handle working faster and faster into her sex.

"Your wish is granted," he told her, swiftly taking away the handle. "But not before you've tasted your own juice."

At his bidding the slave girls released her ankles. One of them went to the front of the pole and dropped onto all fours. Using her as a stool, the corn master stood on her back and lifted the handle to Africanus' lips.

"Now suck," he commanded. "Suck your own cunt juice."

Clodius, aroused at the sight of her lips sucking hard on the handle forced the young slave girl's head to the root of his cock. She almost choked at the rock hard cock filling her throat, but Clodius was too excited to care either way.

"Bring me off," he rasped, keeping his eyes on Africanus now sucking and licking at the juice slicked handle.

"That will do," the corn master announced, jumping from the girl's back.

He went around the pole and gathered the whip tails ready to deliver the first lash. Quintus saw Africanus' face suddenly change from dumb compliance to fear. He guessed that within seconds she would be begging for mercy.

The tails whistled through the air and landed with a loud crack across her shoulder blades. Her spine arched and she jolted forwards thrusting her breasts against the pole. Remarkable, Quintus thought, how much larger a woman's breasts appeared when they were squashed flat. The ample breast flesh pushed out either side of the pole covering the whole of her ribs, then with a delicious wobble settled back on her chest.

"The next lash is for kicking me in the nuts," the corn master informed, sending the tails winging across Africanus' buttocks.

The tails spread as they sailed over her body, each one leaving a thin line darker and more pronounced than the surrounding skin. Her buttocks flexed and squeezed from the sudden rush of pain. Her lungs filled with air then emptied with a whoosh as she fought against the rising pain.

"The next is for even thinking about it," he said, swinging the tails again on her rump.

He gathered the whip with slow deliberation allowing plenty of time for the pain to sink in before delivering the next blow.

"And this is for thinking you could get away with it," he said maliciously.

Quintus winced at the sound of the tails cracking against her back. Yet not a sound had escaped her lips, only a curious hissing noise coming from her nostrils betrayed any sign of suffering. Clearly, the girl had no intention of giving her tormentors the satisfaction of hearing her cry out or beg for mercy. He liked that. It showed self control in the face of adversity, another quality essential in a gladiatrix. But privately he didn't think she could hold out against the next lash heading for the backs of her thighs.

"Would you like her to suck your cock?" Clodius asked cheerfully, falling back in his seat as the girl let his cock slip from her sperm dribbling lips.

Without waiting for an answer the girl was there at once burying her pretty head under Quintus' tunic. One hand lovingly stroked his erection while the other expertly fondled his balls. But Quintus although enjoying the sensation of her hot eager breath wafting across his cock kept his gaze firmly on the whipped slave. Her fine regular teeth were clenched and constantly grinding against the fresh onslaught going on all down her back, buttocks and thighs. So far not a sound came from her, only a series of rapid pants and deep throated grunts which, for some inexplicable reason he found quite arousing in their own way.

Her teeth ground so fast her jaw ached and her bottom seemed to have swelled to three times its size. Bare, hot and throbbing, her bottom cheeks blazed from each renewed lash. She wasn't quite sure whom she hated most, the two masters enjoying the spectacle of having her so unjustly flogged, or the hideous ape lashing her with increasing fury. One of these days, she thought, I'll kill the bastard, but then the whip curled its tails around her sides where the skin was thinner and stretched tight over her ribs.

Quintus suddenly looked up. A harsh piercing scream rent the air. At last her resistance had broken. The threshold of pain could no longer be resisted. The corn master smiled with satisfaction and landed the tails on the crown of her bottom.

It seemed to Africanus that a red hot iron had burnt into the base of her spine. Up to now her solid buttocks and back, her firm fleshy thighs had been able to withstand the constant lashing but now, as the tails struck at the more vulnerable parts of her body the pain had become unbearable.

"Stop, please master," she sobbed. "I've taken enough."

How many strokes had she taken? More than the twenty originally ordered that was certain.

"Give her another half dozen," Quintus said, wanting to see how much more she could actually endure before passing out. "On the backs of her legs," he added, sensing that was where she seemed most vulnerable.

The corn master willing obeyed and sent the first lash searing into the bulge of her calves.

Her feet jerked upwards and her whole body went into a spin, jerking awkwardly at the wrists, crashing against the wooden pole before finally settling to a stop. She hung with one shoulder against the pole, her body at right angles to the wood.

"Give her a lash across the front of her thighs," Quintus requested. "And another on her knees."

"No!" Africanus screamed.

"Yes," the corn master laughed.

And the tails left their fearful welts exactly where he intended them to fall.

Africanus' face was a mask of suffering; flowing tears competed with streaks of sweat, her mouth hung open and slack. Mucus from her dilated nostrils stained her lips and chin. The corn master tossed the whip aside just as Quintus erupted into the slave girl's mouth.

"Take her down," Clodius said dully. "Then have her washed."

"Wait," Quintus said, turning his eyes to his friend. "With

16

your consent, there is just one more test I'd like to see. Who amongst your slaves has the biggest cock?"

"I believe Proteus has that honour. Why do you ask?"

"Now the girl has been flogged I want to see how she holds up to being fucked."

Clodius thought that was funny. "She's hardly in a position to refuse," he smirked.

Africanus was already on her feet and rubbing her bruised and welted bottom. Under normal circumstances, any slave who had been so ardently flogged would have collapsed or fainted, but this slave was still on her feet. Quintus wondered if she could endure another punishment, perhaps more pleasurable if less painful.

"Fetch Proteus," Clodius ordered.

A slave girl hurried out of the grinding room and was almost as quickly back with one of the strangest looking men that Quintus had ever set eyes on. His short legs were hairy and bowed at the knees, his back had a pronounced hump and his face was almost submerged under a mane of wild unkempt hair and beard. Quintus took a step backwards to escape his foul breath.

"From under which stone did this thing crawl?" he asked, still unable to believe the evidence of his own eyes.

"From the stones of Britannia, or maybe it was Gaul. I can't remember exactly. But he has the strength of five men and I use him for hauling sacks of grain. It spares the horses."

"Mate him with Africanus," Quintus said loudly.

A look of pure horror crossed her face. Being whipped was one thing, mated with this animal was quite another. It didn't help her state of mind when he threw off his filthy tunic and growled at her, revealing a cock that had earned him the nickname of 'Horrificus' or one who causes fear. Africanus did indeed look fearful as well she might. Even

Quintus, a man not easily shocked visibly baulked when he saw the size of his penis.

"That's not natural," he muttered.

Africanus fell to her knees in front of Quintus. She now realized it was not her own master, Clodius, who was in control but this stranger.

"Please master, don't let me mate with this beast. I'll do anything you want but spare me this."

"You have held up well against your flogging," Quintus complimented her. "Now I want to see how well you manage with this creature."

There was method in his reasoning. He knew that after combat a defeated gladiatrix might well be offered for sex with a victorious gladiator, or even a whole troop of legionaries. If she provided sexual satisfaction she would be spared, if she failed then death would swiftly follow, so it stood to reason that if Africanus could survive this creature and after such a severe flogging, she would make a good investment.

"I will spare you the ordeal of having a thing of that size in your cunt," he said unexpectedly.

Africanus breathed a sigh of sheer relief. "Thank you, master," she whispered, bowing her head to the ground.

"I said I would spare you having it in your cunt, but not up your arse."

She would have got up then and bolted, but two male slaves held her fast.

"Stay as you are," Quintus commanded. "He will take you now."

"Not up my bottom," she pleaded. "I've never had it that way."

"Well now's your chance to learn how it's done," Quintus remarked. "And if I were you, I'd relax that arse of yours, or the pain will be much worse than any flogging you might

18

receive."

"Why are you doing this to me?" she wept.

A slave who survived a severe flogging might well be held in high esteem by fellow slaves, or even the master, but being humiliated like this would bring nothing but contempt.

"Are you questioning me?" Quintus asked, unused to being answered back.

She could see he was angered and might do something that would do her no good at all.

"No master," she whimpered. "I will obey your command and have that...that thing up my bottom."

Quintus brightened. It was just what he wanted to hear; complete and uncompromising obedience, another valuable asset. In gladiatorial training obedience was everything.

"You may have her now," he said to Proteus, then went back to his seat and joined Clodius where a meal of seasoned quail and shrimps had just arrived.

"I have to get out of here," Africanus thought, dropping on to her hands and knees.

Somewhere behind her Proteus was shuffling between her parted thighs making ready to penetrate her bottom. The slaves who had been turning the wheel had been permitted to rest and enjoy the spectacle. Glad of a break in their labours they gathered in a group, eyes fixed on Africanus' whipped body. In the bright sunshine her black skin shone with sweat. More slaves released from domestic duties elbowed and shoved for a place at the windows, some just gaping open mouthed at Proteus' famed penis, whilst others called out ribald remarks and made lewd gestures. It wasn't often they had the chance to see a fellow slave bum fucked by a thing of those dimensions. One or two even took bets as to how long Africanus could suffer being ridden by him.

19

"Tonight," she thought, "I'll make a break for it. Once I'm over that wall I'll be long gone"

But where was she to run? Home? That was a long way away and she could only just remember it. She knew she came from somewhere on the coast of Africa, a small village by a great river where she had been free. Then the soldiers had come rounding up all the young women and girls, herding them in chains aboard a boat where, packed like bees in a hive, they had remained for eight days until the craft disgorged its thirsty cargo at the wharves of a great city. There she had lived until she was fourteen, working as a slave girl. But life had not been unpleasant as a ladies' maid. She had been treated kindly and well fed. Then as she grew to womanhood she had been sold again, this time to a dealer who in turn auctioned her to a Roman who had set her to work at the wheel. The work was hard and grinding but at least it had kept her fit and her muscles had developed strength she never imagined possible. She had a good sense of direction and was pretty sure that she could find her way to the coast. There were plenty of cargo ships sailing to and fro to her homeland. She reasoned the price of her body was worth exchanging for a passage home.

Suddenly she was brought back into the present. A hard slap landed on her flank and she heard Proteus chuckle as his rough, horny palms spread over her bottom cheeks. His thumbs pressed hard into the softer flesh of her crease and eased it apart. He looked at her tight puckered bottom hole and laughed. Soon, she would be screaming with pain as his enormous rod drove hard into that tight little aperture.

"Get ready, Africanus!" a voice called from a window.

"Don't shit yourself," another called, and the whole assembly burst into hysterical laughter.

"Ride her 'til she's sore," a guard yelled.

Africanus steadied herself against the head of the

enormous cock touching her anus.

"They might've at least greased my arse before he started," she muttered.

Then her nerve failed. The powerful sphincter muscles in her bottom tensed and closed. Her buttock muscles flexed and for a moment both Clodius and Quintus admired the beautiful shapely hollows forming in their sides.

"The girl has a splendid arse," Clodius remarked, wondering why he hadn't noticed it before.

"It shows strength," Quintus agreed, wondering why Proteus had not penetrated her.

He saw him raise a clenched fist and bring it fast down upon the base of her spine.

"Open your arse, you bitch!" he rasped.

Africanus grunted from the blow and squeezed her cheeks tighter. With luck he might abandon the idea, but Proteus had no intentions of abandoning anything, not least riding the magnificent arse now presenting itself for his unbridled pleasure.

He drew back and slapped her left arse cheek so hard the sound echoed around the courtyard. He slapped her again on the right cheek, then on the sides of her thighs. His hand went under her legs and seized her sex mound. Africanus swallowed hard when his fingers slowly closed around her sex, increasing the pressure until her eyes watered.

"All right," she sobbed. "Ride my arse."

Again his thumbs eased open her cheeks and this time the head of his cock pressed hard against her anus. She grunted and felt the head slip into her bottom. His hands left her cheeks and gripped her hips, holding her still while his loins gathered strength for the first thrust.

The pain seemed to come from everywhere at once. Her bottom hole stretched until it could stretch no further. All

21

through her bottom cheeks a burning sensation spread like hot flames. The previous welts left by the whip began to throb again as blood rushed through her veins. She kept her teeth firmly clenched and took deep breaths through her dilated nostrils, blasting air and mucus over her lips and chest.

"I must go with it," she told herself, feeling his swelling organ drive deeper into her bottom.

To the delight of her audience, she dropped onto her elbows, arching her back and lifting her buttocks high in the air. His cock seemed to penetrate more easily, pushing open her anus and filling her to the hilt. His course, wiry pubic hair grazed against the softer surface of her skin. She shivered when his balls slapped into her crease. Learning to relax, she rocked back and forth on her knees, meeting each separate thrust with a backward push of her hips. But the mounting pain increased as his rotating hips screwed faster. His hands roamed over her back, slapping and smoothing the whip welts. Then, obeying the ribald suggestions from the crowd, he leaned right over and grabbed her breasts, squeezing hard, clumsily fumbling for her nipples. A scream, long held in her lungs gave full vent when he pinched her throbbing teats. Tears streaked from her rolling eyes as he in turn rolled and crushed the tender buds. His loins accelerated their pace thumping his pelvis into her wobbling cheeks.

"Go on, give it to her," a shrill voice cut the air.

"He's coming!" a girl shrieked.

Africanus felt his organ suddenly increase its hardness and in a second she was flooded with his hot gushing sperm.

He quickly withdrew and the audience craned their necks to see him come in great globules all the way up her back and into her hair.

A final slap on her buttocks sent her crashing to the

22

ground and she laid panting and sobbing. There were no thoughts in her mind now, just the dull ache in her legs and bottom which would go on throbbing for hours. If her masters' had sought to both punish and humiliate her, they had achieved just that. And she hid her face in shame.

CHAPTER TWO

"Look at the state of her," Clodius said, disgusted. "I wouldn't use her to clean my toilet let alone fight in the arena."

It was true. She hardly looked the sort of material that would inspire confidence in any would-be purchaser. Sand stuck to her sweating skin and a strong smell of body odour tainted the air. Proteus' spending had dried on her skin in transparent streaks. Some of it still gathered at the entrance to her bottom hole. She lay on her side in a crumpled heap, her sex open and wet.

"If you still want to buy this thing, I'm sure we can strike a favourable bargain," Clodius remarked, kicking her rump.

"The girl has many qualities, but now I want her washed and scrubbed," Quintus said. "Have her taken to the baths while we work out a price."

After her ordeal at the whipping post it seemed that she had suddenly been transported into paradise. The wooden tub was filled to the brim with hot, steaming water and lime leaves to sweeten her smelling skin. It was the first time in her life as a slave that she had ever been permitted to take a bath and now she leaned against the rim savouring the soothing liquid swirling around her breasts. After she had soaked for an hour a masseuse would come and massage her punished limbs, but until then she had time to relax.

Slowly the dirt melted from her skin and it took on that wonderful shiny sheen so peculiar to black women. Her hands reached for a cake of soap and rubbed it softly over her thighs and belly. The throbbing in her back and buttocks had subsided to little more than a dull ache, but her anus still hurt from Proteus' massive cock. It was a miracle it hadn't split her arse in half and she wondered how she had managed to take such a pounding. Her legs were long and powerful, but she knew men found her desirable. It was her breasts they found most attractive; firm round globes blessed with large inviting dark nipples. When she was sexually aroused the areolae seemed to quadruple in size, spreading their pimpled discs over half her breasts. Her hands cupped each one, and idly thumbed the nipples sending a sudden thrill travelling through her chest and belly. It had been a long time since she had masturbated. In a place like this where privacy was unknown the chance rarely came to indulge in a little self satisfaction, not to mention the relief it brought.

Dare I bring myself off, she wondered, looking swiftly around the bath house. All the other tubs were empty and there wasn't a soul in sight.

I dare, she thought, and her right hand dipped beneath the steaming surface.

Her fore and index fingers lightly touched the outer lips of her sex now pouting and swollen with excitement. A low moan escaped her lips when the tips of her fingers touched that sensual little bud that had women begging for a male cock.

"Oh, that's so good," she muttered, wiggling her fingers faster and faster.

But she didn't want to come quickly, instead of hurrying her orgasm she pushed her fingers deeper inside her sex, tickling and teasing the sensitive inner petals that thrilled at the slightest touch.

The hand still cupping her left breast lifted, raising the whole shining black globe high enough so her lips could suck on the erect and pulsating nipple. Another swift glance around the bath house told her all was safe from prying eyes. Her lips parted over the nipple, hovered for a second then sucked it in deep. She withdrew her hand from between her legs and reached for the soap cake not discarding it until her palm and fingers were well lathered.

Lost in a private world of ecstasy she flicked her tongue over her nipples, smiling broadly as her lathered hand went between her legs. From then on time seemed to stand still. She left off sucking her tingling breast and opened her legs as wide as the tub permitted. All four fingers of the lathered hand bunched together, the thumb tucked neatly into her palm. Now she was ready to bring herself off, not with two fingers but with her whole hand. Her head went backwards on the rim and she guided her fingers into her sex, moving her wrist in a slow revolving motion until her knuckles were just inside the outer lips. For a moment she held her breath unsure whether her sex could take another shove of her wrist.

Do it, she whispered, fuck yourself with your whole fist.

Her fingers uncrossed and fluttered wetly against her sex tunnel walls. When she felt her own excited juices flowing over her fingers, she gave her wrist a vigorous shove. She had done it. For the first time ever she was fist fucking her own sex. Her arm pumped fast and furiously so much so that it ached but the feeling was unbelievable. Every pore tingled and stung from the tip of her toes to her neck.

This is glorious, she sobbed, ramming her feet and shoulders against the groaning planks of the tub.

Suddenly as her climax approached every muscle in her body grew hard and went into wild uncontrollable spasms. There was no controlling her body now. Her shoulder blades protruded from her back scraping themselves raw on the timber, her legs stiffened, her thighs and calves went as hard as iron. Quickly she reached for her breast and sucked on the nipple heightening her arousal past the point of no return. If one of the guards had driven a spear into her belly, Africanus would not have felt it. Her wrist pumped so fast it blurred, and then she gave vent to a long wailing shriek, so loud and shrill that one of the slaves passing by the bath house stopped dead in her tracks. She thought someone had been murdered but no sound followed for Africanus had come and now lay exhausted in the tub, her arms and legs floated like pieces of drift wood, without purpose, without feeling. She opened her eyes and saw through the steam a dim figure staring down at her.

"If you've finished, I'd like to massage you now," a tired voice announced.

"How long have you been there?" Africanus asked the middle aged woman leaning over the tub.

"Long enough to see your arm half way up your cunt," she replied crudely. "Now get out of that tub and brace yourself for a beating."

"Oh what have I done now?" Africanus sighed, swinging her leg over the rim.

"Done?" the woman asked, surprised at the question. "You haven't done anything. It's all part of the treatment. A good birching makes the blood flow, cleans the dirt out of the pores."

She didn't tell Africanus that she ought to have been birched during intervals in and out of the bath, and then only lightly. She came from behind the tub wielding a sheaf of birch twigs and marched to where Africanus was standing.

"Stand up straight and cup your breasts," she told her. "Legs together and don't move."

The woman walked slowly around Africanus, making no sound except for heavy breathing, punctuated with favourable comments regarding her body.

27

"You have good breasts," she observed, stroking each one with the tips of her fingers. She brushed her thumbs lightly over the nipples, noticing with satisfaction how quickly they responded. "I suppose many men have sucked on these succulent buds."

"No they haven't," Africanus replied, startled at the suggestion.

"What about your cunt? How many men have had the pleasure of that sweet mound, I wonder?"

None of your business, Africanus thought, wondering where all this was leading.

The woman walked softly behind her and ran her fingers along the welts, then through the buttock crease murmuring her admiration for such a strong arse. Then for several moments she patted and smoothed the cheeks.

"What did it feel like, having Proteus' cock up your arse? You must've found it delightful. Eh?"

Africanus shuddered at the remembrance of his huge organ brutally riding her bottom.

"It was fucking awful," she swore.

There was disappointment in the woman's voice when she whispered, "I'm sorry to hear that."

Africanus stared directly at the wall trying to avert her mind from this strange woman now fondling and poking her back and shoulders. She was so close she could feel her breath on the back of her neck and instantly her skin goose bumped.

"What about women?" the woman asked. "Do you like women?"

I don't like you for a start, she thought. You give me the creeps.

"No, I don't like women," she said out loud, wishing the woman would either beat her or leave her in peace.

"Perhaps that's because you've never had the pleasure

of enjoying another woman's flesh," the woman persisted. "Have you never wondered what it's like to feel another woman's breasts or lick her cunt?"

Africanus could feel her temper rising. Now she understood what the woman was really after and she wasn't going to get it. Not with her at any rate.

"I think you need a good thrashing to soften you up a little," the woman threatened, angry at the lack of response in the beautiful black woman standing so wonderfully naked.

She padded softly to Africanus' rear and patted her bottom cheeks. "What about a few strokes on your thighs to begin with. Shall we say eight or would you prefer ten?"

Without waiting for a suggestion either way she cracked the twigs across the backs of Africanus' naked thighs. The blow came from the full strength of her arm and when the twigs struck a fierce pain far greater than she imagined shot through her legs. She hit her again, aiming the sheaf so accurately that both thighs were struck at once, and went on beating her until the backs of her legs were numbed.

"What about your bare arse? Shall we say at least twenty on those magnificent moons?"

It was like being hit with a tree trunk. The whole sheaf smacked and splintered from the sheer force of the blow. Yet oddly, Africanus was beginning to feel aroused from the effect of the heat blazing through her bruised buttocks. But she wasn't going to let the woman know that. Another lash landed on the side of her bottom where the buttocks formed into the delicious hollows that Quintus and Clodius had so admired. Inside her sex Africanus felt a tingling sensation. She knew her clitoris was being teased to arousal and to distract herself she concentrated on counting the blows now swinging under her cheeks. If only the bitch wouldn't hit her there. Every woman alive has her sensitive regions and the underside of the buttocks was where Africanus was most sensitive. The woman noticed that her legs had suddenly gone stiff and she was visibly trembling.

"I can see you like having your arse whipped," she grinned. "Especially here."

And she concentrated on the sensitive skin, not lashing so hard but merely flicking the shattered twigs where she guessed they would have the most effect.

Sweat was breaking out all over Africanus' skin and the sweet smell of lime leaves and soap hung pleasantly around her.

The woman's hand alighted on her bottom fondling and squeezing the place that she had just teased. She moved closer pressing her body against Africanus' back and rubbed her hard nipples into the naked sweating skin.

"I think a few strokes on your belly and tits will have you gasping for it," she observed, sidling around Africanus.

She lashed the twigs over the plump mound of her belly smiling gleefully at the flat hollow sound they made. Then she concentrated on her breasts.

"Keep them lifted and don't move," she commanded.

A strange formation had altered her features, the eyelids were heavy with longing and her parted lips trembled constantly. It was all she could do to keep herself from dragging the black woman onto the marble massage slab and riding her there and then.

The twigs sailed over Africanus' cupped breasts made more beautiful and larger for being held in her hands. The woman's eyes widened at the sight of the quivering flesh and the areolae spreading ever wider.

"Press your tits together," she rasped.

Africanus obeyed and compressed her globes until the nipples almost touched.

The woman, blushing in her desperation lashed both

breasts so hard the twigs snapped and flew in all directions, but every time the nipples were struck by the sharp pointed twigs Africanus heaved a sigh of arousal. Between her legs she was wet, so wet it trickled down the insides of her thighs. Her clitoris pulsated so much she could hardly breathe. Either the woman knew exactly how to arouse her, beating and tormenting her sensitive places, or it had happened naturally, a mounting orgasm brought on by a beating.

The woman could see the effect the twigs were having and cast the sheaf aside.

"I think you've had enough," she whispered, taking Africanus' hands from her breasts.

She kept their fingers locked and lowered her head, her lips sucking on the splendidly aroused teats.

"You taste so sweet," the woman breathed. "I think now it's time for your massage. Follow me."

Almost in an orgiastic trance, Africanus followed her into the massage room and laid herself flat upon a huge marble slab.

"It seems you are all the better for a good beating," the woman said softly. "See how relaxed you are."

That couldn't be denied. All the tension had evaporated. Her tensed muscles now felt soft and light.

"Are you going to do what I think you're going to do?" she asked, no longer despising the woman but finding her oddly attractive in the way that one is mesmerized by a cobra.

"That all depends on what you think I'm going to do," she said huskily.

"I think you want to kiss me."

A rasping laugh echoed around the marble walls. "I'm going to do much more than that," she whispered. "Now let me feel your cunt."

31

Without any resistance, Africanus allowed the woman to part her legs, spreading them over the slab. A renewed surge of pleasure filled her trembling belly and bottom as the woman's hand slipped between her thighs.

"I saw what you were doing in that tub," the woman said, running her fingers through the thick pubic curls. "No need to be ashamed. It's what we all do, but sometimes it is more satisfying if another woman does it for you. Wouldn't you agree?"

Her voice was soft and throaty and when she spoke she looked directly into Africanus' eyes. She realized that the woman was going to fist fuck her whether she wanted it or not, and after having her bottom thrashed to arousal was not entirely surprised to find the idea equally arousing.

"I've never been fucked by another woman," she admitted, unable to control the slow gyration of her hips.

Whatever the woman was doing between her legs was having an instant effect. Without conscious effort, as if the woman's fingers had taken control of her senses, Africanus' hips and pelvis began squirming over the slab. Involuntarily, she reached for her breasts and cupped them, inviting the masseuse to suck on her nipples. But she ignored the invitation and went on worming her fingers into the soaking slit, moving them faster until the sex lips became so soft and pliable that her hand slipped in to the wrist.

Africanus arched her back high off the slab willing the woman's hand to go deeper and faster. In desperation she pumped her hips against the driving fist whirling inside her, forcing herself towards an orgasm that would leave her breathless and satiated. Keeping her wrist turning, the woman moved further along the slab and leaned over crushing her open mouth onto Africanus' lips. Their hot tongues met flicking and diving deep into their throats.

32

Africanus reached over her sweating belly and grabbed the woman's wrist pushing it harder against her sex. In a welter of thrashing legs and arms Africanus rose to her climax.

Suddenly the woman pulled back. "Not yet!" she shrieked. "Not so soon!"

But Africanus was past the point of no return. Her body jerked and twisted from the hot rhythmic spasms darting from her breasts and belly. Her nipples tingled so much they hurt, but it was nothing compared to her trembling clitoris now so sensitive she squealed and shrieked at the slightest touch. She had had men inside her, the guards often took the slave women shackled to the pole, coming behind them, kicking their ankles wide and fucking them from behind while their hands remained tightly manacled, but it was nothing compared to what was happening inside her now.

Her bottom bounced on and off the slab, cries of ecstasy reverberated around the marble chamber and in an instant she climaxed with a long drawn out howl. Trembling with anger, the woman took away her soaking fist and looked savagely at Africanus' exhausted face.

"You came too soon," she hissed, furious at being denied her own climax.

Usually watching a panting girl in the throes of orgasm was enough to bring her off, but this one had come too quickly and now she felt cheated.

"I think you need another thrashing," she grated.

"I think she needs nothing of the sort."

Both Africanus and the masseuse looked round at the man coming into the massage chamber.

"You have disobeyed my orders," Quintus said, glancing at the woman and then at Africanus.

It didn't take much imagination to realize what had just

taken place. He could plainly see the look of sexual gratification on the black girl's face and the tell tale pool of juice between her legs. The air in the chamber was still thick with the aroma of sex and sweat.

"You were instructed to scrub her and bring her directly to me," he said to the woman, anger evident in his tone. "I've been waiting for an hour and when I come looking for her, what do I find? Instead of being freshly scrubbed, she's been fucked by you."

"I'm sorry, master," the masseuse trembled. "I just can't help myself."

"In that case, your sexual cravings need curtailing. Go to the whipping post and prepare yourself for a flogging, and," he grinned, looking at Africanus, "you shall have the honour of delivering it."

Africanus swung her legs off the slab, her face distorted in disbelief.

"But I've never flogged anyone in my life."

Lost in thought, Quintus stroked his chin. He looked first at the black girl then at the masseuse and back to the black girl again.

"You get out!" he barked at the woman. He waited until she went sobbing out of the chamber and seated himself on the slab. Africanus stood in front of him. Suddenly aware of her nakedness, she placed her hands over her sex and kept her head bowed.

Quintus surveyed her beauty, admiring her robust limbs and hips. A smile spread across his face and he patted the empty space beside him indicating that she should be seated. Africanus lowered her bottom to the slab and looked at the floor wondering what was coming next, whether he would have her there and then, or merely content himself with mauling her naked body, but he just sat still marshalling his thoughts.

34

"You have been sold," he told her flatly. "And I am your new master. Your days here are over and from now on you will begin your training as a gladiatrix. Do you know what a gladiatrix does for a living?" Africanus shook her head. "She kills in the arena, like a gladiator." He gave her a few seconds to think about that. "Your training will be long and hard, but the rewards are endless. Fail and you will be sold back to Clodius and spend the rest of your miserable life turning that wheel. Now go to the tub and scrub away the filth left by that bitch and report to the whipping post. I shall watch closely to see how you perform."

He got up and went, leaving Africanus' mind in turmoil. A gladiatrix! But she had never killed anyone, let alone doing it for a living. Then suddenly it fell into place. Having her unjustly flogged then bum fucked were tests to see how she held up. To see how much punishment she could take. Well, if flogging was to their taste she could give them a feast. She went swiftly to the tub and scooped up a handful of water, rubbing it hard between her legs. She knew of men taken from quarries and mines to train as gladiators. The training was hard but to those who succeeded came great rewards; some had even been given their freedom, or had managed to buy it. One thing was for certain, it was her way out of this place, a chance to govern her own fate. No more turning that wheel in endless drudgery but a new life of fame and fortune, providing she wasn't killed. But that would be down to her. Going out of the chamber, she knew that her new master would be watching her and might even change his mind if she failed to meet his expectations.

"I'll flog the bitch raw," she muttered aloud, and made her way to the whipping post.

The masseuse was hanging by the wrists. Her body, pale and slender looked a lot less daunting than when Africanus had first encountered her in the baths. For a woman in her early forties she was in surprisingly good shape, the hips were slim and the buttocks pert and tight, her legs shapely if perhaps a little too thin. Africanus knew at once that she wouldn't stand up to a severe flogging. She guessed that maybe ten strokes would finish her.

Under the awning sat her new master obviously pleased with his new purchase. The contrast between the hanging woman and the magnificently naked black girl dispelled any doubts he might have harboured. Flogging the masseuse would be a good test to see if she could stand the sight of blood and more importantly inflict the wounds that brought it. So far she had passed all the tests he'd set her, now he wanted to see if she could wield the whip without emotion. Killing was a cold blooded business and there was no room for either compassion or weakness.

"Give her twenty strokes," Quintus commanded. "Lay them on hard and fast."

The whip that Africanus had been given dangled limply in her hand. Looking at the bare back and buttocks of the older woman, the lack of flesh with which to sustain the blows left her hesitating. In no time at all the leather tails would cut her to the bone. Somehow, despite her earlier sexual assaults and beating, Africanus thought the wretch didn't deserve such a cruel flogging.

"Please, master," she pleaded, "I don't think she can take a full twenty strokes."

"You will carry out my orders or be sold back to your former master," Quintus said sharply. "The choice is yours."

Africanus was quick to grasp the meaning behind such an order. If she was to prove her worth in the arena there would be no time for sentiment, let alone mercy.

"Very well, master," she agreed, and lifted the whip above her head.

36

It was surprising how heavy it seemed and when she let it fall it took little effort to land it across the masseuse's back. A sickening crack of leather on naked flesh broke the silence and was quickly followed by a heart rending shriek of pain. The woman's thin body went into a spin and when it stopped her whipped back was against the post exposing her flat belly and small, attractive breasts. The dark brown nipples stood out in strong relief against the much paler surrounding skin. It was difficult not to notice the thick, luxuriant amount of pubic hair between her legs. In her eyes Africanus saw sheer terror at what was to come. Beyond her under the awning Quintus was growing impatient and Africanus experienced a wave of panic.

Be strong, she told herself. This is your way out of this hole.

She gathered the whip and sent the tails cracking across the flat, quivering belly. The woman's body jerked from the post and doubled up, the feet almost touching her buttocks as she swung away from the post. Africanus distinctly heard her bottom thump into the wooden pole as she settled back into place.

She gave her three more rapid strokes, aiming low over her slender thighs. Instead of wildly gyrating, her body hung motionless numbed with agony. A forth stroke caught her directly across her nipples and this time her body bent in all directions. Like a drunken puppet whose strings have become hopelessly entangled, her legs bent at the knees, straightened and came together so fast her ankles cracked on impact. Her head rolled from side to side, her tongue hung from her lips, saliva dribbled from the corners of her mouth.

I must be strong and finish the punishment, Africanus told herself, realizing now that flogging a defenceless

37

woman was not as easy as she thought. She would have to close her mind to the endless shrieks and pleas for mercy, shut her eyes to the livid welts forming in terrible lines on the punished skin and look, yes look, as if all this torment she was inflicting meant nothing to her.

"Take that, you dirty bitch," she shouted, lashing into the woman's buttocks.

A deep muted groan came from her throat as the tails curled around her boyish hips sending her into another spin. Africanus quickly gathered the tails and before the woman had stopped spinning delivered another blow into her ribs. She swung slowly back and forth trying to angle her body away from where she thought the next stroke would land. A curious game of cat and mouse ensued with the woman jerking left and right and Africanus landing the whip where it fell easiest. But the woman's strength was failing and she had resigned herself to the remaining lashes which now fell at regular intervals on her buttocks and thighs.

"That will do," Quintus announced, and Africanus dropped the whip and stood still, feeling slightly foolish and wondering what to do next.

"You whipped her well," he complimented, rising from his seat and motioning her forward. "The strokes were expertly delivered."

"Thank you, master," she bowed.

"Now you may free her and take her to the bath house, then return directly to me."

Africanus, aided by a male slave released the wrist shackles and, taking her by the arms, dragged her lifeless body across the courtyard.

"I've done it," she thought, as the male slave dumped the masseuse's body on the marble slab. "I've proved my worth."

A curious feeling of superiority and power passed through her as she looked at the welted flesh. Now it seemed that she was on equal footing with her own masters. Only a short while ago she had been forced to submit to the woman's libidinous ministrations, and might have received another thrashing but for the timely intervention of her new master. Now she understood why slaves feared their masters. The power to punish with impunity was an intoxicating one, but as she looked at the groaning woman she felt a strange feeling of contempt.

The woman opened her eyes and glared malevolently at the black girl. Even though she had been flogged lifeless there was still defiance in her face.

"One day I'll repay you for this," she muttered.

"Not before I've given you my cock," the male slave suddenly blurted.

It wasn't often a male slave could have sex with his female counterpart, unless his master granted permission, which wasn't often. Now he had a wonderful opportunity to slake his lust, and who would know? The black girl had been sold and would not be there to testify against him if the woman complained.

"Open your legs," he said firmly, and climbed onto the slab.

Africanus remained silent, wondering if he knew the woman was not that way inclined, well, towards men anyway.

He threw off his tunic and Africanus nodded satisfactorily at his throbbing erection. In a trice he was between the woman's legs, throwing her ankles carelessly over his shoulders and ramming his cock into the proffered hole.

"Stop him!" the woman shrieked, pounding his ribs with her tiny fists.

But she too well penetrated for him to stop now and

39

Africanus leaned idly against the wall grinning at his pounding buttocks. The woman raised her head to bite him but he was one step ahead and slapped her hard across the face.

"Keep still," he barked, "or I'll drown you in that bath."

Africanus burst into a peal of laughter. That would have been more than he dare do, but the thought was amusing. She went to the head of the slab and grabbed the woman's flailing arms and pinioned them behind her head.

"I'll kill you for this," she spat, rolling her eyes like a demented outcast.

Africanus held her rigid while the male slave smacked his pelvis into her groin. He reached over and squeezed her breast quite oblivious to the welts cut into her nipples. It was all over in minutes and he slithered off the slab and went out happily whistling.

The woman rolled over onto her belly mouthing savage curses and swearing her revenge. Africanus went into the bath house and came back carrying the birch twigs. Silently she raised the sheaf high over her shoulder and cracked it at full strength onto the slim reddened buttocks. The woman let out a howl and clutched her bottom.

"Take your hands away from there," Africanus ordered, relishing her new found power.

Without waiting for her hands to move, she lashed the birch onto her buttocks, then lashed her back until the twigs finally snapped and were useless.

"You want to know why I did that?" Africanus asked her.

The woman looked up imploringly knowing she was totally at her mercy. "Why?" she muttered.

"Because I don't like you," Africanus replied, and went out into the sunshine and suddenly realized that she didn't even know the woman's name.

"You may wear this," Quintus offered, tossing her a tunic. "It will do until we reach the ludus, the official name given to the training school."

"Thank you master," she bowed.

Another unexpected privilege; most slaves employed in menial tasks went completely naked. Wearing a tunic was a sign of importance.

"You may thank your previous master for all he has done for you, and for willingly selling you to me."

Africanus turned to where Clodius was standing and dropped to her knees. "Thank you, master," she said, lowering her head and kissing his toes.

"Get up, girl, and see you serve your new master well."

Africanus got to her feet and bowed. "I shall do everything that's expected of me," she assured him and followed her new master into the outer courtyard.

CHAPTER THREE

She didn't expect the amount of chains, weights and locks, not to mention an iron collar that were fitted to her. Neither did she expect to have to ride in an ox cart. She thought as an aspiring gladiatrix she would have been treated with more respect as befitted her rank.

"Until you have been fully trained and proved successful in the arena, you are still a slave," the driver told her. "And a lowly one at that. Now get your arse on the floor."

Africanus stumbled into the waggon and seated herself on the floorboards, her back against the railings and legs stretched out in front. The driver whose job it was to deliver her intact selected the collar from the pile of chains and fitted it around her neck. At the front and back of the collar were rings large enough for a length of chain to pass through. At the rear he put a length of chain through the ring and locked it to the railings. She put out her wrists and these were fitted with shackles joined with a short chain, not unlike the manacles criminals wore when they were taken to the arena for execution.

"Lift your wrists and put them over your tits," he commanded.

Africanus obeyed and placed her fastened wrists between her breasts. These he secured to the front ring in the collar with more chain.

"Now your ankles," he said, rummaging in the pile for another pair of shackles.

He fitted a shackle to each ankle and chained them together. Just when she thought he'd finished, he lifted a heavy weight from the pile, a solid lump of iron with a ring at the top. This he placed in her hands and passed a length of chain through the ring, wound it around her neck and back to the weight.

"You have to hold that all the way there," he told her gaily. "And if you let it fall the chain around your neck will tighten and you'll strangle yourself. So it's up to you."

Feeling more like a condemned criminal than a trainee gladiatrix, Africanus sat in her barred cage holding the weight tight against her chest. The populace of Marcellum paid her little heed as the cart rumbled through the streets. Just another whore on her way to the cells they thought and carried on shopping. Quintus was taking no chances with his latest acquisition, for one thing, she didn't come cheap, and secondly a girl as fit as her, with legs of that length could run like a gazelle if the chance presented itself. Once out of that cart she'd be up and gone in a trice, better to be safe than sorry.

The training school was about a mile outside of the town and the cart rumbled to a halt under the shade of an olive tree. The driver got down from his seat and unlocked the barred door and climbed inside, locking the door behind him.

"Drink?" he offered, raising a pitcher to her parched lips.

She drank greedily, spilling most of it down her front. The driver watched a stream of lemon water run over her chest and through her breast cleft. She had good breasts with nipples poking invitingly at her flimsy tunic.

"Are you comfortable?" he asked, lifting the weight higher until the top bumped her chin.

"My arse is sore from these fucking boards," she swore. "And this weight is too heavy for me to hold. Does my master know you're treating me like this?"

"Your master ordered me to chain you," he told her. "We've had too many runaways between the town and the school. Now let me see if I can make you more comfortable. Can't have you suffering in this heat, can we now?"

He carefully positioned the weight at the centre of her chest so that both breasts were visible either side of it. They looked incredibly inviting under that sweat soaked tunic. He could even see the darker hue of her areolae showing through the material, not to mention those erect nipples forcing themselves higher and higher. He was always told that when a woman's nipples went hard it meant she was begging for a fuck. There was little he could do about that without releasing all the chains and manacles and that bloody great weight, but he could fondle those beautiful tits. It was the only chance he was ever likely to get.

He reached out and placed both hands on her breasts, taking great care to thumb the nipples rapidly to and fro. They stiffened at once; hard buds of excited tit flesh just longing for an eager mouth to suck them.

"Are you supposed to be doing this?" Africanus asked, wide eyed and breathing fast.

He couldn't answer because his mouth was clamped over her left breast, lips sucking hard on the nipple, so hard it lifted from the areola. She bucked when his teeth bit into the bud.

"That hurt," she protested, and let the weight slip.

An ominous grunt escaped her throat. He looked up just in time to see the chain tightening around her neck and quickly lifted the weight clear of her chest.

"I told you not to let go of that weight," he said testily, and slapped the side of her head.

"How can I keep still when you're sucking my tits," she retorted, beginning to wonder if all this was part of his duties.

He thought for a moment and looked at the position of the sun. A little after midday, he thought, wondering if there really was time to loosen her shackles. Perhaps if he released the chain at the back of the collar and the manacles around her ankles he just might be able to get her on her back with her wrists still secured to the iron weight. It could rest on her chest while he fucked her. She wouldn't strangle herself; he'd make doubly sure of that.

"Do you know the penalty for attempting to escape?" he asked. In her position it seemed a pretty stupid question. "It's one hundred lashes," he told her, keying the lock at her ankles. "And who's to say you didn't try it?" he suggested darkly.

"You shit," she blurted, suddenly grasping his intention. He was going to fuck her, and if she complained she'd get a hundred lashes.

He unlocked the padlock at the back of the collar and eased her shoulders gently onto the floorboards, keeping the weight deftly balanced on her chest.

"Now don't move," he chuckled, "because if that weight slips it's the underworld for you."

They both knew he wouldn't dare let that happen, not with such a valuable cargo, but there was nothing she could do in the way of resistance.

"You've got good legs," he complimented, lifting her calves and resting them on his shoulders.

His erection was massive and throbbing, she could see the veins around the shaft pulsating in time with his heart beat. The shiny purple head nodded as if eager to bury itself inside the dark mysterious crack between her thighs. With a gentility that surprised her, he lowered his bulk over her body and took his weight on one hand whilst using the other to guide his cock into her slit.

"You're wet," he said, plunging hard into her.

"It's the heat," she lied, gasping as he rammed his cock fully home.

Africanus was no virgin, but her sexual experience was

45

limited. The grinding house guards had fucked her while she had been shackled to the pole, and occasionally she had permitted one or two of the male slaves to have her when the opportunity presented itself, but it had all been hurried, over and done with in minutes, hardly worth the effort, when she had come it was more of an accident than a compliment. Now, here in the middle of nowhere on a public road she was being fucked by a driver, a menial no better than herself, but it was the fear of discovery that made her thrill to the cock pounding away at her groin. Holding the iron weight added to the thrill. Her hands on its sides were the only means of stopping herself from being throttled, and there was nothing she could do about it.

His technique was not what she expected; he wasn't riding her brutally, but taking his time, plunging in and out with long steady insertions, touching her clitoris at every stroke.

"Do you always treat your captives this way?" she gasped, blinking from the sunlight.

"Only when they've got legs like yours," he grunted, sliding his arms around her sweating thighs.

"What about my cunt?" she asked. "Can you feel it around your cock?"

She squeezed her vaginal walls, closing the petals around the shaft, feeling the pulse increasing in the veins.

"Your cunt is like silk," he stuttered, angling his hips, spearing her sex tunnel left and right.

Just then a troop of horse came thundering by. The horsemen caught a brief glance at a pair of long, black silky legs pointing to the waggon roof and a pair of buttocks bouncing up and down between them. But there was no time to halt, only to shout a few ribald words of encouragement and they disappeared in a cloud of dust.

They must've seen us fucking like a pair of goats, she

thought, a chill going round and round inside her belly. She wondered who else was going to come along that road and see them fucking inside that cart. In the distance another vehicle approached, a sort of covered carriage drawn by a pair of white horses. Some nobleman or senator on his way to Rome probably.

Africanus locked her heels over the small of the driver's back. Her strong thighs flexed crushing against his ribs. He was riding her faster, working towards his climax, just like Proteus had done, except now there was no pain or humiliation, just the sheer orgiastic pleasure of having a man inside her dripping tunnel. In the stifling heat, he too was sweating. Drops of perspiration dripped from his chest and face plopping onto her belly and breasts. He managed to keep his balance on one arm whilst daring to reach over and fondle her breasts. His fingers squeezed tight, nails digging into the wobbling globes, but the sharp unexpected pain only added to the pleasure of his cock slamming relentlessly into her sex. Underneath, the rough broken boards dug into her back and bottom, splinters pierced her skin like darts. It was coming from everywhere at once. Her whole body seemed to be assailed with pain, even the weight and collar grew heavier and tighter.

"I'm coming," she moaned, unlocking her heels and flinging her legs wide.

Something sharp dug into her buttocks and she tried to lift her bottom but his cock kept her impaled, forcing her harder to the floor. Whatever it was stabbing her buttocks only heightened the pleasure of her orgasm, and she came with a warbling groan, kicking wildly at the waggon railings, drumming her heels on the bars. The driver emptied into her, flooding her sex with hot streams of juice. He managed, even as he came to snatch a quick glance at the passing carriage. Whoever was inside took a furtive look at the amorous couple now uncoupling behind the bars, then closed the curtain and continued on his way.

"You're the best fuck I've had in a long while," the driver told her, hauling her upright.

He had the decency to cover her breasts before shackling her back into position. He let her drink a bellyful of lemon water and let himself out of the cart, locked the door and went back to his seat, joyfully whipping up the ox and adjusting his tunic as the wheels rumbled over the cobbles.

The sun had almost set when they arrived at the gladiatorial training school. An unnatural silence hung over the roofs and buildings, and in the semi darkness Africanus saw the cart pass under a low arch and into a courtyard surrounded by a high wall. The driver unlocked the door and swiftly unshackled his passenger. Africanus sighed aloud at being released, especially from that weight and the collar around her neck. Her bottom still hurt from the splinter that had pierced her skin. Still, she thought, as a shadowy figure advanced carrying a torch, a good hot bath will put things aright. She could hardly wait for the morrow to arrive when she would begin her training. Wielding a sword was going to be fun.

"Come with me," the figure said, turning on its heels.

A door opened and Africanus stumbled in the dim light along a bare stone corridor, lined with studded doors. The figure keyed a lock and the door creaked open.

"Your cell," the figure informed, and Africanus went in.

"What about a bath?" she shouted after the figure. "I'm all covered in dust."

But the figure could not have heard, because the door was locked behind it. A lamp had been left burning on a small cabinet and when her eyes became accustomed to the light she saw a crude bed covered with straw. On the cabinet were half a loaf of bread and a pitcher of water. A pot for night use stood under the bed. An awful sinking feeling went through her stomach. But too tired to think about it, she lay on the straw and fell fast asleep dreaming of the driver and his rampant cock.

The cell door crashed open and Africanus looked up with a start. She was squatting over the pot emptying her bladder.

"You stink like a ferret," the man in the doorway said, wrinkling his nose. "You had better get yourself cleaned before the lanista sees you."

He waited until she had finished before leading her out of the cell, watching her with a leer as her water drummed into the pot. As they were leaving a girl slave came in and collected it. Urine was a valuable commodity and was used by fullers, its acidic properties were ideal for cleaning clothes.

"If you don't measure up," the man said, "that's where you'll be sold."

All the way along the passage he described how slaves spent their lives calf deep in urine tramping with their bare feet on the dirty clothes sent to be cleaned.

"Thanks," Africanus muttered, entering the bath house.

A girl slave told her to stand over a stone sink, whilst another threw a bucket of cold water over her smelling skin. Seizing scrubbing brushes they went to work with a fury, rubbing the stiff bristles over her buttocks and legs, not stopping until all the dust and sweat had been removed and her skin again shone like polished ebony. They gave her a towel to wash her own private parts. Instead of wearing the tunic, she was given a clean white cloth which one of the girl slaves wrapped around her hips. It was short, barely covering her buttocks. If she bent over for all the use it was, she might as well been wearing nothing. Bare breasted, she walked into the courtyard and her first day as a gladiatrix.

The lanista, the gladiatorial trainer, was a former gladiator, now in his late forties, but still remarkably strong and well built. "I am Drucus, your trainer," he told her.

His manner was not unkind, but in his eyes Africanus instantly recognized cold, calculating strength, not a man to cross at any price.

He came up to her and slapped her buttocks and he seemed to be satisfied at their firmness. He slapped her thighs and hips and back. His strong hands manipulated her shoulders and biceps. He slapped her belly and said it was too soft, but that was nothing to worry about; a month of training would get rid of any excess fat. Her breasts stung when his palm slapped each one in turn. Large and well shaped, he told her, nothing to worry about there either.

"She's in good shape," he complimented, squeezing her breast. "But there is a lot of hard work ahead of her before she's ready for combat."

He was addressing Quintus who had come into the courtyard. "You'll need to keep a sharp eye on her," he said testily. "She fucks at the slightest opportunity."

The lanista grinned lasciviously. "If she fights as well as she fucks I'm sure she'll do well. But it wouldn't go amiss to have her paired with another woman. They fight differently from men, and it wouldn't be fair to match her against a trained gladiator."

"I can fight as well as any man," Africanus said boldly.

"Put her to the test," Quintus ordered. "And we'll see if her boasting rings true. Fetch Circo."

The gladiator was fair haired, a prisoner of war from Britannia, solid muscle from head to toe. His biceps and chest rippled with strength. He wore a pair of leather breeches and at the sight of the near naked black woman his cock bulged.

"This is no time for licentious thoughts," Quintus grunted. "Give them the rudis."

A rudis was a wooden sword used in training. Not until a gladiator was judged a skilled combatant was he given a gladius, a real sword.

"Keep up your guard," Drucus advised, handing her the rudis. "Move fast and never turn your back. Good luck my black beauty."

Already he was warming to the girl. A month of hard physical training would do wonders. He wondered if Quintus was speaking the truth when he said she fucked at the slightest opportunity. She looked the sort who liked her cock. There was no doubt in his mind that she could fuck like a stoat if needs must, and with an arse that could crack walnuts, she'd make a magnificent ride.

Africanus and Circo stood facing each other and raised their rudis, crossing them and waiting for Drucus to give the order to begin. He held a long wooden shaft between them, and when it was swiftly raised Circo displayed his consummate skill. He moved so fast it was bewildering, the wooden blade went everywhere at once, in one second it slashed at head height, and in the next cut across her belly. He moved as lightly as a girl, smacking the blade against her rump, then on the backs of her thighs. Her breasts wobbled and slapped when the blade hit both globes in quick succession. A hard thrust poked into her navel and she buckled over only to receive another singeing blow across her shoulder blades. They had only been fighting for less than a minute and Africanus was reeling from blow after blow. Circo could hardly believe what he was seeing in front of him, a tall, magnificent black woman with a body he would readily kill for, leaping in all directions, breasts swinging like huge melons, an arse that wobbled and danced every time he struck it. Normally, matched

51

against such a novice, he would have disarmed her in seconds. But he was in no hurry. No hurry at all.

"Aaagh!" Africanus groaned, as the rudis smacked on her flank.

She turned sideways and another blow whistled into her bottom. It was surprising just how much it hurt, a short wooden sword coming at full speed from a man twice her strength. Try as she might, she just wasn't up to his skill, let alone the speed at which he moved. She ought to have been disarmed minutes ago, but she still held on to her rudis, doing her best to parry each cutting blow. He was playing with her, she knew that. She also knew her strength was failing fast. Her movements were slower and her judgment poor. He was hitting her more frequently, especially across her bottom. He seemed to have a fondness for beating her buttocks. The short skirt was no protection against the rudis and was quickly ripped from her hips. He sent the blade edge into her naked crease and she let out a long howl like a wounded she wolf. Dancing on one foot, she lifted her left thigh and saw the blade swing fast under her legs. It cut clean and deep into her slit so hard her body lifted from the ground. Drucus winced and would have stopped the contest there and then, but Quintus refused him.

"Let her fight 'til she's unconscious," he said. "Perhaps then she'll realize that female gladiators are not made in a single day."

"But she has good qualities," Drucus admitted.

Quintus nodded assent. She had taken a beating but was still on her feet, even though her buttocks were swelling from the constant bruising and welting thrusts.

The final stroke came when Circo caught her across the shoulder blades sending her tumbling head over heels. She lay spreadeagled on the ground, panting like a race horse, her legs wide open. Although it was against the rules of combat, Circo couldn't resist sending the flat of the blade winging into her sex. She grunted and rolled over, sand sticking to her sweating skin.

"You may return to your duties," Quintus said drily, and Circo marched off hoping it wasn't the last bout he'd have with her.

"I think you're right, she needs another woman to fight against," Quintus admitted reluctantly.

She had put up a good fight, but was no match for a man.

"Now you see what lies ahead of you," Quintus told her as he stood over her, wondering if she ever would be fit for the arena. "Drucus will work on your body strength for at least a month, by then I'll have another woman for you to fight, and we shall decide which type of gladiatrix suits you best. After you have washed and had your bruises salved you will take the loyal oath to me and your trainer. From now on you belong to both of us, body and soul." He turned to go, but something went through his mind and he turned on his heels. "Who gave you permission to fuck with the driver? You were supposed to rest on your journey."

"It was the heat," she replied softly, rubbing her aching bottom, and not wishing to betray the man. "It makes me horny."

"In that case I think you need cooling," he said. "This isn't a brothel and you won't be sharing your bed with anyone, unless I give you permission to do so. Is that clear?"

"Yes, master," she whispered, feeling like a cheap whore, and wondering how he could have known she fucked the driver.

"Have her taken to the frigidarium and cool her passion, then beat her," he said gruffly and stalked off, thinking

53

that hiring a professional gladiatrix was going to cost yet more money. He hoped Africanus would be worth the extra expense. If she wasn't, he'd sell her to the fullers. See how she liked wading knee deep in piss for the rest of her miserable life.

The frigidarium was just one of a series of baths ranging from hot to tepid to freezing. Usually the bathers passed from hot to cold, giving the body time to adjust to the varying temperatures. Africanus wasn't given the opportunity to languish in either the hot or tepid, but was hurled head first into the near freezing water of the frigidarium.

At least, she thought, ducking her shoulders under the water, if my arse is frozen, I shan't feel the whip lashing into me. After a few minutes of immersion her body became immune to the coldness, and she leaned against the edge of the bath, arms outstretched along the rim, legs floating on the surface. It wasn't like the tub at Clodius' establishment, but a real bath constructed of stone and marble, large enough to hold twenty or more people. She closed her eyes thinking of the bout she'd just fought. Circo had beaten the shit out of her, almost literally for once or twice she came close to emptying her bowels when he smacked the rudis on her rump. She had a lot to learn; that much was certain, but there was no doubt in her mind that under Drucus' tutelage she would learn fast, but she was certain that there was much more to being a gladiatrix than merely slaying the opponent. In the fullness of time she would learn all there was to know, but for the present all she needed was to soothe away the ache in the freezing water.

She lay still admiring the frescos decorating the walls. Numerous scenes depicting gladiatorial combat had been executed with startling realism. She studied each painted

54

figure, some were heavily armed, others less so, some were bare headed and others wore huge, wide brimmed helmets. There was one that was particularly frightening; a full faced helmet with mere slits for the eyes to see through and shaped like a wolf's head. The depicted gladiator carried a sinister sword bent at the middle. It didn't take much imagination to picture the sort of fearful damage it could inflict. She was studying a gladiator wielding a trident when a girl slave came hurrying into the frigidarium.

"You must get out now," she said urgently. "The mistress wants you. Put on your skirt and come with me. Quickly now."

Mistress, she wondered. What would the mistress want with me? Whoever the mistress happened to be.

She clambered out of the water shivering and, hugging her freezing breasts, ran around the water's edge and into a small, sun filled courtyard. In no time at all the sun warmed her skin and suddenly she felt happy with life. All around the perimeter grew exotic plants with brightly coloured flowers and broad spreading leaves. The flags underfoot were chequered squares of red and white marble, and in the centre a small pond was filled with goldfish and lilies. She never imagined that people could live in such splendour.

"So you are Quintus' latest acquisition," a feminine voice echoed under the portico.

Africanus saw a woman beautifully dressed in a purple robe with gold trimmings. Her hair was curled and piled high on top of her head. It was difficult to guess her age. She could have been anywhere between five and twenty, and forty. Her face was broad with splendid dark, roving eyes, full, wide, painted lips and high cheek bones. She walked tall and erect, taking long, purposeful strides. Her hips seemed to dance with every step. In her right hand she carried a cane, long and supple with which she swished the air as she walked.

"I am the lady Octavia," she introduced. "Your new master's wife and I have the pleasure of delivering the punishment. It will make a pleasant change beating a full grown woman instead of these chits of girls my husband seems to employ. I suppose you are the one who fucked with the driver."

"Yes, mistress," Africanus replied dutifully. "I am she."

She was beginning to think that playful dalliance with the driver was causing her a great deal of trouble and had given the impression that she was little better than a common tart.

The lady Octavia came across the coloured squares and putting the end of the cane under Africanus' skirt, lifted it off her hips.

"I can see you've been in combat," she said, angling her head on one side, closely scrutinizing the marks left by Circo's rudis. "Lucky for you it wasn't a gladius, or you would've been cut to shreds."

"Yes, mistress," Africanus replied, breathing in the lady's scented perfume.

"You know why you are being beaten?"

Africanus nodded dumbly, but she didn't know it wasn't only because she fucked the driver, but because Quintus had underestimated how costly it would be to train her, and he was taking out his anger by allowing his own wife to give her a thrashing. She had a penchant for beating her slaves and making her a present of the black gladiatrix would assuage her anger when he told her he had to take out yet another loan.

"You have splendid buttocks," lady Octavia remarked, placing her soft hand on Africanus' bottom. "And so firm. I wonder how the Gods blessed you with such a beautiful

56

body. It would be a shame to add further blemishes to such smooth skin, so I'll let you off with only ten strokes."

"You're very kind, mistress," she whispered, feeling the hand travel up her back.

"And these breasts," lady Octavia continued, drawing nearer. "Why, they put my young slaves quite in the shade. Your nipples are bigger than some of my slave's tits."

It was an exaggeration, but the point was well made.

"I do have large tits, mistress," Africanus agreed, looking down at the finely manicured nails pinching her nipples.

"I'll cane you now and one of my slaves can salve you directly afterwards and perhaps a little later on you can provide me with some entertainment. Bend over and touch your toes. But first, would you prefer a gag? The cane can be very painful on naked skin, particularly when it is stretched, and crying out is seen as a sign of weakness."

"I would prefer a gag," Africanus said, not wishing to give the wrong impression to anyone who might be listening, especially Drucus whom she wanted most to impress.

"Very well, I will allow you that. Take off your skirt."

Africanus slipped it from her hips and, following her mistress' instructions, wound it into a tight rope. She put the middle of it in her mouth and knotted the ends behind her head, then bent her bare bottom to the cane.

Lady Octavia took a step to the left of her and touched the cane lightly on her bottom, gauging where the first lash would fall. It came with a savage whistle, striking across both cheeks and with such force it dug deep into her flesh. A muffled grunt escaped Africanus' lips and she toppled forward bumping her head on a pillar.

"Keep still and show more self control," lady Octavia advised, smiling widely at the welt already forming on the glistening skin.

The second, third and forth strokes landed above the first with perfect precision, the same distance apart, working upwards towards the base of her spine. The fifth and six strokes came in graceful, yet fast uppercuts, slicing under the cheeks and into the crease where thighs joined to buttocks. Lady Octavia saw the instant effect that produced, but kept silent at the sight of the erect nipples and quivering thighs. It would be worth remembering for later. The remainder of the lashes fell in diagonal strokes, criss crossing over the cheeks, making Africanus grunt and snort at every stroke.

"You may stand up," lady Octavia said happily. "And take off your gag."

Africanus untied the knot and opened the skirt. Her mouth had left a wet discolouring and a sticky mess of nose mucus dripped to the flags.

"Wipe that up," the lady said, displaying a hint of anger. "I won't have my private garden fouled by a slave."

Africanus got onto her hands and knees and used her skirt to wipe up the mess. She stood up and wrapped it around her hips and then placed her folded hands neatly over her groin.

"I think tomorrow Drucus is going to start your training, after you have taken your oath of obedience, of course. At the end of the day you will take your bath and report to me in my private quarters. Do you understand, slave?"

"Yes, mistress," she bowed.

"Now thank me for beating you."

"I am thankful for the beating," Africanus echoed.

And the lady adjusted her plaited hair whilst a slave escorted the gladiatrix back to her cell.

As promised by lady Octavia, a young girl slave appeared with a pot of balm and bottles of aromatic oils designed to heal wounds and soothe bruises. She spread a cloth over the straw and Africanus laid herself on it, hands clasped behind her head. It seemed that taking good care of the gladiators' was all part of the training ritual.

The young slave tipped some oil over Africanus' belly and rubbed it softly into the pores, humming quietly as she did so. She was dark skinned and very pretty; her hair had been tied in a bun at the nape of her slender neck.

"Tell me about your mistress," Africanus said, feeling the oil already cooling her burning skin. During that brief meeting in her private garden Africanus was sure she had missed something, and that something was dangerous, but she couldn't quite fathom what it was.

"She is the wife of Quintus, our lord and master," the girl informed, smiling and revealing rows of perfect teeth as white as orange pith.

"I know that. I want you to tell me all about her. How does she treat her slaves?"

"Oh, she's very kind, especially to us young ones. She only beats us if we've done wrong."

Africanus sighed. "Well I gathered that. What sort of entertainment does she like?"

"Eh?" the girl asked, looking confused. She tipped more oil over her charge's breasts and began manipulating the ample flesh, her slim expert fingers squeezing and pressing. She rolled the nipples between her fore finger and thumb smiling absently all the while.

"Your mistress said that I should provide her with entertainment. What exactly did she mean by that?"

The girl looked even more confused. "Oh, I think she wants you to put on a mock fight. Sometimes the men have to do that, fighting during a party. No one gets hurt. It's all for fun really."

A groan escaped Africanus lips. She had only been there a day and the idea of giving a display of mock combat was absurd. Clearly the girl was either simple or just genuinely didn't understand what she was driving at. Perhaps there was nothing to drive at. The suggestion might have been an innocent one and it was she who was getting suspicious where no necessity existed.

I must learn to relax more, she told herself, and closed her eyes as the girl gently eased open her thighs and tipped more oil onto her pubic mound. Quite oblivious to the gladiatrix' throaty purrs, she wiggled her oil soaked fingers inside the gaping sex, and then when the lips were thoroughly wetted, slipped her tiny hand into the sex tunnel. Her elbow moved slowly to and fro while her wrist twisted from side to side. Africanus was so wet from both the oil and her own juice that she hardly felt the diminutive knuckles teasing her inner petals. But she certainly felt the beating of her heart increasing with each turn of the fist, and the sudden flush of sweat breaking on her brow.

"If you go on doing that, you'll make me come," she warned.

"Come all you like, miss. It'll make you feel better after such a hard day."

"I'd rather have a hard cock," she grimaced.

For a split second the girl hesitated as if Africanus had said more than she knew, but she continued on with her oiling and salving, turning the gladiatrix on her belly and applying generous amounts of oil on her caned buttocks, working it hard into the crease, and still humming that infuriating tune. Her constant manipulating of the muscles and tendons worked wonders and when she finished Africanus had fallen into a deep slumber.

The girl gathered up her bottles and pots and tip toed out of the cell, a crafty knowing grin creasing her lips.

"The mistress is going to love you," she whispered, and crept quietly away like a thief.

At the end of the passage she stopped, her way blocked by the massive frame of Circo.

"Nydia, what are you doing here?" he asked abruptly.

"Oiling the new gladiatrix, master," she answered coyly.

His eyes narrowed suspiciously. It was unusual for a girl slave to be roaming around the gladiators' quarters at this time of night, even if she was speaking the truth, which he strongly doubted. His hand went under her legs, crushing her sex mound and pinning her against the wall.

"If you breathe a word of my being here you little lizard, I'll snap your pretty little neck."

"I won't say anything, master," she gulped, clutching the bottles tightly on her chest.

He growled and dropped her, then for good measure, slapped her face, a blow which left her reeling.

She waited until he had turned a corner and padded silently after him, keeping a respectful distance lest he should suddenly turn. She heard a cell door open and close and came quietly on, keeping well in the shadows until she reached Africanus' cell. The lamp was still burning and through the grating saw the distorted shadow of Circo loosening his breeches. A sly knowing smile went across her face and she crept closer. She stopped and furtively secreted herself in an alcove where she could see everything that was going on.

In that peculiar state of being neither asleep nor awake, Africanus drifted in and out of consciousness, unsure whether the hand slipping between her legs was real or imaginary. She stirred and a hand closed quickly over her mouth. In the dim, wavering light, she looked into the face of Circo. He took his hand away from her mouth and put his forefinger to his lips. She nodded, understanding she was not in any danger.

Her sex still throbbed in the aftermath of the oiling and

61

Nydia's slithering fingers. Circo rubbed his palm into her sex and she moved over the bed making room for his muscular, rippling torso.

"It's all right," he whispered hoarsely. "No one knows I'm here. We can fuck until dawn."

In her alcove, Nydia put down her bottles and wiped away a bead of sweat trickling down her cheek. If Circo discovered her presence he wouldn't think twice about carrying out his threat, but it was worth the risk. She made it her business to know everything that went on in the ludus and this was well worth knowing.

Again, Africanus experienced the tantalizing thrill of illicit sex, the overriding fear of being caught *in flagrante dilecto*, and the punishment that would swiftly follow. Circo was between her open thighs, kneeling up so she could see, even in that poor light, the sheer strength and power of his body. His cock was fully erect, his balls tight with longing. He slid his arms under her knees and lifted them from the bed.

"A woman is all the better when her legs are in the air," he told her, lifting them higher and higher.

Her long, shining legs were dead straight, toes pointing to the cell roof. She understood how he wanted to take her and leaning forward, grabbed her ankles and spread them wide. Circo couldn't help but utter a low whistle at the beauty of her thighs and paused, giving himself time to caress the long length of silky skin. It was too much to resist and he slipped backwards and dropped his head between her legs. A musky aroma of feminine sex wafted into his nostrils. The heat coming from her open sex warmed his face. It was a long time since he'd had a woman and he was seized with a desire to explore, touch and kiss every inch of her body. Hard man though he was, made brutal and savage in the arena, he still knew how to treat a woman. He would take his time and not leave until her body was sexually wasted. He placed the tips of his fingers inside her sex and parted the lips, taking time to feast his eyes on the quivering petals, the soft pink skin and stream of juice running freely into her pubic curls. His tongue flicked around the lips tasting the sweet essence of her excited sex. Her belly shook and creased deeply across the navel and he heard her moan.

"Please fuck me now. Please, I want your cock."

But Circo only pressed his mouth harder, letting the tip of his tongue tease her clitoris until her head rolled uncontrollably and her loins shook with longing. Her juices were running over his tongue like a river, coming from the depths of her sex in a rich creamy flood. He swallowed her juice and licked his lips. There was nothing like the earthy taste of a woman in heat to savour on the palate.

"Give me your cock," she pleaded, letting go of her ankles and grabbing his hair.

She almost ripped it from the roots before he took his mouth from her dripping sex and threw himself over her body.

His hands went straight to her breasts, rolling them under his palms, squashing them so hard it hurt. The pain going through her drove her wild and she reached down, closing her hand around his throbbing shaft.

"In my mouth," she gasped. "Let me suck you."

Circo hesitated. In the heat of passion her voluptuous lips could easily suck him off and that was not what he wanted.

"Slowly, girl," he whispered, aiming the purple glans into her mouth.

She sucked it in and ran her tongue around the deep, sensitive groove at its base, tasting his earthy aroma. For a while he held her head still, not letting her take in his whole length, just allowing her to suck and lick the swollen head. When her passion abated he let her take in his cock, her hot mouth gliding slowly down the shaft, then back again to the groove where her tongue flicked and curled.

"Suck my balls," he whispered, easing his shaft out of her mouth.

Africanus opened her mouth wide and, using her fingers, pushed his throbbing scrotum gently between her teeth. Taking care not to cause him pain, she nibbled at the fruits filling her cheeks, rolled them over her tongue and soaked them with her hot saliva. Between her legs her sex lips were quivering and so sensitive the merest touch would have had her screaming, but they both knew that would be fatal. Instead, he slipped his balls from her mouth and kissed her full on the lips. They did not stop kissing until their lips and tongues ached. Then, when she lay panting and breathless, he plunged his cock into her sex and filled her with one mighty thrust of his loins.

"How you fuck!" she sobbed, throwing her arms and legs around him.

He was caught in her powerful limbs and she clung like a limpet, pressing her sweating body against his own heaving torso. Locked in a tight embrace, they rocked to and fro, unhurried, prolonging the delicious moments of deep, satisfying sex.

Nydia had left the alcove and crawled on her hands and knees to the grating, through it she saw Circo's buttocks gyrating ceaselessly against Africanus' sex, heard her low moans and whimpers as he thrust harder and deeper.

"I want it too," she whispered, jealous of the black girl now impaled on Circo's massive organ.

It was all she could do to stop herself from slipping into the cell and begging him to fuck her. She reached for one of her bottles and slipped it into her sex. Her other hand closed over her budding breast and squeezed it hard. Her hand pumped fast and she came in seconds, so fast her head swam. She put her fingers inside her and wetted them then sucked them into her mouth. The bottle fell from her other hand and smashed on the flags. She froze; cold, clammy sweat formed under her arms and she looked tentatively through the grating. Circo paused, listened and went on thrusting his loins. A gush of air whooshed from Nydia's lungs and she crawled back into the alcove her sex dripping its juice in a slimy, glistening trail.

Africanus lifted her bottom off the bed and thrust her hips furiously against Circo's groin. His cock was deep inside her but she wanted it deeper.

"Bite my tits," she wailed, clawing at his head.

Circo's head plunged over her breasts and, placing his strong hands either side of the wobbling orbs, he pressed them together and sucked both nipples into his mouth.

"Don't suck. Bite. Bite them hard," she sobbed, longing for the increased pain that would heighten her arousal.

Circo obeyed and closed his teeth over the erect buds, rolling and crushing the tender teats until she her fists beat against his ribs in pain.

"Fuck me harder," she shrieked. "Fuck me 'til my cunt throbs."

She was losing control and shouting at the top of her voice. Circo quickly closed his hand over her mouth, stifling her shrieks. In the darkness, Nydia saw his other hand reach for her thigh, pinching and clutching at the abundance of flesh quaking beneath. Africanus was going wild at the fresh onslaught of pain going through her thighs and belly. The more pain he inflicted the greater her orgasm. He knew what she wanted and returned his mouth to her nipples, biting so hard tears flowed down her cheeks, yet all the while she gasped and panted, thrashed her legs and arms with wild abandon. No one had ever taken her with so much passion or force. His cock was spearing her vaginal walls forcing them wider from his manic thrusts, but she closed her legs around him, crushing his ribs between her flexing muscles. Circo could hardly breathe but fought hard against her shaking thighs.

"I'm going to come," he rasped, putting his arms around her shoulders and flattening her breasts against his rippling chest.

Their nipples touched and they both let out a long groan. Circo gave three gigantic heaves of his pelvis and erupted into her. Africanus slammed her hips against his middle and with one colossal shudder reached her climax. They lay entwined, panting and moaning, still locked together as the final drops of love juice oozed from their sexes. They lay there until the heated sweat turned cold and sticky. Circo uncoupled from her writhing body and lay still beside her staring at the ceiling. He didn't have the courage or heart to tell her that his master had sold him and they would probably never meet again.

Africanus slid her thigh across his middle and he reached for her bottom, smoothing the cheeks and patting the splendid moons of her arse.

"You're a glorious fuck," he told her honestly. "The Gods have favoured you well."

But she did not reply. Her breathing came regularly as she lay in contented sleep in the arms of the man she wanted to be with for the rest of her life.

Nydia crept out of the alcove and made her way along the passage, moving silently like an assassin, looking neither left nor right, but moving quickly as if she feared the approach of dawn.

CHAPTER FOUR

"I give my life and soul to my master," Africanus chanted, taking the oath of loyalty and unswerving obedience, "I shall not fear death but embrace it willingly should the Gods claim me for their own. I look upon death with contempt and my master with reverence. His word is my doing even until death."

She bowed low and prostrated herself at Quintus' feet. He touched her on the shoulder with a rudis and bade her arise.

"As from now your training begins in earnest," he said. "Work hard and well and you will be rewarded. Fail me and you will suffer my wrath. Now go and may the Gods be with you."

Tears filled her eyes, not only because of the glory of the moment, but because she had been told that Circo had been sold to another ludus in the south. The profit from the sale would be used to hire a contract gladiatrix, a woman who had sold her freedom for five years in order to pay off debts or rise to fame in the arena. She had contracted with Quintus to train Africanus and would arrive at the ludus as soon as Africanus had built up her body strength. It was left to Drucus to ensure that was accomplished, and he began immediately by setting her to work.

She was harnessed to a long heavy chain which ran over a wheel at the top of a tall wooden frame. On the other end of the chain was a heavy weight which she had to pull to the top of the frame, and when she had achieved that, she would let go and begin again until her leg and arm muscles were solid. It would also build up her softer stomach muscles until they rippled with strength.

Groaning under the weight, Africanus struggled forward

one agonizing step at a time. The leather harness was tightly fitted around her torso and generously moulded to cover her ample breasts. She was wearing her short skirt and Drucus watched admiringly as her thighs and calves strained every inch of the way. Her dark skin, covered with a fine sheen of sweat, shone in the sunlight. Her progress was slow and steady, but for Quintus watching from under the shade of the portico, it was not fast enough.

"Use the whip on her," he called to Drucus.

Drucus gathered a whip of plaited hide and stood behind her, lashing her near bare buttocks and naked back, driving her like an animal until the weight reached the top of the frame. At his signal the chain was released from the harness and the weight crashed to the ground.

"Again," he said, ignoring her parched lips. "This time I want to see you move faster, or I'll flog your arse until you can't sit down for a week."

It was no idle threat. With his master, Quintus watching her every move had no choice but to urge her on. Whipped and driven, she worked at the weight until Drucus was satisfied. At the end of the day she collapsed in the sand and lay staring at the sky, exhausted and gasping for water.

"You did well on your first day," Drucus complimented. "Tomorrow we shall put you on the rack. Now go and take your bath."

She got to her feet and staggered across the courtyard wondering if her body could take so much punishment. But it was all part of her training and she knew that if she was to succeed she would have to bear it.

It was Nydia who came to massage her tired and aching limbs, carrying her bottles of oil and a small sheaf of twigs to beat the dirt from her pores.

"You have such a beautiful body, mistress," she fawned, rubbing the sweat from Africanus' back. "And your legs, so powerful, your thighs so…"

"Shut your trap," Africanus snapped, in no mood for flattery.

All day she had been brooding on Circo and the way he had fucked her. He was the first real man who had got between her thighs and left her wanting more. The memory of his hard cock pounding inside her tingling sex was now making her agitated and frustrated. The last thing she needed was that simpleton Nydia prattling in her ear.

"I want you to massage my arse," she ordered. "Make sure you use plenty of oil."

The lashes that Drucus had sent winging into her buttocks had left her feeling sore and it would be difficult to sleep with that ache going on all night, let alone the remembrance of Circo.

"Yes, mistress," Nydia said. "Your wish is my command."

She tipped a whole bottle of oil over the lash welts and another into the buttock crease. Her tiny hands rubbed hard onto the welts until the oil had been well rubbed into the pores. She placed her fingers into the crease and pulled the buttocks apart. Africanus' chest bucked off the marble slab.

"What the fuck are you doing," she asked, looking over her shoulder.

"Oiling your arse, mistress," she replied, worming three of her slim fingers inside her anus. "It will help take away the ache and you'll shit easier."

"When you've finished putting your fingers up my arse, I want you to oil my tits. That harness gave me hell," she grunted, placing her head on her folded arms.

When Nydia had finished poking and prodding her bottom, Africanus rolled over and gazed idly at the girl now oiling her breasts. There was something about her eyes that repelled her, a curious glow that she found unsettling and her mind seemed constantly engaged elsewhere. It might have been that she was just bored or simple, and as her fingers manipulated the nipples, Africanus' thoughts turned to Circo. A flutter passed through her belly and she sniffed back a tear.

"Suck my nipples," she said suddenly.

Nydia smiled artfully, knowing what was going through the gladiatrix' mind. She laid herself on top of Africanus and puckered her lips over the dark, erect buds. Her cheeks fanned in and out as she sucked and Africanus heaved a sigh of satisfaction. Her cunt was quivering with longing, the juice already weeping from her lips.

Then without knowing why she did it, she slapped the girl's buttocks, and went on slapping until her arm ached.

"I want you to make me come," she whispered. "Use your tongue."

"I can't do that, mistress. There isn't the time. The lady Octavia is expecting you in her quarters."

"Oh, fuck the lady Octavia," Africanus thought, shoving the girl away.

Nydia gathered her bottles and scurried out of the baths with Africanus following reluctantly, muttering silent curses.

She was still muttering and swearing when she passed through the atrium into lady Octavia's private rooms. A full moon had risen and bathed the room in its silvery rays. Incense burned from copper dishes filling the room with its delightful fragrance, a sweet smelling combination of sandalwood and pine. A banquet had just taken place and slaves of both sexes hurried to clear the tables. Lady Octavia looked resplendent in a white robe trimmed with red linings. Her hair had been dressed with rows of pearls and gold trinkets and her face painted and creamed. Suddenly Africanus felt very vulnerable in her near nakedness, aware

70

that she was dressed only in her short skirt which she had not had time to change. She looked all around the room at the painted frescos depicting acts from Roman mythology, and a huge mural of Isis, Egyptian goddess of fertility whose cult many Roman women now belonged to.

On a dais were seated several local dignitaries equally as resplendent in finely woven togas and robes, all being waited upon by young naked girl slaves whose faces had been painted and made up. Their nipples and areolae had been darkened and made to look larger than they really were. All of them had been shaven between their legs and their pubic mounds scented and oiled.

"It is customary to provide entertainment for our guests," lady Octavia informed, leading Africanus by the hand into the centre of the room. "Normally we stage gladiatorial combat between our most skilled gladiators and our slaves. I need not tell you the outcome. But tonight my guests require something different. Something a little unusual. Have you heard of the land of the Hermaphrodite?" Africanus looked blank. Lady Octavia permitted herself a half smile. "No, I didn't think you had. Do you know what a Hermaphrodite is?" Again Africanus looked vacant. How the hell would she know what it was?

"A Hermaphrodite is a very special kind of woman, or man, depending on how you look at it," Lady Octavia explained.

The assembly on the dais laughed at the still blank look on the black girl's face. A slave came over carrying a tray bearing a bottle of wine and a goblet.

"Please, help yourself," lady Octavia offered. "It is customary to offer refreshment to our entertainers before they begin."

Bemused, Africanus waited until the slave filled the goblet and lifted it to her lips. It was the first time she had

71

ever tasted wine and to her surprise it tasted mellower than she imagined.

"The entertainment will begin as soon as you have finished your drink," lady Octavia informed her, and leaving her standing alone in the centre of the room returned to the dais and sprawled full length upon a couch. A slave knelt before her and placed a tray of nuts and sweets at her disposal.

From somewhere in the shadows came the plaintive tones of a flute accompanied by a slow rhythmic beating of a drum. A curtain drew back and a woman sidled into the room, swaying her hips to the sound of the music which seemed both eerie and sinister. Her limbs exhibited a curious snake-like motion when she walked which Africanus found very unsettling. She was wearing a long brown robe of deer skin and on her head a pair of horns, not unlike the sort worn by the barbarians in the northern lands. Her hair had not been plaited or curled but hung down her back in magnificent coiling tresses. It was difficult to guess its colour but as she passed under a lamp it gave the impression of auburn. Around her wrists and ankles were bracelets which jingled rhythmically as she moved. She went all around the room, gyrating her hips and buttocks in a fantastic, almost dreamlike motion.

"Is that black woman the gladiatrix you told me about?" a voice whispered in lady Octavia's ear.

"That's her, Glaucus, my husband's latest money making venture," she said bitterly.

"How much did he pay for her?" he asked, studying the black girl.

She was almost too embarrassed to answer. "Two thousand sestertia," she muttered.

"Phew," he whistled, seating himself beside her. "No wonder the ludus is almost bankrupt."

72

There was nothing she could say to that. Glaucus was a sponsor who organized and paid for the games in the arena. It was a risky business. If any of the gladiators were maimed or killed he was liable for the cost of replacing them. If no injury was sustained he made a hefty profit from a cut on all the bets taken by the book makers, not to mention the entire political enhancement they brought. He had sponsored Quintus' gladiators against combatants from his rival, Polonius, and many had been killed or totally incapacitated. Now he was reluctant to have anything to do with Quintus' school. But he had fallen in love with his wife, Octavia and together they were hatching a plan of which Africanus was the lynch pin. If she proved her worth, he would sponsor her independently as a contract gladiatrix just like the one coming to train her, and Octavia would get her share of the profits and hopefully share his bed into the bargain. It wouldn't take much to woo Octavia into bed, especially where money was involved. With luck and a little persuasion, Quintus could be coerced into parting with Africanus and the ludus in lieu of his mounting debts. Glaucus had already prepared the paperwork. Tonight's little entertainment was merely an opportunity for him to view the girl, with a bit of sport thrown in.

A slave advanced and took away Africanus' skirt rendering her completely naked.

"She has a fine body," Glaucus remarked. "And an air of confidence about her."

"We shall see how confident she is when she sees what Leda has to offer," she smirked.

Leda, still fully robed danced around Africanus, snaking her long arms above her head and drawing attention to her splendid hips. Slowly she loosened her robe; first at the top, letting it fall from her shoulders and breasts. Half naked she tugged at the cord around her waist and the robe fell open, but she quickly pulled it together again under the pit of her stomach. Africanus watched her movements with a critical eye. She assumed that when the woman was completely naked they would be expected to engage in a wrestling match or perhaps a stand up fist fight, the usual sort of entertainment the Romans liked at parties. Leda broke into a series of angular jerks and turned her back to both Africanus and the assembled company. The robe fell with at her feet and, kicking it away, she suddenly turned, throwing her arms wide.

"Oh, no," Africanus gulped, eyeing her groin.

"Oh, yes," laughed the lady Octavia.

Glaucus didn't speak a word, but stared agog at the huge penis rising from Leda's thick wiry pubic bush.

Africanus stared at the woman, or man, standing in front of her. She wasn't quite sure what it was, a human being built like a woman with magnificent rounded breasts, pert feminine buttocks and a huge rampant male cock. If the hideous Proteus could see that he would have been consumed with jealousy. It was as long as a baby's arm and of the same girth, if not thicker.

Lady Octavia rose from the couch and the music stopped abruptly.

"Tonight, we hark back to the mythology of ancient Greece," she addressed the assembly, in shrill, silvery tones. "And we are pleased to give you a re-enactment of the legend of Persiphae and the Bull. As you know Persiphae fell in love with a bull and the result of their union was the Minotaur. For the purpose of tonight's entertainment, Leda will play the part of the Bull and Africanus the part of Persiphae."

The assembly arose from their seats and broke into a deafening cheer.

"Are you sure she can take a cock of that size. It will

surely kill her," Glaucus observed, looking at Africanus' terror stricken face.

"If she can take that, she can take anything," lady Octavia replied. "I did hear that one of the tests my husband subjected her too was mating with a man famed for his large cock. Look upon this as a further test of a similar kind, and a laugh for us at the same time."

But Africanus wasn't laughing. As soon as the implication of lady Octavia's announcement sank in she felt sick. She was expected to degrade and humiliate herself with this creature, and in public. There seemed to be no end to their disgusting perversions. She glanced quickly around the room. Every doorway and entrance was heavily guarded, and there were enough willing slaves to bring her down if she attempted to flee. She only wished that Circo were there to defend her, but that was wishful thinking. He could not have defended her even if he had wanted to. Disobedience was rewarded with death.

"What am I supposed to do?" she whispered, as Leda advanced towards her.

"Make love to me," she whispered in return, then she said aloud, "Get on your hands and knees, Persiphae; we are going to beget the Minotaur."

Not on your fucking life, Africanus thought, taking a step backwards and clenching her fists.

Lady Octavia's eyes narrowed with anger. The girl was supposed to submit, not put up a fight.

"I'm sorry," she apologized to Glaucus.

"No, no. I like surprises, and it shows the girl has spirit. I'm interested to see the outcome."

"Stop fooling around," Leda hissed. "You're going to have my cock whether you want it or not."

She was a slave like Africanus and knew the penalty for failure. Lady Octavia was getting impatient. Leda could

75

see the knitted brows and glowering expression as she motioned her forward.

"Look, you stupid bitch, if you don't spread your arse, we'll both be for the drop. They'll have us both in the arena. They'll crucify me and mate you with a real bull. So stop stalling and get on your knees," Leda hissed, sliding her arm around Africanus' waist.

Everything she said made sense. The Romans were a volatile people and not used to disobedience. When thwarted they could be very unpredictable and dangerous.

"All right, I'll have your cock," Africanus surrendered. "But just go easy with that thing."

She still wasn't sure whether the cock was real or false, but it looked real enough. There were no strings attached to it or any other means of keeping it there if it were faked. She put her arms around Leda's shoulders and their bodies met in a loving embrace, belly to belly, thigh to thigh, breast to breast they hugged each other close and kissed long and slow, tongues diving and searching into their mouths. Africanus could see and feel the relief on Leda's face as she submitted to her amorous caresses. Their hands slithered down each others backs and grasped their buttocks, pulling them close, grinding their sexes together. The cock rearing up against Africanus' belly felt hot and throbbing, pulsating with life as its heat spread through the pit of her stomach. It was real! By all the Gods, the creature really was half man, half woman!

A wave of sexual excitement passed through her, a curious combination of lust and exploration of the unnatural. She never imagined that such creatures could exist, a female with a male sex organ was something that belonged in the realms of mythology, now here she was, breast to breast, belly to belly, holding what was undoubtedly a woman, yet between her legs throbbed a

76

rampant cock that any woman would give her life for.

"What do I do?" Africanus whispered, fully warmed to the idea of being male fucked by a person of her own sex.

"Just obey me," Leda breathed, relieved that the stupid bitch was not going to knock her senseless after all. "Get on your back and spread your legs."

Africanus slithered to the floor shaking her buttocks and breasts, playing up to the assembly. Lady Octavia beamed her approval and shot both participants a loving smile, also relieved that the act would go well.

Leda, snaking her hips, fell over Africanus, opening her legs and swinging her thigh over the black girl's face. Her own head went between the parted thighs, slipping her tongue into the hot juicy slit. Africanus sucked in the cock, stretching her lips around its enormous girth. She knew that she couldn't possibly engulf it all, sucking it right to the back of her throat, so she concentrated on the dark purple head, playing her lips over the silky surface, licking and lashing it with her tongue. Suddenly they were all fingers and tongues, searching and probing, licking and sucking. Leda slipped her fingers inside Africanus' sex, working them fast while she teased the clitoris, making Africanus buck and squirm her hips and buttocks. Her hand was around the shaft, rubbing it up and down, still marveling at its size, while she sucked it deeper into her mouth. Her jaws ached stretched over the glans but, holding her breath, she plunged her head upwards letting her lips slide into the groove. Another plunge and she sucked it as far as she could, her mouth fully stuffed with throbbing cock. Leda had stretched Africanus' sex as far as she dared, pulling open the fleshy sex lips, getting her tongue and all four fingers of her hand inside the dribbling tunnel. They continued pleasuring each other until Leda dismounted and rolled Africanus onto her belly.

"Up on your knees," she whispered, and Africanus was there at once, on all fours, rocking on her hands and knees, longing for Leda to penetrate her tingling sex.

"I think she's going to take it," Glaucus said, his face set and serious.

Lady Octavia rested her hand strategically on his thigh. He was hard as a rock. She could see the bulge expanding under his toga. She thought that after the entertainment it wouldn't take much to get him in her bed and strike the lucrative bargain that would make her rich.

Leda positioned herself at Africanus' rear, opening her legs and sliding herself between the spreading thighs. Africanus lowered her buttocks and thrust backwards just as Leda guided her cock into the gaping sex. The whole assembly was watching now, standing up, looking over the shoulders of those in front, and peering around pillars and curtains.

Africanus' buttocks went into a devastating orgiastic gyration, the buttocks wobbling and shaking so fast the flesh rippled.

"Look at that arse," Glaucus cried, his throat dry with despair.

"It is beautiful," lady Octavia remarked, gripping his cock under the toga.

"It's brilliant of you to discover her," he complimented, as her hand crept towards his balls.

"Yes," she said, thankful that Quintus was away on business.

Leda was up on her hands, arms as straight as spear shafts, her calves clinging into the curve of Africanus' hips. Her pelvis moved fast, pumping her organ into Africanus' sex. The cries of agony and pain her cock usually brought forth from any hapless, unsuspecting victim were noticeably absent. Instead, Africanus panted like a mare in heat, harsh stentorian groans grunted from her throat, coming faster and faster, and a sound which Glaucus found unbelievably sexual. There was nothing more arousing and guaranteed to give a man a hard on than the groaning and grunting of a woman in the throes of fucking her heart out. He wondered if lady Octavia made such a din when she was being fucked. He was also thinking that if she wanted his money to sponsor the gladiatrix, he was entitled to his share of the goods.

Leda threw back her head gasping for air, her back was arched so much it was a wonder her spine didn't crack. It wasn't often she had the opportunity to fuck a woman whose cunt matched her own outsized organ. In response, her lover was thrusting her hips and buttocks, making the arse cheeks wobble and slap so loudly that Glaucus could hear the rapid bap, bap, bap sound they made as each cheek collided with the other. He could also see her massive breasts swinging from her chest, going to and fro unison, so large that her nipples almost touched the floor. That was another thing he found amazingly sexual; a woman sitting astride him, fully penetrated and leaning forward so she could swing her tits over his chest letting the nipples just flit lightly on the skin. Lady Octavia had good tits, he thought, and slipped his hand inside her robe, groping her breast.

Her hand had stopped just short of bringing him off. "You can have me tonight," she whispered.

He almost replied that he'd rather have the gladiatrix sitting on his rod, but stopped himself just in time. He drew lady Octavia's head close and kissed her full on the lips. Her hand gripped his cock tight, and in the shadows, unseen by anyone, Nydia was watching everything that was going on. She saw her mistress and Glaucus kissing passionately, the strange Hermaphrodite fucking that black girl who had slapped her bottom, she hadn't forgotten that, or when she had fucked with Circo who'd threatened to snap her pretty little neck. She stayed in the shadows watching both the actors reach their climax; the black gladiatrix grunting like a wounded bear, her strange companion emitting a piercing shriek and collapsing on her back, still writhing like a serpent, the horns on her head twisted into a funny angle. Africanus fell forward and landed with a smack on her belly. She had mated with the bull and felt content, smiling at the thought of giving birth to a Minotaur.

"Well done both of you," lady Octavia applauded.

The two women stood up and Leda raised Africanus' arm high in response to the deafening cheer rising from the assembly.

A guard escorted Africanus back to her cell, on the way she took a bottle of wine that a slave offered. Leda returned to the brothel from which she had been fetched hoping it wasn't the last time she'd mate with that beautiful black girl.

Lady Octavia and Glaucus retired discreetly to her bed chamber. He was in the mood for a night of torrid sex.

Nydia smiled slyly and went off to her room. There was much she had to report when her master, Quintus returned.

CHAPTER FIVE

A mile away from the glittering villas of Quintus and Glaucus lay the poorer areas of the city; a warren of dark unlit narrow streets and alleys inhabited by thieves, criminals, prostitutes, and runaway slaves. No respectable citizen would be seen dead there, unless he had wandered into it by mistake. It was here that the entire underworld dealing in stolen goods took place, along with murderous plotting and every other crime imaginable. It was also a good place to make money if you knew the right people, or spend a night with a prostitute in the numerous lupanars, or brothels. Despite their lowly existence, the prostitutes who worked in them were still protected by Roman law. They had to wear a red robe denoting their trade, but still had the right to refuse a client if they chose, or could haggle over the price of their services. Most of them lived in their own rooms and came and went in and out of the lupanars as the mood suited them.

In the House of the Olives, a lupanar tucked discreetly at the end of a blind alley, a tall dark man was telling one of the prostitutes he was a successful trader in gold and silver. The prostitute was listening intently and had just told him her name was Claudia.

Both of them were lying.

They were seated in a corner of the room where drinks were served, hardly visible to one another in the gloom. A guttering oil lamp cast its wavering shadows over their faces; the prostitute had a broad face with dark, heavily painted eyes, wide painted lips and high cheek bones. Her hair, wild and unkempt, was partially covered under a red shawl. She had good breasts which were mostly visible in the dim light. The man was unshaven with a running scar etched down one side of his face. He was handsome in the rugged threatening way that some women found sexy. He told her his name was Plutarc and ordered her another drink.

The prostitute noticed his eyes kept wandering all over her body. When he spoke he addressed his words to her breasts rather than her face. He was also looking at her legs splendidly bare now that the robe had parted. He liked the look of her thighs and made no attempt to disguise his hardening cock. The prostitute crossed her legs and he nearly dropped his cup. A man would kill to get between those thighs, let alone bury his head at their apex. He reached out and cupped her breast, giving it a soft squeeze. She grabbed his cock and stroked it, and then lifted her cup and stared at him over the rim with seductive, smouldering eyes. He looked back then at her cleavage which had become more exposed. He could see right into her cleft and saw her breasts quiver when she moved. He couldn't quite see her nipples, they were still covered but the teats were hard. He couldn't miss that. He always thought a woman looked very sexy with hard nipples poking at a flimsy dress or robe or whatever it was she was wearing. His cock was throbbing so much he had to reach under his tunic and let it stand up against his belly.

"You've gone hard," she observed, whispering in a low husky voice.

She didn't smile or lick her lips like the other whores in this dump, neither did she open her legs and invite him to feel her cunt. He was beginning to think she wasn't the ordinary sort of whore one found in this part of the city. She certainly wasn't in a hurry to get on her back or in any other position her client demanded. He liked that, showed she wasn't a common tart but more discerning with whom she slept. In a place like this that was very unusual, most of the tarts fucked at least ten or fifteen men a night. He knew of one who had got through thirty and so far had not been beaten on that tally.

"So, you trade in gold and silver," she said, resting her hand on his knee. "I wonder why you bother with a place like this. A man in your position could have the pick of the lupanars in Rome."

"I prefer to conduct my business in Marcellum," he replied, putting his hand on her thigh.

"You like the women of Marcellum?" she asked, moving her hand in slow circles.

"I like you," he whispered, opening the top of her robe so all of her breasts were exposed. "You've got good tits." He reached under her thighs and stroked her rump. "And a nice arse."

"You're very muscular," she complimented, closing her hand around his cock, and wondering how a man who was supposed to be a dealer in precious metals had such a finely toned body. Only men used to hard physical labour had muscles of that size. He was also swarthy and sunburned.

"How did you get this?" she wondered, running a fingertip along the running scar.

It was a bit of a gamble asking a question like that. He could easily slap her in the mouth and tell her to mind her own fucking business.

"One of my customers refused to pay up," he said, and grinned at her.

Normally she would have just nodded and carried on with her banter, but this one made her shudder, not only because she knew he was lying about being a trader, but also she was actually beginning to find him intriguing.

"I like men who won't take any nonsense," she said. "It shows strength."

"You like strong men," he grinned again, putting his hand under her bottom and almost lifting her from the bench.

83

A shiver went through her loins. In the half light he looked both amazingly handsome and dangerous, the sort of combination that women found attractive in gladiators.

"Have you ever fought in the arena?" she asked suddenly, without thinking.

"A long time ago," he muttered, ordering more drinks.

The room was filling and more prostitutes and their clients crowded the benches and tables. The air was thickening with ribald conversation and a heavy overtone of sex. Some of the whores were half naked, blatantly displaying their wares to anyone who cared to buy them; others were fully robed and leaned invitingly against the walls. Younger and inexperienced whores rushed up to any man that entered the room and threw their arms around them. But the high class whore and the bogus precious metal dealer sat quietly sipping their drinks, hands resting on knees and thighs.

One of the men coming into the room grabbed one of the young whores around the waist and lifted her high in the air. She shrieked as he threw her over his shoulder and carried her up the rickety staircase leading to the squalid rooms above, slapping her bare rump as he went.

The high class whore's heart skipped a beat. She liked men who treated their women rough; the feel of course stubble on her cheek or thighs, especially on her thighs, and the tight grip of hands on her hips as he penetrated her, and then being ridden long and hard. The man she was with seemed to be the sort that liked a long hard ride. Yet strangely, he wasn't in a hurry. Most men who came in here wanted to get inside the first willing whore they came across, and perhaps one or two, or maybe three after that. This man was sitting beside her, arm now around her shoulder and warding off any competition with an icy glare.

"I think it's time we went upstairs," he said suddenly.

84

"Oh, do you," she replied, lifting her finely arched brows and going wide eyed. She was also aware of a sudden wetness between her legs, which didn't happen all that often with clients. It took the right man to make her go wet. Her shoe slipped to the end of her foot and balanced precariously on her toes. The hand that wasn't groping his cock began stroking her left thigh.

"You haven't said how much you're going to pay me yet," she half whispered, and leaned closer into his shoulder.

"That's because you haven't asked."

"How about a gold bracelet?"

"I can get ten whores for that," he said abruptly.

It was probably true. Some of the whores in this part of the city sold themselves for less than the price of a loaf of bread.

"Supposing you tell me what you really do for a living," she whispered, turning her shoulders so the robe slipped from them.

Her breasts were almost bare and he could see her dark nipples rising proudly from her breasts.

"I'm a contract killer," he said starkly, without a smile or even a twitch of his lips.

She looked around the room and back again. "I don't believe you. You're making it up."

"Do I look as if I'm making it up?"

His eyes narrowed and he stared straight at her, ignoring her naked breasts and begging nipples. He did not look as if he were making anything up. In his eyes she saw no emotion whatever. His face, handsome though it was might have been set in stone, and she knew he was telling the truth.

"Let's go upstairs," she said. "You can have me free."

He bought a bottle of wine and they headed up the stairs and along a corridor so dark and narrow they could only walk in single file. She led the way into a small dingy room lighted by a single lamp. A bed stood against graffiti covered walls and under it was an earthenware bowl of stagnant water. He closed the door and shot the bolt.

"Take off your robe," he said unceremoniously.

"Are you usually this coarse?" she asked, slipping the robe from her shoulders.

It fell to the boards with a soft rustle and she stood entirely naked, except for her shoes. His tunic came off and sailed over her head. For a few moments they said nothing, but just stood admiring each other.

"Is it really true?" she asked. "You do kill people for a living?"

"Only when I'm asked," he said flatly, and came forward putting his powerful arms around her shoulders, crushing her to his chest.

By Jupiter, my cunt's soaking, she thought, and opened her mouth wide.

They kissed for what seemed a very long time, then without warning he scooped her up in his arms as if she were a child and tossed her on the bed. She had almost reached an orgasm even before he touched her. She lay naked and open, eyes closed, waiting for him to dive between her legs and penetrate her with his rampant organ.

"I suppose you've fucked half of Marcellum in here," he said dully, lifting the bottle to his lips.

She opened her eyes and saw him standing naked like one of the massive statues that supported the entrance to the arena. His cock was hard and nodding gently.

"I've had my fair share," she replied, startled at the question and fixing her eyes on his massive torso. "Everything from senators to boys," she added with a wicked grin.

"Do you do everything that's asked of you?"

"Within reason," she said softly, wondering what he had in mind.

He went to the window and opened the shutter. A cool fresh breeze sweetened the fetid air. "Come over here," he ordered.

She got off the bed and joined him at the window, resting her arms on the ledge and looking out over the rooftops. Her body was bent at the waist thrusting out her bottom.

"Keep still," he said, and upended the bottle neck between her shoulder blades.

The wine trickled down her spine, gathered in a small pool where her hips swelled, and ran through her bottom crease. Slowly the liquid soaked into her pubic curls mingling with her own juice. Her skin tingled all over her body.

"Open your legs," she heard him say.

Slowly and deliberately, she opened them, spreading her shoes wide over the floor. She heard him move and the bottle was put down. He was kneeling behind her, putting his arms around her thighs. He picked up the bottle and angled the neck into her sex, moving it from left to right. She shivered as the contents trickled down the insides of her thighs.

"No one's ever done this before," she whispered, then jolted as the tip of his tongue ran up her thighs in one long sweep.

Her sex was fully open and dripping wine and sex juice, plop plopping to the boards, a sound which made her even wetter. Her nipples, squashed against the window sill, tingled so much she was almost in tears. Then his tongue was in her sex, licking at the lips, going deeper into her, savouring the wine and her own more earthy taste. He licked and sucked her until her orgasm came in a flood, covering his mouth and chin with a fine creamy liquid.

"Will you fuck me, please," she begged.

There was no reply. The silence in the room was savage. On the other side of the street a door opened onto a balcony and a whore with her client came out to take the air. She was unashamedly naked and leaned over the edge looking into the street below. The high class whore wondered if they could see her, arms folded; bare breasted and desperately wanting the throbbing sex organ rearing up somewhere behind her. But her client, the contract killer, held her legs rigid while he swept his tongue up through her bottom crease, and kept on sweeping it all the way up her back. He stood up and aimed his organ into her sex, grabbed her hips and pulled her backwards.

"Oh!" she grunted, and felt his full length sliding further and further into her dripping tunnel.

She leaned over the sill sweating even in the cool breeze, breathing in short, sharp pants, thrusting her bottom against his pelvis. On the other side of the street the young whore and her client had gone back into their room and closed the door, plunging the night into darkness. Behind her, he pumped his loins with a savage ferocity, taking his cock to the brink of her sex then ramming it in with full force.

"Oh Jupiter, save me," she gasped, his hands gripping so tight she was held fast against the sill.

"You're a good fuck," he complimented. "Not bad for an older whore."

She would have returned the compliment, but he had moved closer and, gathering his strength, actually used his thighs and loins to lift her bodily upwards. Now she was suspended on his cock, impaled on the hard rod of man flesh spearing her to the hilt. The constant thumping going on at her rear pushed her further over the sill until she clutched at the sides for support. Her sex oozed from the sheer ecstasy of being so well fucked, and the frightening prospect of tumbling head over tits onto the cobbles below. Her arms shot out baring her whole chest and breasts to anyone who cared to look up. She let out a scream as her whole body lurched forward, arms flailing the air. Her middle was resting on the sill, while he continued his relentless thrusting. His cock was rubbing her clitoris so fast her head swam. If he released his grip now she'd fall to her death. She was totally at his mercy and the idea made her come in torrents.

"In you come," he rasped, hauling her over the sill, standing her upright on the floor.

She looked a mess, hair tumbling over her face now flushed with fear and in the glowing aftermath of orgasm. Her sex and thighs were soaking, stained with wine and sex juice.

"I feel dizzy," she laughed, relieved that she was back on firm ground.

"Get on your knees," he ordered, ignoring her smile.

"Now?" she gasped. "But I…Aghhh."

The slap he delivered nearly knocked her unconscious. "Now," he said dangerously.

She dropped to her knees bringing her head level with his cock. He was still hard even after what must have been a good hour of ceaseless fucking. There was no need to ask what was expected from her, and she opened her mouth, guiding his cock to the back of her throat.

"You need showing who's master in here," she heard him say, and he slapped the side of her head.

No one ever dared treat her like this. The last client, a drunken tailor who had raised his hand had been sent crashing down the rickety stairs. This man was different. He was treating her like a slave, abusing her, fucking her rotten whilst teetering her on the edge of death, ordering her around like a menial, and now slapping her into the middle of next week. And she loved every bit of it. His body exuded strength and male virility, every muscle rippled; his unshaven face bristled in the dim light and she wished he would rub the stubble into her throbbing sex.

She sucked hard on his cock, wanting him to fill her throat with his hot juice. She reached under his legs and cupped his balls in her palm. She'd had men of all shapes and sizes in her hand, but his balls were hard inside the tight sac she now gently fondled.

"Squeeze harder," he told her. "Let's see what you're really made of."

Her hand closed around his balls and squeezed as hard as it dared, expecting him to cry out with pain. But not a sound came, just a muffled grunt as he erupted into her mouth. He kept her there until she'd swallowed every drop of sperm, then let her go and reached for the wine.

"Get on your back," he gulped, indicating the bed.

Another slap landed on her shoulder and she went crashing onto the bed, wondering just how much more of this animal sex she could actually take. She opened her legs and pointed her toes to the ceiling, splitting her sex wide. He knelt between her thighs and tipped the last of the wine over her belly and sex. Then, while she gulped for air, he fell on her, licking every pore of her skin, nibbling and sucking her clitoris until she cried out for him to stop, but inwardly hoping it would go on until day break. When her sex was soaking he plunged into her, crushing her ample breasts under his hairy sweating chest. His hands grabbed tufts of her hair and forced her head backwards. In an instant his mouth was on her nipples, biting and rolling the teats, sending fierce darts of pain shooting through her chest. She could feel the coarse stubble rubbing and grating her soft skin, going all around her breasts, then up through the cleft and onto her neck. She was on fire from the stubble ripping against her face. Her whole body was one uncontrollable mass of tingling pins and needles.

"Fuck me hard, you bastard," she screamed, thumping her fists into his ribs.

"You call me a bastard, you dirty whore," he rasped, slapping her face.

"Bastard," she cried again, and turned her head as his hand smacked her cheek.

"You filthy whore," and his pelvis jerked so hard she went breathless.

"Ride me hard, you shit," she shrieked, reaching up and grasping her ankles.

"I'll punish you for that," he told her, and started slapping her thighs so hard the pale flesh turned red. She could even see the livid imprints left by his fingers.

He rode her till he came, then without ceremony or the slightest thought for her feelings rolled her over on her belly and slapped her bottom until she sobbed.

Leaving her for a moment, he went to the door and yelled along the passage for one of the brothel servants to bring more wine. She looked at him through tear filled eyes. In that state he could have done anything he wanted, no matter how revolting or perverse, but he merely paid the servant and bolted the door.

"Drink," he said, shoving the bottle into her belly.

She sat up and took what he offered. "You said you killed people for a living," she belched. "Would you kill someone for me, if I asked you to?"

He took the bottle and swallowed half its contents then eyed her suspiciously. "Maybe. But I don't always kill for a living. I just make people disappear."

"Ooh," she purred. "A magician, then."

"If you're trying to be clever, I'll piss all down your back," he warned.

Her jaw dropped. She wasn't sure whether he meant that. But then again, looking at his flashing eyes he could be capable of anything.

"I'd rather you fucked me again," she invited. "But before you do, tell me honestly, how do you make people disappear?"

"Easily," he said. "Now sit on my cock."

He swung his legs off the bed and she stood over him, straddling his middle. Lowering her hips, she reached under her legs and guided his organ into her sex. Her arms went around his broad shoulders and she sat on him throwing back her head, open mouthed as he penetrated her. He leaned back and grabbed the bottle, drinking its sour contents while she rode him with a steady motion of her hips and bottom.

"More?" he offered, holding out the bottle.

When she went to take it, he moved his arm away and, taking another hefty draught, sent a long hissing stream cascading over her face and breasts, then laughed so loudly the flimsy partitions seemed to shake. When he stopped laughing he passed her the bottle and let her drink her fill.

"It's nice being fucked by a real man," she gasped, forcing her sex hard onto his cock.

"You're a good piece of fucking flesh yourself," he complimented, rolling her tits under his palms. "And in good condition for an old woman."

"I'm not old," she protested, and rode him faster.

He took hold of her hands and lowered her backwards until her head almost touched the floor. His cock was touching her clitoris and she cried out, throwing her calves behind his back, locking them tight while he thrust his pelvis on and off the bed. He wondered who she really was. Not a common whore, certainly, but quite a dirty bitch in her own peculiar way. He guessed she was probably a widow or divorcee making a few coins on the side. There were a lot of them in this town. They went on riding until they both came and her legs slipped from his back and she hit the floor, groaning as her arse thumped on the boards.

"Your turn," he said, collapsing on the bed.

She struggled to her feet, still wearing her shoes. "For what?"

"To fetch another bottle."

She reached for her robe, but he tore it from her grasp. "Go as you are."

"Naked?" she gulped.

"Naked," he confirmed, and pointed to the door.

Her feet padded across the boards and she went out into the corridor, bawling along the passage for the servant.

"Go and fetch it yourself," he ordered from the bed.

She turned to look at him. "Please, I can't go down there like this."

"Why are you so bashful all of a sudden? Half the town must've seen you in the raw. Now get downstairs."

She went along the passage and halted at the top of the stairs. The room below was packed, but luckily at this hour of the morning most of the occupants were either so drunk or sleepy after spending the night with the whores that very few paid her attention. She didn't summon the servant, but snatched a bottle from the nearest table and hurried upstairs. He was looking out of the window when she came in, watching the first rays of dawn peeping over the roofs. She stopped to admire his strong back tapering to a pair of tight masculine buttocks, and for the hundredth time that night her sex felt wet. She noticed a scar on his shoulders that could only have come from a gladius or lance.

She joined him at the window and they stood side by side, drinking and belching, spitting onto the pavement below.

"Who are these people you want disappearing?" he asked suddenly, heading for the bed.

She had to think about that. It would be unwise to give away too much at this stage without knowing more about him.

"Just people I know," she shrugged. "I just wondered if it could be done, that's all."

"Oh, it can be done all right. All I need are their names, a description and where they live."

"And then what happens?"

"That depends on just how far you want to go, and how much you're willing to pay."

"I can raise the money. I just want to know what actually happens to them."

"They disappear. I know of men working the oars in slave galleys who only a short while ago were in the senate, and women working as slaves in stone quarries who were once married to rich landowners. So you see, it doesn't necessarily involve killing."

Her face screwed in thought. "I've let you have tonight free. Would you accept that as payment?"

"I only work for money," he informed bluntly. "Now supposing you tell me who you really are."

She told him she was just a penniless widow down on her luck and had been robbed of her inheritance and wanting revenge. He seemed satisfied with the explanation and they fell into each others arms just as the sun's rays angled into the room.

"Next time we meet I'm going to whip you," he promised. "After I've fucked you so hard you'll need a stretcher to carry you home."

And he got up and left.

94

CHAPTER SIX

It was at the end of her first week's training that Quintus summoned Africanus. She had done well and was beginning to build up her body strength. Her stomach muscles were harder and her biceps more pronounced, but she still retained the very essence of feminine beauty. Her bottom, hips and breasts were still shapely and her legs magnificent with their gorgeous contours. She came over from the training apparatus and bowed.

"You sent for me, master."

Quintus folded his arms over his chest and eyed her speculatively.

"In my profession I have had to deal with many a disobedient slave, but I have to say that you are by far the worst that has ever incurred my displeasure. After you allowed the driver to mate with you, you were warned that from then on coupling with any man was strictly forbidden. So why did you allow Circo, the gladiator I was obliged to sell in order to hire a gladiatrix to train you, access into your cell?"

Africanus looked at his stern face, wondering how in hell he could have known that. She was sure there wasn't another soul in the place.

"I have nothing to say, master, except admit my guilt and give you my solemn promise it will never happen again."

"Ha, your promises aren't worth the lips that utter them. You took an oath of obedience and have broken it, and I am fully aware that flogging your backside has no effect whatever. If anything it increases your carnal cravings and makes you even more determined to satisfy them. Therefore, on this occasion I shall make the punishment fit the crime. Report to the gladiators' quarters at sundown."

And he stalked off, making a mental note to reward Nydia for her trouble.

Africanus returned to the apparatus, a horizontal wooden pole, not too dissimilar to the one she used to turn in the grinding house, except this one had chains fixed to it at about knee height and when the pole turned at high speed the chains whipped from it and she had to jump over them as they spun round. All designed to test her speed and agility. It had taken three whole days to master that and the backs of her calves still pained.

Another test she had to undergo was the rack, a strange looking wooden bed to which her wrists and ankles were fastened. Slaves turned a wheel at its base and slowly her arms began to wrench from their sockets. Her task was to use all her strength resisting the wheel and prevent her shoulders from dislocating. It was all the slaves could do to concentrate when Africanus, naked except for her short skirt strained and heaved at the axle. As her bottom lifted from the bed so the skirt rode up her thighs, giving them a splendid view of her pubic mound and parted slit. In the heat her body sweated and glistened and more than one slave, feigning heat stroke, went off to the toilet to masturbate.

Once or twice the Lady Octavia came into the training area and, seating herself under the cool shade of an arbour, delighted in watching the black gladiatrix being put through her paces. Now that she was getting more muscular her body was taking on a much more ravishing appearance, and it would be a strange man indeed who did not find her sexually arousing. Soon, when she was fully trained she might be worth her weight in gold, even in the literal sense of the words.

At the end of the day, Africanus, after taking her bath

and having eaten her meal duly reported to the gladiators' quarters. As a general rule she was never allowed anywhere near the gladiators, nor they near her. There were about twenty men undergoing training or already fighting in the arena, and they had just finished bathing when she passed through the arch into their training ground.

The barrage of hoots and shouts never came for they were highly disciplined men and each one remained silent, coolly appraising her body thinking to himself what he would like to do with her given half the chance. Unbeknown to them, that chance had come. Only Galba, the champion had received Quintus' instructions, and he ushered her into their common room where the table was being cleared of plates and cups.

"The master has instructed us to punish you," he said flatly, and he ordered one of the gladiators onto the table.

He lay naked on his back, with Africanus eyeing his erection. She wondered why all gladiators had such enormous cocks. Something to do with their training, she supposed. A hand came behind her and whipped away her skirt, leaving her completely naked.

"I suppose you're all going to have me," she sighed, fearing the worst.

"Correct," Galba confirmed.

"And he's first, I suppose?"

"Well, sort of," Galba smirked. "Now get on that table and straddle his cock."

When she swung a long shapely black thigh over his middle the men couldn't resist but utter their approval in low, sinister murmurings. Her bottom hovered above him while she reached under her legs and grasped his cock. He penetrated her easily and she gasped as her buttocks sank onto his thighs. Months of total abstinence had given them rock hard erections, and it was only because of their iron training and discipline they didn't rush forward and take her there and then.

Africanus leaned forward, taking her weight on her hands, placing them on his chest and rocking back and forth on her haunches.

Maybe this punishment wouldn't be so bad after all, if all she had to do was fuck each man in turn. She thought she could handle that and smiled to herself thinking how stupid her master was if he thought this would put her off having sex.

"Lie over him," Galba ordered. "Flat on your breasts and belly."

Grunting, she lowered her body, squashing her enormous breasts on his chest. A pair of hands grabbed her ankles and spread them over the table.

"Nice arse," Galba remarked, patting each buttock. "Nice bum hole too," he added, struggling against the laughter threatening to burst from his lungs.

At his signal another gladiator clambered onto the table. On all fours he crawled between her open legs and stopped short of the cock embedded deep in her.

"Put your hands on your bum cheeks and part them," Galba told her.

She did as she was ordered and placed her hands on her buttocks easing them open at the centre of the crease. The gladiator was on her at once, aiming his cock into her anus, giving vigorous shoves of his loins, not stopping until he was fully immersed in her bottom.

"I have to take two of you at once?" she shrieked, feeling both cocks ramming inside her.

"Well, sort of," Galba grinned.

Then he ordered another man onto the table, this time kneeling at her head.

"Open your mouth," Galba said, and this time he really

did erupt into laughter.

Africanus clenched her jaw. Having men in her cunt and anus simultaneously was bad enough let alone another in her mouth.

"You need persuading," Galba said, no longer laughing as he slipped off his belt.

A loud crack echoed around the room and Africanus' thigh went rigid. Her thighs were the only part of her body he could readily lash and he wasted no time in convincing her that resistance was pointless.

"All right, I'll suck him," she wailed, and her jaw dropped open.

"I've never seen anything like that in my life," one of the men remarked seriously. "A woman having three cocks at once."

"This is only the beginning," Galba told him. "Our master has given me strict instructions that she is not to be released from our custody until she's heartily sick of having so much cock."

"She'll be sick all right, after she's got a belly full of spunk."

There was more in that observation than he realized. They had as much time as they wanted to slake their lusts and it was probable that each man could get an erection at least three, perhaps four times before his strength failed.

Africanus lay sandwiched between the two men, her bottom cheeks spreading under the weight of the man riding her arse and her breasts crushed against the man beneath her. It seemed she was drowning in a sea of sperm flooding her sex, arse and mouth. She coughed and spat out a globule of spunk. The man at her rear had finished and pulled out of her. Already her bottom was sore and her cunt ached from the twin assaults going on inside her belly.

"Have mercy, for pity's sake," she pleaded. "I can't take

all of you, not in my mouth and bottom."

"You'll have what the master orders," Galba said gleefully.

"Fuck the master," she blurted, wiping her lips with the back of her hand.

Galba ignored that and ordered another three men onto the table. "You're going to have all of us whether you like it or not, so you may as well shut your trap," he said, stroking his chin in thought.

While another three men mounted her he whispered to the nearest gladiator. "I'll wager you fifty denarius she can take both of us in her mouth."

"It's not possible. No woman could have two men at once."

He shook his head. "That woman could satisfy a horse."

They waited patiently until the next three men riding her had dismounted and ordered her onto her knees.

She climbed off the table and dropped to the floor.

"Please I need the pot," she pleaded.

"You can piss after you've had both of us in your mouth," Galba said roughly.

Not for the first time did a feeling of complete helplessness overwhelm her. Her master had sent her there as a plaything, and there was nothing she could do, or anyone who would come to her aid. She only wished that Circo was there to defend her. But more and more he was becoming a distant memory. All she could do now was suffer the constant humiliation and pain inflicted by her tormentors.

She opened her mouth and felt Galba's cock glide effortlessly between her lips. Once inside her mouth, he angled his body sideways, making room for his companion. Lacinius stood beside him watched by the rest of the gladiators staring in disbelief at his cock gliding in beside

100

Galba. The throbbing cock heads touched and her cheeks swelled, stuffed full of the two cocks pushing against them. Slowly the men rocked on their heels, letting her mouth gently ride their erections, but keeping well inside her hot, soft lips.

"I told you this bitch could have a horse," Galba remarked. "Now let's see if we can both come at once. That'll give her something to swallow, eh lads?"

Involuntarily, she reached up and held both organs in her hands, steadying the throbbing shafts now pressing deeper in her throat. She flicked her tongue over the pulsating tips, teasing the shining, delicate skin, working her tongue under and over the grooves.

"The bitch knows how to use her tongue," Galba remarked, grinning.

Lacinius said nothing, but stared at the widely stretched lips, creasing at the edges, wondering how she could take so much male meat in her mouth at one time. In a way he was beginning to admire this beautiful black gladiatrix. She certainly had courage if nothing else. Even the most seasoned whores in the lowest lupanars of Marcellum would have baulked at taking three men at once, let alone have two in her mouth. He hoped she wouldn't choke when they both filled her throat.

"The rest of you can come over her face," Galba suggested, seeing the frustration on their faces. "Or if you prefer, you can use her tits as target practice. First one to spatter her nipples gets to fuck her mouth."

Africanus let their juices slither down her throat, swallowing in great gulps as they came in unison. It was Lacinius who fetched a jug of water to wash her mouth. She grunted and shook her head. A dull ache spread through her lower jaw and she rubbed the side of her face to ease the pain. Galba allowed her time to gargle and spit the water from her mouth.

"Now you can have her," he said to other gladiators, in a tone of disgust.

"I need to piss," she reminded them, as they gathered in a semi circle.

"Do it here," a voice commanded. "On your feet and open your legs."

"Let her piss in peace," Lacinius intervened. "The girl has a right to some privacy."

He was not as well built as the others, but there was something quietly menacing in his tone that commanded instant respect. Even Galba nodded his assent and she went off to the toilet alone and unescorted.

She squatted over the communal bowl still tasting their spunk on her tongue. What she assumed was going to be a glittering career, winning both fame and fortune was proving the worst form of slavery imaginable. Even when she toiled at the wheel she had not been subjected to this appalling degradation. It seemed that life had become one long round of punishments. Even having sex was considered a crime. She got up and wiped herself wondering if it was worth her while to fail and be sent back to her old master. But failure was a sign of weakness and she would not give them that satisfaction, and Quintus had hinted darkly that failed gladiators were sometimes sent defenceless into the arenas as sword fodder for the real, fully armed gladiators.

I shall die with honour, she told herself, and went back to where the men were waiting.

"On your knees," one of them said, already grasping his hardened cock.

Africanus dumbly obeyed and they formed up around her.

"Open your mouth," a tall, shaven headed gladiator

rasped. "And put out your tongue."

A ripple of laughter broke the silence. This had to be the very depths of humiliation, kneeling naked, thrusting out her bare breasts, keeping her mouth open while they jerked off all over her body. Already she felt degraded and soiled. But that she realized was all part of Quintus' plan, to break her spirit and leave her numbed and obedient. After this display of total abasement, she made up her mind never to have sex with anyone again, man, woman, or that strange creature that her mistress had matched her with. From now on she would become exactly what they wanted, a ruthless, cold blooded killing machine

She closed her eyes and waited.

As if in a dream she heard their hands urgently working on their cocks, their breathing coming in rapid pants as they rose to their climax. One of them, the first to come grunted and shot his load. In a flash she opened her eyes and saw his spunk shoot in an arc and spatter on her chest.

"Missed," he laughed, as it trickled through her breast cleft.

The next stream landed directly on her right nipple and a cheer went round the room. She closed her eyes and felt two more hot jets of spunk splash over her breasts. Then another quickly followed landing on her face. She grimaced and turned her head as another jetted in the well of her throat. So far not one of them had managed to come anywhere near her tongue. Suddenly she burst out laughing.

"Is that the best you can do?" she taunted.

The good natured banter abruptly ceased. If there was one thing calculated to incur their wrath, it was being held to ridicule by a woman, and a slave at that. Looks of simmering anger darkened their faces and they went into a huddle murmuring about how they should punish her.

Quintus had given strict orders not to beat her, but only

to humiliate her sexually. Spanking, they concluded, could be allowed if it was deemed sexually humiliating. If she was going to behave like a precocious girl, then they would treat her like one.

"Over my knee," one of them commanded her, seating himself on a stool.

Africanus obeyed, stretching her long legs behind her, she rested her belly on his knees, offering up her bottom for the punishment she knew would soon follow. A spanking would be nothing compared to what she had already undergone.

"Did you ever see such a splendid arse?" he called out, placing his hand on her cheeks. "Such fine skin and so smooth, and strong," he added, kneading the buttock flesh. "And her cunt," he said, working his fingers around her labia, "the finest in all the Empire, but much trafficked judging by the size of her hole."

He spanked her cheeks with the precision of an expert, not hitting her hard enough to leave a mark or cause any pain, but lightly, going all around her crease and pubic mound, spanking her with gentle slaps.

Africanus couldn't understand why he wasn't slapping her arse a lot harder, making her scream and her eyes water. The top half of her body hung limply over his knees, her breasts hanging by their full weight swung to and fro as she jerked and squirmed each time he spanked her. Another hand had gone between her open legs and was playing with her sex, cupping and squeezing the mound until her belly went cold. Slowly the hand was working her towards an orgasm; the sight of her impending arousal was not lost on the rest of the men gathering at her rear. Her breathing started to come in swift pants and her legs went rigid, as straight as spear shafts and devastatingly beautiful to see. Her thighs hardened, the muscles flexing as the spanking increased. Her nipples were fully erect and tingling, pointing their hardened buds to the floor. Her hands formed into clenched fists beating the floor with loud, hollow thumps.

"I'm coming," she wailed, choking back a sob.

Then the spanking stopped and the fingers working inside her slipped from her soaking slit. It seemed as if the whole world had stopped, leaving her breathless on the very precipice of orgasm.

"Please, don't stop now," she begged. "I'm so close."

The men gathered at her rear watched fascinated as her sex lips trembled and quivered. A mere trickle of sex juice dripped from her gaping sex. The slightest touch would have had her screaming in ecstasy, but none came. A pair of hands went under her chest and started fondling her breasts, teasing the nipples and manipulating the wobbling flesh.

"Why don't you bring me off?" she shrieked, suffering agonies of frustration.

"Because we like seeing your cunt winking at us," a voice taunted.

Then it began again. The same hand slapped her bottom, going under the cheeks where the bottom and thigh crease was most sensitive, spanking the fullness of her buttocks now glistening and shining with sweat. She bucked when one of the gladiators thrust his hand inside her sex. Now he started fist fucking her, marveling at the size of her cunt, making lewd comments about how a horse would be hard pressed to satisfy her. More hands grabbed her legs, squeezing and pinching her thighs and calves, smoothing their whole length and wondering at the smoothness of her skin. Suddenly their hands were everywhere, going all over her body, but mostly paying close attention to her breasts, buttocks and thighs. Even the roughest of them knew where a woman's secret places of arousal lay. But there was nothing secret about what was happening to her now. Her whole naked body was on display, offered up for anyone who chose to abuse and finger it, and every time they heard her betraying signs of coming anywhere near an orgasm they stopped and left her panting and gasping. She wanted to cry out for it to end but her mouth was dry and her tongue thick. Her sex was aching and it seemed as if a heavy weight had formed inside her belly.

"Please," she croaked, biting on her tongue. "Make me come."

"Not yet," Galba teased. "Not until you've learnt your manners. What would you say to a rock hard cock riding your cunt? Would that make you happy?"

"It's what I want," she pleaded, digging her fingernails into her palms.

"Then let's hear you beg for it," he taunted, spanking the tops of her thighs and backs of her knees.

"Please, fuck me," she wailed, tears trickling down her cheeks.

"Louder."

"Please, I want fucking," she groaned.

Hearing her begging for their cocks made the gladiators go erect and Galba shot them a sly grin.

"You heard the bitch. She wants fucking. Decius, you're first."

Africanus spread her legs willing the throbbing cock to penetrate her frustrated sex. It would only take a minute to give her the satisfaction that her body desperately craved. He positioned himself between her quaking thighs and gently rubbed her sex lips with the tip of his cock. Africanus held her breath waiting for him to thrust hard into her tunnel. Her fists had clenched so hard the knuckles turned white. But he just went on playing the hot glans around her labia, pausing every now and then to touch her throbbing clitoris.

"Now it's Avitus' turn," Arius announced.

"Please, get on and fuck me," Africanus shrieked.

"Not yet. It's only fair that everyone has the chance to play his cock around your dripping cunt," Arius told her. "It's all part of the gladiatorial code, everyone gets an equal share of the spoils, and that includes you, my frustrated slave."

"I'll take them all," she offered. "But just get on and fuck me."

He spanked the sides of her arse cheeks, then the backs of her thighs while two of his companions tickled her labia with their cocks. One penetrated her, gave a brief shove of his loins and swiftly withdrew. The sight of her quivering cunt was amazing as the swollen lips sucked and quivered, the inner petals flowering in front of their very eyes.

"I think one of us should finish her," Lacinius said, looking at the terrible agony distorting Africanus face. "The poor bitch has suffered enough."

"Very well," the man holding her agreed. "We'll give her what she wants. Bring a wine bottle, someone."

"She wants a cock, not a bottle," Lacinius said firmly.

"So she might, but she's not going to get it," Galba ordered maliciously.

"Perhaps we should ask her," Varius suggested.

Arius gave her rump a hard slap. "All right, which would you prefer, a bottle, or a nice hard throbbing cock?"

"I want cock," she wailed, knowing how much they all enjoyed baiting her.

"But you're not going to get it," Arius told her. "Unless you're willing to take all of us."

"Give it to her both ends at once," a voice suggested.

"What about her arse. I think she needs her bum fucked. Look at those cheeks just ripe for fucking."

Arius smoothed his palm over her bottom. "All right, my beauty, are you willing to have it up your arse?"

"I'll have you any way you want me to have it," she said, past caring what they chose to do with her.

A pair of hands hauled her off Arius' knees and she was dropped onto all fours.

"Brace yourself for the biggest fucking of your miserable life," she heard Arius say, and his cock sank into her sex.

A hand grabbed her hair and lifted her head. Her mouth opened and was speedily filled.

"Now ride us, you dirty cow."

Her hips and head broke into a rocking motion, riding and sucking on the cocks filling her sex and mouth. After all she had suffered; she wouldn't have been a bit surprised if they withdrew without giving her the completion she needed. But being forced to beg and plead for anyone to fuck her made her feel cheapened, no better than a sex crazed slut eager to satisfy her lustful cravings.

Arius finished quickly before she had a chance to come and left his cock inside her, smiling grimly as it went limp. There was nothing more frustrating than having a cock that couldn't bring her off. Inside she felt its hardness wilt and then its soft fleshy stem shrink from her quivering sex walls.

The man at her mouth came just as quickly before she could even savour his hardness.

"You bastards," she hissed.

"Temper," Arius chuckled, sliding out of her, and slapping her thigh.

"That's enough," Lacinius intervened, and he pushed Varius out of the way and rammed his own pulsating weapon hard into Africanus' sex.

No one tried to stop him riding her, and no one used her mouth. They just stood and watched as she panted like a

108

galloping mare. Her breathing was deep and raucous, almost like a death rattle as she worked herself to orgasm. Her hips and buttocks pounded against the man at her rear who in turn was giving her just what she wanted, a rock hard cock slamming against her clitoris and sex walls. Her cunt made a sucking sound as the vaginal walls closed around the shaft. She was so tight that Lacinius had difficulty keeping up his momentum. He knew that she was no longer in full control of her body and it was her sex that ruled her emotions. He went with her, keeping his cock fully embedded in her belly, holding still while her hips thumped against him. Her arse cheeks wobbled and danced in a way he never thought possible, squeezing hard one second, then going softer the next, and all the while the sweating ebony skin constantly rippled and shook. She came with a great cry that rose to the rafters and then she tumbled forward and lay still.

"The girl's finished," Lacinius said softly. "Now let her sleep in peace."

And they left her alone curled in a ball, hugging her knees and snoring, thankful that Lacinius had at least shown some signs of pity.

CHAPTER SEVEN

At the end of a month's training Drucus judged her fit for combat with her new trainer, Fortuna. She was shorter than Africanus, but only by an inch or two, well built with good breasts and wonderfully honed limbs. Her red hair fell in curls around an oval face blessed with fierce green eyes and a generous mouth. She had a reputation for moving fast. Some said she was the fastest gladiatrix in the Empire. So far her tally of slain opponents numbered twenty. She was also highly paid and had her own modest villa on the outskirts of Rome and a couple of slaves to wait on her. At Quintus' ludus she was given her own room and was assigned a young female slave to fetch and carry. A male slave unloaded her personal armour and weaponry and carried it to the store room.

"Let me have a close look at you," she said, after Drucus had formally introduced them.

Africanus bowed, pleased now that her hard physical training had ended. Now she would be looked upon with greater respect engaging in real combat. She had also refrained from having sex with anyone, although she did masturbate in her bath occasionally. The lesson that Galba and the others had taken such delight in teaching her had sunk in. After that she thought she'd had enough sex to last her a life time, unless of course, Circo happened to come into her life, but that, she thought was just wishful thinking. From now on it was dedication to duty, absolute obedience and total subjugation to those who owned and controlled her.

"You've trained well," Fortuna congratulated. "A good body and strong limbs. No fat that I can see. Your tits are large, but a tight fitting breast plate will take care of that

110

little problem, or should I say, big one. Have you used the rudis?"

"I haven't used any weapons," Africanus replied testily.

"Well, that's why I'm here, to train you in the art of swordsmanship and all that it entails. But first we must decide exactly which type of gladiatrix you are best suited for. You are familiar with the different types of gladiatorial combat, I suppose?"

Africanus shook her head. No one, not even Drucis had mentioned them.

"I think we can narrow you down to either a Retarius or a Secutor," Fortuna mused. "The former wears no armour except for a face guard, a sort of metal plate worn on the shoulder behind which she ducks for cover, and carries a net and trident. The Secutor carries a shield, sword and wears a helmet. I think the Secutor will suit you, but first we'll test your speed and ability to guess where the next blow's coming from. Many a good gladiatrix has been chopped because she failed in that quarter."

"That's really comforting," Africanus mumbled, beginning to realize that the red headed woman was a lot more deadly than she looked or sounded.

"We'll begin with a warm up session," and she summoned a slave to fetch over the necessary equipment.

While they waited for it to arrive, Africanus had a good opportunity to assess her new trainer. She was wearing only the customary short skirt which floated around her pert buttocks. Her legs were nicely tanned and shapely; her waist slim and tight, her breasts firm and with large brown areolae. They were also liberally sprinkled with freckles as was her neck and face, which lent her a girlish appearance, useful when deceiving opponents into believing she was a pushover.

"Ah, here we are," Fortuna said, when the slave arrived.

111

"We shall only be using the very basic weapons to start with, and we shall fight naked, see if that fine rump of yours holds up to a beating."

The slave placed two small shields on the ground, no more than a foot in diameter, two long stout canes and a length of chain with wrist shackles fixed to either end. The slave fitted a manacle to Fortuna's right wrist, then the other to Africanus. He handed them the shields which had loops fitted at the back with which to hold them, and then the canes, long and supple with thicker handles.

"But I thought we might at least use a sword," Africanus protested.

"Oh, you stupid cow," Fortuna sighed. "If we had real swords, you'd be dead in the twinkling of an eye. All you have to do today is stop me from welting your bare arse, or anywhere else that takes my fancy."

They stood at the chain's length, Africanus shadowing Fortuna when she raised her shield at breast height. Their knees and backs bent, and for a full minute they circled each other like cats ready to spring. Without warning Fortuna sprang forward and lashed her cane hard across Africanus buttocks. When her opponent retaliated, she put up her shield and Africanus' cane bounced harmlessly off the rim and she came back quickly, lashing her cane across the black girl's thighs. Africanus shrieked and stumbled and in a flash Fortuna put out her foot sending Africanus crashing into the dust.

"That wasn't fair," she hissed. "You tripped me up."

"By all the Gods, do you think that when you get into the arena your opponent is just going to stand there while you beat the living shit out of her," and she sent her cane whistling into Africanus' back.

"On your feet," she snapped, her green eyes glowing with anticipation. "Now when I lash you again, use your shield to stop me."

She raised her cane, then suddenly as Africanus was distracted, tugged on the chain and pulled her forward. The cane sailed in a beautifully described arc catching her opponent under her legs.

Africanus bellowed in pain, then she lost control and charged at Fortuna like a madwoman, lashing her cane in all directions, but Fortuna effortlessly parried each lash and sent her own cane winging into Africanus' bare rump. A broad sweep of her shield sent the black girl into a demented spin and a sharp tug of the chain had her hitting the ground at full speed. Just for good measure, Fortuna gave her six rapid lashes across the shoulder blades and one across her belly.

"You're fucking useless," Fortuna said drily. "If we had been fully armed, you'd have been dead long ago."

"If we'd been fully armed, I would've killed you," Africanus retorted rashly.

"Oh, really," Fortuna replied. "In that case we shall put it to the test. Slave, fetch me two full size shields and helmets. You needn't bother with either a rudis or a gladius. I think I can make my point with the cane, but you can release these shackles."

Quintus and Drucus came into the training area, along with lady Octavia and that infuriating little lizard, Nydia. Africanus didn't know why or how, but she had a strong suspicion that she was somehow responsible for getting her abused by the gladiators.

The shields duly arrived along with a pair of elaborate bronze helmets, wide brimmed and with eye holes protected with a grill. It was a lot heavier than she imagined and when the slave fitted it over her head everything went dark. The eye holes were small and she could only see directly in front of her. With such restricted vision it would be necessary to turn her head to see either side. The shield was elaborately painted with serpents and scrolls and had lots of dents in it where previous combatants had come to grief. It too was much heavier than it looked and when she slipped her left forearm through the loops her arm nearly dropped off.

"Ready!" Fortuna called in a voice sounding both muffled and hollow behind the confines of her helmet.

"This ought to be interesting," Quintus remarked, seeing both women heavily attired.

"The black gladiatrix thinks she can kill her opponent now that she's wearing a helmet," Drucus said dully.

Lady Octavia said nothing but watched with detached interest as both women began again their encircling movement. The combat lasted longer than most of the onlookers imagined it would. Suddenly, Africanus, although unused to having her normal vision blocked, and her arm growing tired from the heavy shield, discovered new found strength and courage. Now that she actually looked like a gladiatrix, she felt like one and instead of rushing at Fortuna and burning up all her strength, she wisely kept out of harm's way, carefully dodging each lash of the cane and bringing her shield into play, deflecting each blow as it came. She even managed to catch her trainer off guard and sent her cane whistling into her pale, pert buttocks. A muffled grunt came from behind the visor, and when she quickly retaliated Africanus put up her shield and swept her cane in a swift downward motion, lashing it over both Fortuna's breasts. But this time there was no muffled grunt of agony. Through the eye holes of her helmet Africanus couldn't see the raging fire burning in her trainer's eyes. Artfully and with consummate experience and skill, Fortuna led her on into a sense of false security, ducking and diving at every blow that her opponent

114

delivered, occasionally letting her get the better of her by deliberately exposing her naked arse and taking a lash or two on her buttocks and thighs. But Africanus was getting too confident. Unexpectedly, Fortuna crashed her shield into that of Africanus, and with such force she sent her reeling. While she tried to regain her balance Fortuna got in with six lashes, each landing with the full strength of her arm. Africanus' bottom blazed from the pain eating into her buttocks, but her trainer sent another four strokes across her back. The lashes seemed to be descending everywhere at once, and with terrifying speed. Africanus now made the fundamental error of turning her back on her opponent and no matter how she twisted and turned, Fortuna always seemed to be behind her. The pain was unbearable, a blazing furnace of criss crossed welts that drew agonized cries from behind the visor. Her eyes stung with flowing tears and she was temporarily blinded. She knew only that her vision and strength was no match for her trainer and there was little choice but to suffer the cane lashing expertly onto her thighs and breasts.

Hot and sweaty, she bared her blazing bottom to the cane. The onlookers could plainly hear the sharp crack of each lash as it landed on her naked rump and thighs. Africanus gritted her teeth determined to see it out to the bitter end. The lashes came with increased ferocity, landing one on top of another making the welts deeper and the pain greater. Her nipples and breasts throbbed from the fiery heat spreading rapidly through her body. She made one final desperate attempt to floor her opponent. Her shield crashed against Fortuna's with a loud, hollow clang and for a second it seemed that Fortuna would hit the ground, but she quickly rallied and sent her cane whistling across the backs of Africanus' knees. She buckled and fell in a crumpled heap, not even bothering to raise her shield against the measured strokes lashing her swollen bottom.

"She still has much to learn," Drucus acknowledged censoriously. "But she put up a good fight."

"She has to be ready within a month," Quintus grunted, omitting to mention that that was when the money lenders would call in their loans, but he did applaud when Africanus struggled to her feet rubbing her welted bottom.

"That's enough for today," Fortuna said, handing her helmet to the slave. "You fought hard and well. I think now you deserve your bath. I shall join you later."

"Thank you, mistress," Africanus bowed, and she hobbled towards the baths, wondering how much longer it would be before her master sold her to anyone who needed a slave to wade calf deep in urine, or empty the pots of piss at the nearest brothel.

"You did well," Fortuna complimented when they were alone together in her room. "I had you heavily armed to show you how much you have to learn, and I whipped you to test your strength and speed. I think that in a month or so you will be ready for your first real combat. You demonstrated great resilience. I was surprised how much of a beating your arse can take."

"Thank you, mistress," Africanus replied, relieved to hear that she had done better than she imagined. "Have you always been a gladiatrix?" she asked.

"By the Gods, no. I was a slave like you. Now I fight on my own account. Perhaps one day I shall have my own ludus and train my own fighters. But it costs a lot of money. I was lucky I suppose because my former master liked me and in return for having my body he made sure I was trained well."

"They've had my body here too," Africanus confessed.

"A slave is expected to do her master's bidding. I

remember how my master used to fuck me every night and whip me into the bargain, but it did no harm, if anything it strengthened me and I of course, I enjoyed it."

"What happened?" she asked, intrigued that she wasn't the only one who everybody wanted to fuck.

"He always used to whip me before having sex, and I soon learned that a good whipping made me more eager for his cock. It was always the same. I used to lie belly down on his bed with my arms and legs reaching for the bed posts. He tied my wrists and ankles with rope, pulling the knots tight until I couldn't move. More often than not I was gagged with a ball of cloth stuffed in my mouth. Then I would offer up my bottom for his pleasure. He didn't always use a whip, sometimes he used a rope or a cane and he really knew how to lay on the stripes. I used to writhe in agony, squirming like an eel, my arse flogged raw and my thighs red and burning, and you'd never believe it, but I used to have orgasm after orgasm. When I was hot and ready off came the ropes and he'd turn me over and give it to me there and then. His cock was enormous after he'd thrashed my arse and his balls fully loaded. I had to lie on my back with my legs in the air while he pumped his stuff. He used to suck on my tits until I begged for more. If he'd come and I was still hot for it, he'd use a candle on me, pumping it in and out until I came. But it was the lash I loved most of all. It was a single length of leather hide which he kept well greased and supple, and it did hurt. I forget how many strokes he gave me, no more than fifty at one time, but enough to have me gagging for his cock. Sometimes I had to kneel on the bed and have my wrists tied to the post, then he'd thrash my arse and watch my hips dancing. That made him up for it as well and it wasn't unusual to have his hard cock up my arse. The more I was whipped and fucked the better I could fight, so I suppose

117

my success is down to my old master."

"I've been told not to have any more sex with anybody unless it's with my master's permission," Africanus said sadly. "But that's the trouble, you see, the more I'm whipped the more I want fucking. I just can't help it."

"None of us can," Fortuna agreed. "It's in our blood. Every woman wants fucking after she's had a taste of the whip."

"I've gone without it for weeks and thought I'd got over it, but after that combat I knew I wanted it as soon as my arse started throbbing."

"I'm sure my slave could oblige you. She must know of someone who could be relied upon to keep his mouth shut."

"Lacinius," she said. "He was the only one who showed any mercy after the rest of them had wanked all over me."

"Would you like him to fuck you now?"

Africanus let out a long sigh. To give way would be a sign of weakness, but her cunt ached for a man, even if the memory of Arius still pained. And what about her oath of obedience? Could she betray that solemn promise of celibacy? Inwardly she was struggling against her own physical emotions. A battle she knew she was losing.

"Can you also trust your slave to keep silent?" she asked, already wet at the thought of having Lacinius between her thighs.

"Leave everything to me," Fortuna said, and left the room to summon her young slave.

The girl bowed as befitted her lowly status and ran off to do her new mistress' bidding. It was some time before she returned with Lacinius.

Fortuna opened the door when he knocked softly on it and let him in.

The young slave hovered in the darkness.

"You have done well," Fortuna said and gave her some

118

coins. "What do they call you?"

"Nydia, mistress. Thank you," the slave said, smiling broadly.

Lacinius saw both women had been waiting for him, stripped naked in the humid night air.

"But I thought…"

"Never mind what you thought," Fortuna cut in. "We're both willing to have sex with you. It's all part of the gladiatorial code. Everybody gets an equal share of the spoils."

Lacinius saw the joke and laughed. "That's fair," he smiled. "So who's first?"

"You have to take both of us at the same time," Africanus said. "If you can manage it."

Lacinius had the distinct impression that both women were mocking him and his eyes flashed in anger. He might be merciful, but he certainly had no time for precocious women getting above themselves.

"You get on your hands and knees," he said to Fortuna. "And you, lie on her back, belly up," he ordered Africanus.

The women obeyed, Fortuna got on her hands and knees, whilst Africanus laid herself on her back, throwing open her long silky legs. Lacinius knelt behind Fortuna and entered her at once, dipping his cock in and out of her cunt and at the same time embracing Africanus' thighs.

"You've done this before, you artful swine," Fortuna grunted, as his cock eased deeper into her sex.

"How else can a man take two women simultaneously?" he asked, folding his arms tighter around the dark sweating thighs.

He waited until he heard Fortuna start to pant, then took away his cock and plunged straight into Africanus.

"Urgh," she grunted, not having had a hard cock for some time.

119

Soon the air was heavy with their grunting and panting, the harsh groans of Africanus mingling with the higher pitched rasps of Fortuna. Lacinius found it easy to penetrate them in turn now that his cock was slicked from both their juices.

"I'm so wet," Africanus breathed, writhing her shoulders over Fortuna's back.

Lacinius could see that right enough. The black girl's cunt was wet and dripping, the juices flowing from under his cock and over Fortuna's arse.

"I can feel her juice running into my cunt," Fortuna said crudely, wiggling her buttocks.

But both women were fully aroused, not only from the attentions of Lacinius' cock but from the sensual writhing and squirming of their own bodies. Under Fortuna's body, her breasts swayed to and fro as she rocked in time from Africanus' bouncing buttocks. A heady aroma of hot feminine sex filled the room and drifted into the still night air. But in the shadows Nydia sat listening to every sound, her own pert nipples erect at the thought of what was taking place inside that steaming room. Her slim girlish body shivered in the night air, but her skin was hot with longing. She too was prohibited from coupling with any of the male slaves, but that didn't stop her from craving a hard cock inside her. She crept to the window and peered over the ledge. Lacinius' manly buttocks were thumping between Africanus' shimmering thighs, then, just as she started to pant, he slipped out of her and penetrated Fortuna. Nydia's own breasts, small and pert by the standards of every other female slave who worked there, tingled and ached. Her nipples stood up like young strawberries. If there was one thing she could boast about it was her nipples. Now, as she heard the two women inside the room rising to their orgasms she was consumed with frustration and jealous rage. She waited patiently until the noise abated and crept back to the courtyard entrance which Lacinius had to pass on his way back to the gladiators' quarters. On her way she was sure she heard someone's bottom being slapped and the giggling that followed.

A door furtively opened and was as quietly closed. The laughter inside the room ceased and soon came the sounds of contented snoring and murmurings.

"I can find my own way back," Lacinius rasped, shocked at finding the young slave lurking in the shadows.

She sidled up to his powerful frame. In the dark he seemed massive and towered over her like a statue of Mars. Her slim hand went under his tunic and groped clumsily for his cock which was still hard.

"I want your cock," she whispered, stroking the shaft, working her hand up and down, her heart throbbing at the prospect of riding him.

"I don't mess with little girls," he said condescendingly. "So why don't you run off and play with yourself."

"I'd rather play with you," she simpered, flashing her eyes.

He had to admit that she was pretty with her hair tied up behind. He wondered how old she was, probably older than she looked, somewhere about eighteen or twenty he guessed. But he preferred more mature women with ripe, full bodies who knew how to fuck.

"Go back to bed, before I put you over my knee and slap your bottom," he said, not unkindly, and walked off.

"You won't slap me," she whispered. "Not now. I know all about you. I know everything."

CHAPTER EIGHT

After the re-enactment of Persiphae and the Bull, Glaucus had given the matter a lot of thought. He had paid the occasional visit to Quintus' ludus and seen the black gladiatrix in combat against her trainer and was satisfied with her progress. She had now reached the stage where her trainer had judged her competent to use the rudis, the wooden sword, and she had got used to wearing a helmet with its restricted vision, and to carrying a shield to defend herself against her opponent. He also liked the look of her physically. Her black skin looked both sensational and sexually alluring when it took on that shimmering gleam. Fighting almost naked would definitely attract the mob seated in the arena. As far as he knew there wasn't another black gladiatrix in any of the training schools, which gave him a definite advantage over the other sponsors. He'd heard through the political grapevine that the new emperor, Domitian, who had just succeeded Titus, son of Vespasian, who had commissioned the mighty Colosseum, was eager to stage a number of games including battles and combats between gladiatrices. It seemed that women fighting naked or semi-naked was drawing in the crowds, and Glaucus knew there wasn't a moment to lose if he was to act as sponsor. Even the emperor's envoys had been sent to his villa asking when he could stage his next show. He looked out across the Justinian Hills with their vineyards and farms and felt that life was good, and would be even better when Octavia arrived that very afternoon.

Octavia's carriage laboured up the hill towards his villa and she saw in what splendour he lived. Numerous slaves toiled in the gardens tending the flowering shrubs and keeping the ponds free of weeds. She shielded her eyes against the sun reflecting off the whitewashed walls and envied him.

"When will she be ready for real combat?" Glaucus asked her, when they were seated under the shade of the portico.

"Her trainer thinks she'll be ready in about six to eight weeks," Octavia replied, sipping a delicious vintage.

"As long as that!" he returned disbelievingly, and stood up pacing the floor. "We haven't got that much time, Octavia."

Then he told her all about the new emperor, his desire to stage female naked combat and the urgency if he, Glaucus was to act as sponsor.

"We have to get in first and beat off the competition. In a month it might be too late, especially if Polonius gets wind of the emperor's intentions, if he doesn't know already."

Now it was Octavia's turn to pace the floor. She looked splendid with the sun shining through her transparent dress, her curvaceous legs moving in long, purposeful strides, and her breasts quivering with every step. But this was no time for sexual thoughts. There was the matter of Africanus being fit for combat and it had to be resolved here and now.

"I think it would pay to send her into the arena in Marcellum," Octavia suggested, "I'm sure you could sponsor a combat, perhaps with one of the women criminals or thieves from the gaol, after all they're only sword fodder, and it would enable us to judge her ability in a real arena, and perhaps make some money into the bargain."

There was a lot of sense in that suggestion. Fighting against her trainer at the ludus was one thing, engaging in combat before a large crowd with all its attendant distractions was quite another. It would also give a good indication of just how competent she really was. If she could pass muster in a provincial arena it might be just possible to pack her off to the Colosseum itself, and most importantly win the favour of the emperor together with all the benefits that would bring. But there was still the other little problem of Quintus.

"He's fucking penniless," Octavia swore bitterly. "He told me only the other day that he has to go to the money lenders for yet another loan."

"So he's hardly in a position to dictate the terms," Glaucus reflected. "I will sponsor the girl to the tune of four thousand sestertii. If she's wounded or killed then I'll foot the bill. It's a make or break situation, Octavia. Of course, if she wins, we'll reap the rewards. I calculate making at least double the cost of the sponsorship, maybe more."

"She'll win," Octavia said darkly. "How soon can you stage a show at Marcellum?"

"Shall we say, in about a week, and assuming she's victorious, we shall be looking at the Colosseum in about two weeks after that."

"I can't wait," Octavia said joyfully, and she pressed her body against him.

Glaucus had no scruples about fucking the wife of his friend. There is no sentiment in business and Octavia, as far as he was concerned, was all part of the deal.

"I think we should go to my private quarters," he suggested, leading her by the hand.

They walked through the villa, Glaucus eager to impress her with its sumptuous surroundings, and Octavia seemed to be suitably impressed. She looked agog at the expensive furniture and magnificent frescos adorning the walls. His bedroom was no less impressive with its large window overlooking the valley below, and fragrant smells from the flowers wafting in on the breeze.

Without a moment's hesitation she peeled off her robe

124

and stood naked in the sun. Glaucus went to remove his own tunic but she moved forward and loosened his belt, casually tossing it aside. Her hands slipped the garment from his shoulders and went straight to his shaft, already huge and throbbing. She stroked it lovingly with a grip so soft it could have been her sex around it instead of her hand. Her fingers moved slowly up and down, squeezing at the base, then gliding up to the purple head and rolling it between forefinger and thumb.

"You're good enough to do this for a living," he joked, and didn't catch the sudden look of apprehension on her face. But it was gone as soon as it came and she dropped to her knees, placing the cock head on her lower lip. Her wet tongue flicked over the tip making it more sensitive to her hot breath caressing his shaft. Her mouth opened wide, hovered for a second then completely engulfed him. Down she went, still breathing hot and heavy, pressing her soft lips into his wiry pubic hair. Glaucus heaved a deep sigh as her fine pearly teeth nibbled the base of his shaft. He could feel a sudden inrush of blood swelling his cock even harder. Her mouth came up again, sucking like new born babe on its mother's teat. He looked down and watched her wide, voluptuous lips puckering and sucking, the lower lip trembling around the shaft, wet and glistening now from the ministrations of her tongue. Her lips sucked into the groove and sucked harder drawing his whole shaft deeper into her mouth. Then, as if a thought had suddenly invaded her mind, she drew back exposing his naked cock.

"Do you have any wine?" she asked, passing the trembling head under her chin.

He left her briefly and fetched a bottle. She took it and filled her mouth with rich, amber liquid. Her head was on his cock at once, sucking him in deep. For a moment he couldn't breathe, but held his breath as she sloshed the liquid round and round inside her mouth. His naked cock stung as her wine soaked tongue lashed around the shaft. At the corners of her lips the wine gathered then trickled down her chin. Breathless he watched it drip onto her chest and trace its course down over her breasts. The effect on her nipples was instant. The teats sprouted from the surrounding areolae which pimpled and shriveled, getting larger and expanding over the pale surrounding flesh.

She slipped his shaft from her lips and again reached for the bottle. She drank greedily and swallowed his shaft, but this time her hand pulled it gently downward until it was in line with her arched throat. Then, inhaling a deep breath she engulfed his whole length. Her hands signaled a riding motion and he didn't need to be told twice what she wanted.

"I'll ride your mouth till I come," he told her, and rocked gently on his heels, taking time to ease his shaft in and out of her mouth and throat.

Her tongue flicked rapidly at the shaft and lashed at the head when it rested momentarily on her lower lip. Then he rocked again and watched his cock disappear inch by inch between her sucking lips. Octavia shuffled forward on her knees until her breasts were level with his thighs. With the erect nipples only just touching, she began to snake her shoulders, moving them in a slow circular motion, shaking her breasts and pressing the nipples lightly over his skin.

Glaucus almost wept at the feel of her tongue and breasts. A lesser man would have come down her throat at that very moment, but he was determined to hold back. Having a woman like Octavia sucking his cock was an experience not to be thrown away in an instant. She pulled back and, taking the bottle, upended the neck over his cock. The liquid ran fast into his hair and her mouth was there at once, sucking in his wine drenched scrotum, passing his balls from one side of her mouth to the other, but not for an instant did her teeth graze the crinkled skin.

"It's like being in your cunt," he said, clutching fistfuls of her hair.

"Maybe that's where it should be," she returned, expelling his balls and pulling him to the floor.

They rolled over and over, joined at the middle, jerking and thrusting their hips, slamming hard into one another. It was Octavia who ended up on top, sitting astride him, his cock fully embedded in her sex. She reached for the bottle and passed it to him. He sat up and drank, but before he had the chance to swallow she told him to squirt it over her breasts. That was something he'd never done, not even with his slaves. The liquid hissed from his lips and splashed all over both breasts staining her skin with its bright amber hue.

"Now lick it off," she purred.

Her arms went around his neck, hugging him close as his tongue lapped at her breasts and nipples. He drew them in deep, sucking the wine from her teats. Her skin soon turned hot and sticky and smelt strongly of the vintage.

"One day, when that black gladiatrix has made our fortune, I'm going to bathe you in wine," he said seriously.

"You can tip it all over me and lick it off bit by bit," she returned.

They kissed long and hard and, taking her by the hips, he bounced her up and down on his cock, not stopping until they both climaxed. He held her still delighting in her hot sex juices flowing from her lips and drenching his balls.

"You make a lot of love juice," he complimented.

"That's because you inflame me, my darling. Every day my cunt longs for you."

"Soon I shall be filling it every night," he assured her. "We'll keep on fucking until we fall to pieces." He looked at her wine stained skin. "Where did you learn that trick?"

127

She shrugged, and then laughed. "Oh, that's my little secret."

Then she looked over his shoulder at the blue hills beyond and thought how wonderful it would be living here.

"I don't think she's ready," Fortuna said, when Octavia told her everything she had discussed with Glaucus the previous day. "She's fast and uses her armour well, but I shall have to work on her for another month before she's fit for the arena."

"There isn't the time," Octavia snapped. "The sponsor is arranging a show in Marcellum in less than a week."

"Who is she fighting against?"

"The usual scum, riff raff from the prison. Female thieves and petty criminals, nobody she should worry about."

"Will they be armed?"

"I think Glaucus mentioned that they might be given a sword or lance. I very much doubt if they'll know how to use them, and besides, they'll be no match for a trained gladiatrix. So stop fretting and work on her."

Fortuna shook her head at the mercenary minded bitch striding out of the training ground, and wondered what had suddenly brought this on. As a rule no gladiator or his female counterpart ever took to the arena without being fully trained, but she reasoned, if she was only matched against common criminals she would have a sporting chance, and maybe it wouldn't do any harm to test her anyway. In Rome it was a regular occurrence, emptying the prisons and sending their hapless inmates to their deaths in the Colosseum, pitching them defenceless against fully armoured gladiators, having them slaughtered in droves. It was the women she pitied most, running around the arena, naked, chased by sex starved men with huge erections, then fucked in public. A woman was entitled to some privacy, after all. But this was no concern of hers. What she had to do now was make sure that Africanus was fully trained and ready.

"The arena!" Africanus exclaimed. "You mean I'm actually going to fight in the arena?"

She was shaking at the prospect. Her first public display of swordsmanship. She was almost in tears now that the moment had finally arrived.

"We still have a few points to work on," Fortuna told her. "You're not quite up to speed with the gladius, and you don't maintain your guard nearly as much as you should. I'm going to use my cane to teach you a few important lessons."

With a willing heart and mind, Africanus stripped off her skirt and went into the centre of the training area. She had got used to fighting naked, except for wearing the obligatory helmet and carrying her shield, and in a way she secretly delighted showing off her honed body with all its rippling muscles and curves. There was also the added bonus that the men in the audience would be just itching to fuck her senseless but wouldn't even have the chance of getting anywhere near her. They'd just have to go home and toss themselves off dreaming about her. Serve the bastards right, she thought, slipping her arm through the shield loops.

Fortuna too, was naked, except for a length of silk that had been tied around her waist, passed under her legs and knotted in front. It was enough to keep her sex hidden yet display the rest of her body. She knew that men found her freckled chest attractive and delighted in large breasts and dark brown nipples. She had already taught Africanus the art of thrusting out her bottom more than was necessary and shaking her enormous breasts every time she wielded the gladius. It's what men come to see, she told her, bare arses and tits wobbling all over the place together with the added bonus of combat. And she lashed the cane hard into Africanus' buttocks.

"Keep that shield in front of you, for fuck's sake," she swore.

The more intense the training, the worse the language became. It was a way of relieving the tension and keeping the mind sharp.

The cane sailed into Africanus' unprotected buttocks and she let out a long howl. She span round and skilfully brought the shield into play, deflecting the next blow.

"Better," her trainer acknowledged, and then sent it lashing across her back. "How many times have I told you not to be distracted when I compliment you," she barked. "Ignore what's going on around you and just concentrate on the cane. When you get into that arena it'll be a real sword you'll be up against."

"Yes, mistress," Africanus agreed, and parried the next blow.

Octavia watched from the arbour, proud of the black girl's progress. There was no doubting her fitness and skill as well as her magnificent body. How that dark skin gleamed and shone in the sunlight. And those buttocks! Once the word got around that she was being fielded in the arena men would be queuing all the way to the docks to get a seat.

The cane whistled through the air, but Africanus saw it coming and knocked it clear.

"Now you're learning," Fortuna called, and whipped the cane towards Africanus' breasts.

This time she ignored the compliment and concentrated on the cane. The shield came up quickly and it bounced off it flying out of Fortuna's hand. She went to retrieve it but Africanus got there first.

130

"Now I'm going to whip you," she laughed.

Fortuna consented and strapped on her shield.

Octavia stood up to see how much of a whipping she could deliver.

Africanus bent her back, thrusting out her buttocks and letting an imaginary audience have full view of her wobbling breasts. She moved slowly like a predatory cat, going in a semi circle, then suddenly striking with full force and for once her trainer was caught off guard. The cane lashed into the small of her back and again across her buttocks.

"Better!" Africanus joked, but Fortuna was too busy rubbing her arse to notice the next blow winging in under her legs.

"Aaagh..fuck!" she screamed, her body jolting from the searing pain biting into her sex.

Even Octavia thought that amusing and clapped her hands in glee. "Well done, Africanus!" she called.

Africanus turned and saw her mistress then gave a polite bow. "Thank you, mistress," she acknowledged.

Then she tumbled forward as Fortuna kicked her savagely on the rump. The cane was whisked from her hand and fell in quick lashes over her belly and breasts. Africanus rolled over but the cane fell on her buttocks with the full savagery of Fortuna's strength. The smack of cane on bare flesh echoed around the walls. She managed to bring up her shield and deflect the next series of singing blows, whilst artfully reaching out and grabbing her trainer's ankle. A sharp tug brought her to the ground and Africanus sat astride her, smiling triumphantly.

"You move fast," Fortuna said softly. "I think you're ready after all."

Then without thinking, Africanus leaned over and kissed her full on the lips.

"Thank you, Fortuna," she whispered. "If I'm ready, it's all because of you. You have trained me well."

"Let's go to our quarters and rest," Fortuna smiled. "We have done enough for today."

They went directly to the baths and washed off the sweat and dirt. It felt good to be clean again.

"Have you ever seen the Colosseum?" Fortuna asked, pouring Africanus a cup of wine.

"Never," she said, putting the cup to her lips.

"Oh, you should see it," Fortuna said seriously. "Fifty thousand Romans watching every move you make; waiting for you to strike the final blow, the hush before you deliver it and the noise afterwards. It rises like a great storm as if the God of War had entered the arena." Her face was flushed with the greatness of it all. "Now your training is over I shall be taking my leave soon, but perhaps we shall meet again. Who knows, after enough of your opponents have perished, you too may win your freedom and be as I am, a gladiatrix fighting in her own right. The rewards are good, plenty of money and all the men you can fuck."

"I have to prove myself here first," Africanus reflected.

"I shall be watching you. Have you made your devotions to Nemesis?"

"I've never heard of her."

"The Goddess of fortune, chance and revenge. Every gladiator prays to her and makes a small offering before he enters the arena. She will bring you luck and good fortune."

She went to a corner of her room and opened a cabinet. She reached inside and brought out a statue and placed it on the top. It was an image of Nemesis, made of pure gold.

"It was a gift from a wealthy patron after I won my last fight. I shall offer a gift on your behalf; now pray to her for victory."

132

Africanus got to her knees. "Nemesis, bring me the victory I deserve," she whispered. "Give me strength to overcome my foes and give long life to Fortuna."

She leant forward and kissed the feet of the statue, then stood up, her eyes filled with tears. The night sky had darkened and thunder clouds blackened the sky. Suddenly a crack of thunder boomed across the heavens quickly followed by a flash of lightning.

"See, the Goddess has answered your prayer. One thing I promise you," Fortuna said softly, "after your victory I shall make love to you as my parting gift."

"I wish we could fuck now," Africanus replied, putting her arms around Fortuna's shoulders.

"No. Sleep now, and may all the Gods favour you."

Africanus went to her room and bolted the door. She did not want to be disturbed.

The arena at Marcellum was nowhere near as grand as the Colosseum. It seated about two thousand people and had a covered seating area for the dignitaries of the town, and unlike the Colosseum the seating arrangements were not divided according to status or class. The townsfolk sat wherever they pleased. Only slaves were banished to the worst seats. At one end of the arena a door opened into the cells below where the gladiators waited their turn. Quintus and Octavia sat under cover out of the searing heat, waited on by a couple of slaves. Glaucus was keeping a low profile and sat at the other end of the arena on a seat specially reserved for sponsors. Polonius was also fielding several pairs of gladiators who were now at that moment battling each other. But Glaucus' mind was on Africanus and Octavia; the first because so much was riding on her success, and the second because he wanted to ride her. After she'd left his villa he was totally besotted. He knew of no woman who could suck a man off in the way she could. Her tongue was like a living serpent coiling around his cock, and the way she sloshed that wine in her mouth was out of this world. He was still wondering who had taught her that, or perhaps it had just come naturally; some women were like that, inventive and just downright dirty.

Quintus had agreed to Glaucus' terms that he would put up the money to stage the show providing he was allowed to keep half of the profits. He had little choice but to agree, teetering on the verge of bankruptcy. If Africanus failed, he would be finished. Octavia had remained strangely silent throughout and just gazed with cool nonchalance at Glaucus seated on the other side of the arena. It wasn't wise being too friendly, at least until their real plans came to fruition.

Africanus, blissfully unaware that so much depended on her success, sat alone in a cell deep below the arena, although she could hear the cheering crowds above and the whimpering of the female convicts in the adjoining cells. She was nervous and it didn't help her state of mind when a man dressed as Mercury in a sinister black cloak and mask passed by her cell on his way to dispatch the wounded. The hammer he carried looked particularly ominous.

I can only do my best, she muttered, polishing her shield to take her mind off things.

A stream of wounded gladiators went by followed by their opponents flushed with victory. She looked up and almost fell from her seat.

"Circo!" she called, jumping up.

The man turned and looked strangely at her. He was not Circo. She sat down again and went on polishing her shield more determined than ever to win, and wondered where and what Circo was doing now.

"It is your turn," the arena master announced. "Go and

prepare yourself. When you get in the arena face the town governor, raise your weapon and say, 'Hail, we who are about to die salute you!' And try and die with honour."

"Thanks," she muttered, heading off to the armoury.

The armourer selected a helmet, wide brimmed and high crested but without a visor which meant that she could see a lot more clearly. Well, that was something anyway. He wrapped strips of leather around her forearms and calves offering some protection but not inhibiting her speed. He took a long thin strip of leather with a broader gusset in the middle and fitted it around her waist. The thin strip went deep into her buttock crease and under her legs. Only the gusset covered her sex. All in all little better than a thong. In her hand he placed a stout leather whip as thick as her middle finger.

"But I'm supposed to be armed," she said aghast. "Of what use is a whip against a sword?"

"Not on this occasion," he told her, then slapped her on the shoulder and wished her good luck.

And Africanus walked up the cold stone stairway and into the bright sunshine.

Her heart almost stopped at the immensity of the crowd now on their feet and chanting her name. Glaucus had seen to that. Hundreds of hand bills had been distributed around the town proclaiming her prowess. Octavia couldn't help but wave to him in exultation.

Africanus raised her arm in salutation and repeated the words the master of the arena had told her. She turned and saw a group of naked women entering the arena; convicts and whores from the local prison released to do battle with the gladiatrix. For a moment she stared at them in disbelief. Where were her armed opponents with whom she was supposed to fight to the death? The women were only lightly armed with short blunt lances.

The master of ceremonies rose to his feet and the crowd fell silent.

"Today we bring you the exploits of Zenaida, famed queen of Persia who, armed with only a whip defeated a band of wild female savages in the barren desert of Mesopotamia."

The crowd roared their approval and Africanus realized now why she hadn't been armed. This was no fight to the death or shedding of blood but the sexual thrill of seeing naked women whipped in public. Nevertheless, she was outnumbered and in the right hands those lances, even though blunted could inflict considerable damage, even death if she didn't watch herself.

The band, numbering about eight came nervously towards her. She didn't know it but her appearance was frightening. Tall and superbly fit, armed with a shield and whip, helmeted into the bargain, she represented a fearsome spectacle. But she knew she must keep her eyes riveted on her opponents and not be distracted by the crowd, not even by Fortuna who was seated at the front beaming her approval. It was all in the mind; floor the first one who attacked and the rest would disperse, and then finish them piecemeal.

Her plan worked to begin with. The boldest of them, a hard faced whore from the pits of Marcellum rushed at her screaming like a demon. At twenty paces she hurled her lance which bounced off the shield, and then Africanus uncoiled her whip and lashed her brutally across her naked rump. The howl that followed had the audience leaping to their feet. The noise was deafening but Africanus stepped forward and kicked her hard in the groin and she rolled over groaning and clutching her sex. Another lance sailed through the air and missed its target by miles. Africanus snatched it up and snapped it over her knee. Two more

136

women rushed at her waving their lances and hurling them at full speed. One ricocheted off her helmet; the other glanced off her shield. She snatched up the nearest lance and with deadly precision returned it into the thigh of the astonished criminal. The edge of the blade might be blunt but the point was sharp enough. The woman shrieked and crashed to the ground, hopelessly wounded.

Now she had an edge over her opponents. Two of them were disabled and the rest dispersed, running naked around the perimeter, desperate to escape the fearsome gladiatrix, whom it seemed, was indestructible. The men in the audience weren't the slightest bit interested in the fate of the criminals; they were more interested in the wonderful display of bouncing breasts and bare buttocks and legs running hither and thither. Africanus thrust out her gorgeous rump and wiggled her hips. Her breasts shook ponderously under their own weight, and amid roars of approval she advanced quickly on the slim female cowering at the entrance. This was no time for mercy and she sent the whip lashing into her thighs. The woman made the fatal mistake of turning her back and reaching up, trying to climb out of the arena. Africanus flogged her mercilessly, criss crossing her bare back with bright red welts. Paralysed with fear, the woman clung by her fingers to the parapet, swinging to and fro from each renewed lash. Out of the corner of her eye, Africanus saw a lance darting through the air. She ducked and more by luck than judgment it pierced the left buttock of the clinging woman. Africanus pulled it free and broke it over the woman's head. She slipped from the parapet and lay unconscious.

Now with three of them gone the odds were much more in her favour. It took only minutes to disable another two by lashing the first insensible and knocking the second unconscious with her shield. The remaining three went into

137

a huddle, not knowing what to do next. As if seized simultaneously with the idea of making a last ditch attempt to be rid of her, they all hurled their lances at once. Two of them shattered against the wall, but the third caught Africanus unawares and glanced off her ribs, not going in deep enough to inflict a wound but the point was painful. She grunted and rushed over aiming a kick in the groin at the tallest one who buckled against the wall and passed out.

Only two left, but one of them looked extremely dangerous. She was short and wiry with blazing eyes. She kept her distance while Africanus flogged her sole remaining companion. She rolled over and over, screaming from the whip lashing into her back and belly. Africanus flogged with the assurance of a professional, landing the lash between her shoulder blades, then another only a finger's width below it and again and again until her back was a ladder of livid red welts. She struggled to her feet and Africanus, deaf to her pleas for mercy lashed across her thighs and belly. The woman fell against the wall, still on her feet while the whip did its evil work. She tottered and fell, still conscious but defeated.

The last remaining woman had deftly retreated to the other side of the arena and had picked up one of the lances. She stood completely naked and it wouldn't have taken much to knock her out of the contest, but Africanus sensed that she deserved a sporting chance and slipped her arm from the shield, and discarded her helmet. She dropped her whip and picked up a fallen lance. The woman looked at her from under a great mop of unkempt hair and nodded her gratitude. Africanus motioned her forward into the arena, a gesture much appreciated by the audience who now had a clearer view of both combatants. The shorter woman was very pale from being locked up for so long which made her thick bush of black pubic hair and dark nipples all the more emphatic. Her breasts were pert and round, and like her slim legs, quite beautiful in their own way. Her arse was small and tight, almost adolescent in its shape, tapering outwards to her slender hips and curving in to her slim back. She was a well known thief in Marcellum and many of her victims were in the audience overjoyed at last that the thieving bitch was about to get her just reward. Fortuna leaned forward in her seat. She recognized a difficult opponent, even if no one else did. The woman was shorter and nowhere near as powerful as Africanus, but she could move as fast as a ferret if needs must and could kill if she had to. It would be interesting to see how Africanus dealt with her.

A hush went through the arena. It was easier to concentrate on a one to one combat and already the bookmakers were taking bets. The younger men in the audience were gazing at the naked beauty of both women and noting the contrast between them. Their arms stretched to each end of the shafts and they began by parrying the lances, each trying to knock the other's out of their hands. They moved in circles, Africanus bending her back to the shorter woman who in turn reached upwards. But the shafts were not made for such a constant battering and soon snapped. Now they were both disarmed, but to their surprise the master of the arena came over and handed them each a long thick leather strap. Now the contest could begin in earnest and on equal terms.

It was Africanus who struck the first blow sending her strap winging against the woman's buttocks. She let out a howl, her body twisting and writhing from the impact as a broad red welt spread across her pale cheeks. The audience loved that and cheered the gladiatrix on to beat her senseless. But the shorter woman knew how to take

139

advantage of her taller opponent and whirled round lashing her across the tops of her thighs. Africanus grunted and sent her strap lashing over the woman's nipples. She struck again; lower this time under her breasts where the flesh was softer. The pert orbs lifted and she stumbled backwards throwing out her arms. Africanus hit her with full force on her belly and again on the pit of her stomach. She moved fast and grabbed the woman under the legs crushing her sex with her powerful fingers. The woman screamed in anguish and took hold of her assailant's hair, tugging it with all her might. She was a lot stronger than she looked and tears trickled from Africanus' eyes. Only a swift jerk of her elbow prevented her hair from being ripped out of her scalp.

Temporarily winded, the woman retreated clutching her stomach, but when Africanus moved in to finish her, she ducked and sent her strap winging up between the gladiatrix' legs. Her sex was open and the leather went deep slamming the thong up into her slit. Her belly heaved and her hips shuddered from the impact. If the woman had quickly followed with more lashes she might have won, but Africanus came back whirling the strap around the woman's thighs. She tried to tug it free and the woman span and fell flat on her stomach. Africanus kicked her legs open as wide as she could and lashed at the parted buttocks. She turned at an angle and sent the leather directly along the arse crease. The woman writhed and squirmed on the sand as the end of the strap whipped into her open sex. The men in the audience could see what was happening and were on their feet watching every move of Africanus' strap. The woman tried to roll over and curl into a ball, but Africanus kicked her back again and began lashing the tightly clenched buttocks, not stopping until the pale skin was blazing red. She put one foot on the burning buttocks and pinned her to the sand. The woman moaned for the strapping to stop but Africanus had gone beyond feelings of mercy. Even though her opponent was beaten, she lashed her back and thighs, delighting in the punishment she was delivering, yet feeling strangely aroused at the sight of the whipped flesh. It was the woman's helplessness that had her breasts tingling. Her own sex was wet and she hoped that the skimpy thong would prevent the audience from seeing just how wet she was. But the more astute men noticed how hard her nipples were and the way she kept clenching her buttocks. It didn't take much imagination to see how aroused she had become and how close she was to her orgasm.

"On your hands and knees," she commanded, kicking the woman's ribs.

With a painful groan, she obeyed and got onto all fours. She remained still until the strap whistled into her buttocks, a blow that sent her scurrying forward. A major part of gladiatorial combat was to win the crowd, get them on your side and increase your popularity and good standing with the rich and famous and one way to do this was to make the loser suffer. Africanus wasn't wholly aware of that, but she did realise how much the audience roared their approval when she started whipping the woman around the arena, driving her forward like an animal, lashing her again and again across her back and buttocks. She reached the place where the consul was seated and gave one final blow sending the woman sprawling. She groaned and rolled over, looking at Africanus through misted eyes and then fainted.

"You have done well," the consul complimented, and tossed her a silver coin.

Africanus bowed low and gathered up her helmet and shield. Octavia was on her feet applauding her success as was Quintus. Glaucus was nowhere to be seen, he had gone to the atrium to collect his dues. It was Fortuna who came below to the darkened cells offering her congratulations.

"You might be disappointed that you were not given the chance to use a sword, but look upon it as a real test of your mettle. If anyone of those women had known how to use a lance, you would've been dead. You dispatched them ruthlessly and quickly, the true mark of a gladiatrix."

Africanus wiped the sweat from her brow. "Does this mean you're leaving now?"

"Quintus won't keep me here longer than necessary. He knows you're fit and ready, but there is just one more thing we have to do."

She smiled and there was no need for words or explanations. They both knew what they wanted.

"Tonight," Africanus smiled, and lay down to rest. The sound of her name being chanted still rang in her ears.

CHAPTER NINE

Nydia was wearing a dark cloak and hood and was standing in the shadows; waiting. That little scenario with Lacinius had been the final insult. Who did he think he was treating her like a school girl, threatening to put her over his knee and spank her, then pack her off to bed, not that she would have minded being put over the knee of such a muscle rippling man and spanked. But he hadn't. He was just like all the rest, treating her with utter contempt. By the Gods, she was seventeen years old and a grown woman. She deserved respect. Even that black gladiatrix, Africorus, or whatever her name was had slapped her, and the man who'd fucked her, Circo. She remembered his name all right. He'd threatened to snap her pretty little neck. Now she was fetching and carrying for that freckled faced bitch, waiting on her hand, foot and finger. Only her master, Quintus had never abused her. He was very pleased when she reported everything she saw between the black woman and Circo, and told her to keep her eyes open and report anything else she saw going on in the ludus. She had an inkling that her mistress, the lady Octavia had something going with Glaucus, but needed to substantiate it with fact, not guesswork. If her master was to confront his wife he must be able to lay it all before her, times, dates, places and people, and eye witness accounts of her misdemeanors. Quintus had hinted that Nydia might even be granted her freedom if she proved a reliable witness. She was determined that in the end, she would bring them all down. Then she would see if they held her in contempt then.

The door to her mistress' private rooms opened and she came out making for the main entrance that led to the street. And so it began; the mistress moving with a swift and rapid stride; the girl slinking behind her in the darkest shadows, ducking into doorways and corners whenever the mistress paused for breath. But where was she going at this time of night? The girl kept up her pace, stopping when her mistress stopped, and when she moved on, crept stealthily forward, but never allowed herself to gain on her. They passed through the Forum and the great temple of Jupiter, and into a warren of alleys and dark, narrow streets, getting closer and closer to the river and the places where few people were seen after dark. Only the destitute, the drunken and homeless lurked under some cold arch or slept on the pavements. But the mistress walked on knowing exactly where she was going. The walls of the warehouses rose dark and oppressive above the dense mass of roofs and hovels made less distinct by the mist rising from the river.

Nydia stopped at the end of a blind alley. Wherever her mistress was going it had to be into one of the houses. There was nowhere else she could go. Lights burned in the windows and the girl heard the high pitched shriek of drunken feminine laughter. A door opened and a man staggered onto the pavement, tottered and fell senseless. A woman, dishevelled and half naked stood in the doorway shouting abuse. Above her, a sign board swayed and creaked. It was just possible to read the sign and see a picture of a bunch of olives. A lupanar! A brothel! Her mistress was going into a brothel! The girl crept forward and peered through the window. The place was packed, but she just caught a fleeting glimpse of her mistress seen for the first time in the light. She threw back her red hood and revealed a mass of wild, unkempt hair. Her face was painted with cheap powder and the eyebrows were darkened with soot. Her lips were glossed with bright garish paint, but she still looked beautiful even in that state. But what was she doing there? A high born, rich lady consorting

144

with thieves, prostitutes and cut throats, it didn't make sense. But she evidently knew the man who had joined her. He put down a jug and a couple of cups and then they were lost from view.

"Got you!"

Nydia almost wet herself. A pair of strong arms had gone round her shoulders and pinned her to the wall.

"How much to fuck you?" the man asked, breathing a heavy mixture of wine and beer into her startled face.

Nydia couldn't reply at once. Her first instinct was to run. But where was she to run to? The man naturally assumed that any girl hanging around outside a brothel was either a whore or a beggar, and both would fuck for the price of a meal. He clearly liked the look of this one, dark skinned and slender with small tight bum cheeks. His hand moved to her breasts and squeezed them.

Nydia stood like a frightened rabbit, looking over his shoulder at the house opposite. Another lupanar with noisy, drunken tarts and loud aggressive men. She looked swiftly up and down the street. Every house was the same. Every house was a brothel, and every woman a whore. And right in the middle of it was Nydia.

But she was quick thinking. She certainly didn't want his dirty tool grinding away inside her sweet cunt. Only the Gods knew where that had been.

"I'll toss you for two sestertii," she whispered.

He thought for a moment and nodded. That was a bargain. She reached for his tool, eager to get the rotten business over and done with, but he grabbed her hand and hauled her into a side alley not much wider than a man. It was so dark she could hardly see her own hand, let alone the rigid cock bursting from his filthy tunic. But she certainly felt another pair of hands grabbing her waist. Her cloak was stripped from her shoulders and ripped from her back. She

145

spun round and it fell to her feet. The man lifted her as if she weighed no more than a bag of strawberries and suddenly she was naked. All around her she saw shadowy figures lurking in the darkness. For a moment they seemed content to grope and fondle her nakedness, work-hardened hands assailed her from all sides, gripping her breasts painfully hard, stroking her buttocks and trying to fumble between her clenched thighs. Then two arms went under her knees and lifted her. She fell back with a scream and two more arms went around her back and she was carried bodily to the end of the ally where a festering pile of sacks lay in a heap.

Naked and trembling she looked at the darkened figures gathering around her. Tunics were coming off and one of the figures fondled her bottom.

"Never felt such a tight little arse," he croaked, squeezing her cheeks.

"Good tits as well," another complimented, pinching her nipples.

"And what a pretty bush," a voice remarked, as a hand groped her pubic mound.

"Please, I'm not a whore," she pleaded. "I'm on my way home and got lost. Please let me go."

"You said you'd toss me for two sestertii," he reminded her. "So stop telling stories and get on with it."

"I think she's playing hard to get," a voice chuckled. "These young whores always like to think they're the Gods' gift."

"Well, she can stop playing hard to get and have my cock in her mouth."

"Oh, please, I'll toss you, I promise, but don't make me suck you," she sobbed.

"You'll do as you're told. Now on your knees and open your mouth before I slap you."

146

"Maybe that's what she wants, a fucking good slapping. And these cheeks are just made for it."

A hard, horny palm slapped onto her buttocks and she would have fallen flat on her face were it not for the two arms holding her upright. She screamed and the echo reverberated along the alley.

"Gag the bitch!"

A piece of sacking was ripped from the pile, rolled into a ball and stuffed into her mouth. Then they all started slapping her on the bottom, belly, thighs and breasts.

"A lump of fucking flesh is always the better for a good slapping," a voice suggested, bringing a hand down hard on the backs of her slim thighs.

"She's a nice little morsel though, fresh and clean. I wonder what her oyster tastes like. Salty, I'll bet."

"Oh, please, don't," she wailed, as she was dropped onto her back. "Please don't put your tongues in me. I'll toss you as much as you…uurgh.."

A rampant throbbing cock was shoved crudely into her mouth and her stomach heaved.

"Now stop jawing and suck on that, you little cow."

There was nothing she could do, except everything they wanted her to do. She wished now she'd never left her room. But it was too late for that. She was trapped in a dark alley with at least six men determined to have her and there was not a thing she could do about it. Even if she managed to escape she could hardly run naked through a place like this. It would be only minutes before another mob of rampant males grabbed her and hauled her into another stinking back alley.

She had no choice but to suck on the cock riding in and out of her mouth. It was so large her jaws ached and her lips felt as if they were splitting at the edges. Her hand went up and gripped the shaft, holding it still while her

147

lips sucked and smacked over the pulsating head. Her legs were lifted and spread wide open and a face thrust between her thighs. She could feel an unshaven chin rubbing coarsely against her labia. A tongue wormed into her sex and started flicking all around her sex walls. More hands groped her breasts, teasing the nipples, making them go erect. Then two pairs of lips began suckling her, nibbling and biting the teats, grinding the enlarged buds under their teeth.

"You're hurting me," she wailed, taking the cock from her mouth.

"It'll hurt a lot more if you don't suck me off," a voice threatened.

"I'm doing my best," she sobbed.

"If your best doesn't get a lot better, you're going to get a lot worse."

It took a few seconds to work that out. She put the cock back into her mouth and sucked much harder, guiding her mouth as far down the shaft as she could, then sliding back up again and all the time gently stroking the throbbing veins. His loins shuddered and his cock went hard, even harder than it was already. She knew he was coming and whipped it from her mouth just as he shot his whole load. Fat globules of sperm splashed onto her mouth and face. He swore and aimed his cock between her parted lips but all in vain. His balls had emptied and his cock sagged sadly on her chin.

"You cheating bitch!" he roared, slapping her face hard.

For a moment the earth went into a spin and she thought she was going to be sick. The man with his tongue in her cunt had had his fill and had given way to the next. Another cock, rock hard and throbbing was thrust into her mouth.

"Now swallow, this time," she was told.

She nodded dumbly and guided the shaft into her throat.

148

She was on her back, slim shapely legs pointing to the dark sky above. Her nipples were still being ravaged. It seemed they couldn't get enough of her gorgeous teats. A tongue flicked and probed her sex and all the while she sucked on the cock now forced to the back of her throat. A light appeared in a window above her head and a shutter opened blasting hot sweat-laden air into the night. A whore, bare breasted, leaned over the sill and breathed in the night air. She looked down and smiled at Nydia as if it were an every night occurrence, a young whore being had by a bunch of men on a pile of stinking sacks. The shutter closed and Nydia's writhing body was plunged into darkness.

She gulped and gasped at the cock nudging the back of her throat. The man shuddered and shot his juice into her. It slithered into her belly and she sat up heaving and grunting.

"Have you all finished now?" she asked plaintively.

"Not 'til we've had your cunt," she was told, and her legs were thrown over the shoulders of the man kneeling at her thighs.

"Uurgh," she grunted, and threw her legs wide.

He filled her with two massive thrusts and fell over her body, kissing her sperm soaked lips.

"It's too big," she sobbed. "I can't take a thing like that."

"Your cunt is tight," he agreed.

It occurred to the man that this was unusual in a whore. Most of them had been so well fucked that a cock just wallowed inside them.

It made a change fucking a tight whore. He began to wonder if she was telling the truth. Perhaps she was a young slave who had wandered into the nether regions of the town and had got lost. On the other hand it could be just a ploy. After she was fucked she'd probably ask for more money, coming out with some story that she would be whipped

149

for getting home late and deserved some recompense. But she wasn't going to get it. Not a single sestertius. The whores around this neighbourhood had protectors who willingly ripped the heads off their clients if they failed to come up with the goods. This little whore didn't know a soul. And he smiled smugly and rammed his cock hard into her sweet wet cunt. His lips closed over her nipples and flicked the erect teats on the tip of his tongue. She had the most succulent nipples he'd ever sucked on and he stopped riding her and took out his throbbing cock and held it over her breasts.

"Now you can toss me," he told her. "And make sure I come over your tits."

Nydia held his cock over her chest and rubbed the sides with her fingers. The purple head swelled and trembled as he rose to his climax. Looking down at it, it seemed even more enormous than when it had been spearing up into her insides, the head was as big as a ripe plum and she could barely get her tiny hand around the shaft. She closed her eyes and touched her nipples with the quivering cock head, passing it round and round the teats. He erupted over her, piling his thick juices over her nipples.

"Now lick them clean," he told her.

They stood around her; leering faces barely discernible in the gloom, watching her chin drop on her chest, her hands cup her pert breasts and lift them to her trembling lips. Her tongue lapped over the teats licking at the freshly delivered sperm with its salty essence tingling on her lips. The sight of a young, pretty whore licking her own spunk-soaked tits was too much and she was suddenly thrown onto her belly. Her legs were forced apart and two hands grabbed her arse cheeks. Fingers went into her crease and pulled open her buttocks. She jerked and someone pushed her face hard into the sacks. Her muffled pleas for mercy went ignored and unheard as a cock rammed into her bottom hole.

Her pert bottom was just too good to be left unfucked and the man rode into her, angling his hips left and right, opening her anus wider and wider. Nydia gritted her teeth and prayed for it all to end. If only she could get inside that house where her mistress had gone she would be safe. But then again, how could she explain her presence. Whatever her mistress was doing there she certainly didn't want her slave poking her nose in. She would just have to grin and bear it. She only hoped her arse wouldn't split as his cock rode her bottom with short fast thrusts. Hands were all over now, smoothing her calves and thighs, going under her shoulders and groping her breasts, under her legs and fingering her cunt. She heard a chorus of heavy breathing and panting as hands frantically jerked along stiff cocks in the dark and then it happened. Streams of hot juice cascaded over her back and buttocks and the man was still riding her arse oblivious to his companions jerking over her.

Then all of a sudden it ended.

She felt a rock hard tool gliding out of her punished throbbing bottom and she was rolled onto her back and staring wide eyed at the sky.

"Not bad for a whore who lost her way," one of her tormentors taunted.

"She's given us a good ride," another added seriously, putting on his tunic.

"Now thank us for fucking you so well," the man who had first encountered her said sternly.

"I have to thank you for all this!" she replied aghast. "Look what you've all done to me!"

"Be thankful you got off lightly. If our ship wasn't sailing on the next tide, you'd've been fucked much harder."

She sat up and wiped away a tear. "I hope you're going

to pay me," she sobbed. "I deserve at least ten sestertii for having you all."

"By all the Gods! Did you hear that? The whore wants ten sestertii."

One of the sailors reached for a leather purse and tossed a small silver coin onto her naked belly.

"There's one sestertius," he said grimly. "Now pass me that cloak."

He wrapped it around his shoulders and commented that it would fetch a good price.

Nydia's hands flew to her breasts. "You can't take that. I've nothing else to wear."

"There's enough sacks to cover your body," he replied gruffly. "You'd look good wearing one of those."

"You're cruel," she sobbed.

"I wouldn't argue with that," he said, and gave her bottom a hearty slap. "If you take my advice, next time you go whoring take the money before you open your legs, and don't go up dark alleyways with men you don't know. Now you can go in that corner and cry."

They went off in a gaggle laughing that she was the best fuck they'd had in a long time and cheap too.

Nydia lifted one of the sacks and nearly died of fright. A rat bolted from the rotting heap and went scurrying along the wall. She stood shivering naked in the night, shaking the sack, hoping to rid it of its crawling vermin. She wrapped it around her middle and tied it with a piece of twine. She looked more like a barbarian than a Roman slave girl. At the end of the alley she saw more shadowy figures coming and going. Even though it must be well past the midnight hour the lupanars were still doing a roaring trade. She would just have to sit it out and wait until the crowds drifted home and the streets were silent. She hoped she could at least get home before daybreak

She sat on the sacks and curled into a ball rubbing her aching bum.

"Come back for more of the same, have you?" Plutarc asked, filling the high class tart's cup.

"I've come back to discuss business," she whispered, ducking her head as a bottle sailed over the heads of the crowded room.

Whilst Nydia was outside trying to negotiate her way out, her mistress and the man she'd seen were making their way up the rickety stairs. They went into a different room this time, one that faced the street. It was larger and more airy. The shutter was open and a cool sea breeze diluted the air.

"What business?" he said, loosening his tunic. "The only business I have with you is your cunt."

She threw her red robe over her shoulders but remembered to leave her shoes on. "You said you could make people disappear," she reminded him, putting her long white arms around his brawny shoulders.

"For a price," he said, placing his hands on her hips.

She looked into his eyes and felt her sex quiver. "I like your chin," she whispered, rubbing the backs of her knuckles against the coarse stubble.

"I like your arse," he said, slapping it.

They kissed long and hard. Business could wait. They had other things to do.

She looked down at the hard shaft prodding the pit of her stomach and felt herself moisten. He seemed to bring something out of her that no other man could, a sort of girlish sense of fun that was so decidedly lacking in the arms of her husband or Glaucus for that matter.

"I think I'm in for a rough time," she giggled, and hugged his massive, masculine frame, feeling the hairs on his chest

153

grazing against the softer flesh of her breasts. She loved it when their nipples touched.

"You're in for a dirty time," he told her, and put his hand under her bottom crease, squeezing her pubic mound.

"I like dirty men," she giggled and slapped her forearm, then her upper arm in quick succession. She clenched her fist and her forearm shot up as she shouted, "Go!"

He didn't need telling twice. He'd had a few whores since their last meeting but none quite like this one. When the lupanar whores were foul mouthed it just sounded common, but when this one swore it sounded amazingly sexy.

"I'm in a dangerous mood," he warned her.

"I like it when you're dangerous," she said in a husky voice.

He rummaged under the fallen tunic and drew out a leather belt.

"Oh, you're going to beat me," she said, trembling with anticipation.

"Wrong. Now get on that bed."

She climbed onto the creaking frame and reached up to the bed end and clasped her hands, doing just as he ordered. He wound the belt tightly around her wrists and tied the ends to the top railing. She hung there, arms straining, head and shoulders off the pillows, wondering what he was going to do next. Beneath her bottom the sheet was soaking. She only had to look at him and she almost had an orgasm. Remarkable she thought how one man could be so ordinary, and another so muscular and sexy. Life with him would be just one long orgasm. And she shuddered.

His erection was massive, like his chest and arms.

He took hold of each ankle and spread them wide apart, then tore a strip of cloth from the sheet and tied her left ankle to the post. He did the same again and tied her right ankle. He snatched one of the pillows from under her shoulders.

"Lift your arse."

She heaved her hips off the mattress and he pushed the pillow under her buttocks. Naked, bound and totally under his control she shivered with longing. She hoped he would fuck her soon or she would orgasm even before his cock as much as touched the lips of her cunt.

"I told you I'm in a dangerous mood," he said, reaching for the solitary candle.

He inserted the unlighted end inside her sex and, with the flame still burning, worked it slowly in and out.

"Be careful you don't burn me," she smiled nervously, feeling the heat against her pubic curls and insides of her thighs.

He did not smile in return, but pushed the burning candle deeper into her, stopping when the flame flickered at the entrance to her gaping sex.

"It's hot," she murmured, and wriggled her bum.

"It's going to get a lot hotter."

He left the candle where it was and leaned over her quivering belly and kissed her nipples, rubbing the stubble of his chin hard into her soft breasts. She shivered and tugged at the belt, longing to put her arms around him. Her hips squirmed and she arched her back.

"That fucking flame's getting closer," she said, not smiling.

"It's going to get closer still if you don't shut your mouth."

He lay across her breasts, flattening them under the weight of his chest and kissed her full on the mouth. She could feel his chin rubbing against her face. One of his hands went to her side and squeezed the flesh below her ribs. She never knew how sensual and sexy that was; having her flesh squeezed like that, especially when she was being kissed. With her husband it was in over in minutes. Hardly worth the effort of going to the baths and washing it all off. With this one she wouldn't mind staying unwashed for weeks.

"That fucking flame's burning my cunt," she writhed.

He reached down and pulled the candle a little way out of her.

"If you don't keep still," he told her, "I'll let your cunt roast."

She caught her breath. He would never do that to her, but the threat made her belly heave.

Standing beside the bed and turning her head to the side, he placed the head of his cock on her lower lip, running it back and forth along her mouth, just keeping the silky glans resting on the tip of her tongue.

"Now suck. But don't move or your curls are going to go up in smoke."

She could feel the dull heat of the candle flame warming her pubic mound and drew his cock deeper into her mouth. How to suck a man like that with a massive throbbing cock and not move, just keep dead still, not even a twitch, just suck and suck until he came. A fine bead of sweat trickled down her temples. Her brow was sweating and more ran through her eyebrows stinging her eyes and running over the bridge of her nose. Her chest was soaked in sweat, and somewhere between her legs the heat increased.

"Please take that candle out of me," she asked, pushing his cock from her mouth with her tongue.

"Not until you've sucked me right off."

She sucked him again, working her head up and down the shaft, getting faster and lashing her tongue in and around the groove, anything to make him come before her cunt went up in flames. Her mouth opened wide and engulfed his cock. She could feel it throbbing on her tongue. Then he came gushing down her throat and she coughed and swallowed.

"Will you take that fucking candle out of my cunt!" she swore, getting frightened.

He leaned over and blew out the flame. Someone knocked at the door and he shouted for whoever was outside to enter.

A brothel servant came in, saw the whore tied to the bed with a smoking candle protruding from her thighs, and placed a bottle of wine on the table. Plutarc paid him and the boy left never batting an eyelid, one never knew what one would come across in a place like this.

"You gave me a fright," she laughed.

"You said you like me in a dangerous mood. You also said you liked dirty men," he reminded her.

She didn't know how dirty until he drank half the bottle, belched and stood over her aiming his cock directly at her naked chest. A fast stream of urine rushed from his cock and splashed over her breasts. She giggled helplessly. It went everywhere, a steaming pool of piss gathering in her navel and soaking into her curls. Her breasts and belly were dripping. She closed her eyes when he shot it over her face and hair. Her wrists and ankles tugged and strained against their bonds. She hoped he would mount her.

"You're an animal," she laughed, and clenched her buttocks against the orgasm quaking in her sex.

He took a knife from his pouch and slit the strips of cloth. The belt was taken from her wrists and she sat up and hugged him. Her body was still dripping with his water.

"I need a piss," she said, reaching under the bed for the pot.

"You don't need that," he said, kicking it away.

"Please, my belly's bursting."

157

"Then hang your arse over the window."

"You want me to piss in the street?"

"Either that or your gut bursts."

She padded to the window and looked nervously below. One or two drunks staggered by, and on the opposite side of the road a whore was servicing a client standing against a wall, balancing on one leg, the other wrapped around his thighs.

She turned and sat on the ledge clinging to the window shutters for support, then eased her bottom over the sill. A jet of urine hissed from her and hit the pavement with a loud smack. Someone shouted that she ought to have more respect, baring her arse to all and sundry. Plutarc laughed when he heard that and dragged her into the room.

"Get down on your hands and knees," he grunted.

"You want me to lick up my own piss?"

"Either that or the candle goes back in your cunt. And this time it stays there."

She got on her hands and knees. He strolled over and sat astride her back, raising the bottle to his lips. He squirted the wine from his teeth, making a loud hissing as it splashed between her shoulder blades. Then he slapped her ribs.

"Giddy up," he smirked, digging his knees into her sides.

Her back bent under his weight as she crawled around the room, going through the yellow puddle and across the floor. At the bed she stopped and he slithered down her back and over her bottom. He reached over her and grabbed her hair.

"Open your thighs."

At last. This is what she really wanted. He was going to ride her hard from behind. What did they call it; mare and stallion? He certainly had an erection like one. She could feel its hard length sinking into her arse crease. She shuffled her knees over the boards and dropped onto her forearms, thrusting out her bottom. Penetration was always so much deeper and satisfying that way. His hands gripped her hips and held her rigid. His cock went around her sex lips and up through her crease.

"Ohh," she grunted, and rocked on her elbows.

He was so hard she wanted to scream, but his hand had taken a length of her hair and wound it around her face passing through her mouth on the way. He tugged on it as if it were the reins of a mare he was holding. Then he rode her hard, smacking against her cheeks and slapping her thighs and back. He took another mouthful of wine and swallowed half of it, the rest he sent whistling into her hair. She was soaked in wine and urine, her hands and knees were raw and black from the dirty floor, but she couldn't get enough of the manly cock slamming into her sex. Just the feel of his hands squeezing the flesh above her hips was enough to make her squeal.

"You're treating me like shit," she swore, loving the sound of the word.

His balls emptied into her sex and she screamed in release as he pounded into her even harder as he came. Then he thrust her away from him and she crawled forward shivering from her orgasm. She had never felt so dirty or wasted, or so satisfied.

"You said earlier you had some business you wanted to talk about," he said.

They were lying on the bed, her head rested on his chest and her fingers were tugging gently at the hairs. Her right thigh lay across his middle and he stroked the curve of her hip. Her skin seemed permanently pimpled from the thrill of his touch.

"I want a couple of people to vanish from the face of the earth."

"Mm, mm. Who are they?"

She hesitated, swallowing hard. Once the decision had been made and the contract agreed there would be no going back. She had thought of nothing else and had made her mind up irrevocably.

"One of them is my husband who owns the ludus. The other is just a business associate."

He was silent. His arm went around her shoulder and stroked her hair. He was thinking so hard it almost gave him a headache.

"I see. Who exactly is your husband?"

"His name is Quintus Varus, and the other is called Glaucus Severus."

The names meant nothing to him. "And when do you want them removed?"

She had thought about that too. That would take some careful planning. It wouldn't be wise to move too fast.

"Soon," she said evasively. "My husband first. Then the other one."

It all depended on Glaucus and Africanus. As soon as she was ready to be fielded independently and Glaucus was ready to buy out Quintus she would make her move. Her husband would meet with an accident, or simply vanish and according to the laws of the Senate, she would inherit, and any debts he had incurred would be wiped out because she was not officially a signatory to the business. The ludus and Africanus would be hers. Glaucus would sponsor her in the Colosseum, and when she had made enough money out of him he too would meet with an accident. Then she could sponsor her own gladiatrix and the other gladiators. All the profits would go straight into her purse. Nothing personal about it. Business is business.

"I'll let you know when," she said, and stroked his cock.

"I need details of their movements," he said.

"I can give you that when the time is ripe. Now please

160

fuck me."

He got off the bed and stood upright, pulling her after him and swinging her around so that she stood against the wall and put her arms around his shoulders He penetrated her and she swung her legs around his hips, locking her ankles over the small of his back. She looked over his shoulder and hugged him close. A tingling thrill went through her now that her breasts were crushed against his chest. His hands were under her buttocks supporting her weight as he carried her across the room and rested her arse on the window sill. She didn't care who saw her bare arse. Her legs tightened around his middle and they hugged so close they could only breathe in short, jerky pants. Slowly, she eased forward until her whole weight was suspended on his cock. She caught her breath and ran her hands over his muscular back.

"You're all muscle," she whispered, jiggling her bottom.

"You've got lovely thighs," he said, putting his hands under them and pinching them.

He was a man she could so easily fall in love with, but common sense told her to keep him at arm's length. She could fuck him whenever she wanted, and when she was rich and independent she could have him without having to masquerade as a prostitute and creep through the streets in the dead of night. But she had to admit being a part time prostitute was exciting, a world away from the watchful eyes of her husband and all the pretence of being a respectable citizen's wife. And the man who was pounding her sex really knew how to fuck.

"Next time we meet I'm going to piss all over you," she promised.

"The last time we met I promised you a sound whipping, and you're going to get one."

The thought of that made her work her arse so fast they

came before they knew it, and he carried her to the bed and threw her bottom up over the filthy sheets. She saw him pick up his belt and coil the buckle end around his fist. She spread her legs wide and he lashed her buttocks at random, letting the belt fall where it would, now on the backs of her thighs, then across the centre of her cheeks, and under her legs, catching the pouting sex lips begging for the pain and ecstasy that followed.

"Hit me harder, you useless turd," she shrieked.

He sent the leather cracking into her arse so hard it left an instant welt, so clear that he could see the pattern in the leather forming on her pimpled skin.

"You dare insult me, you old whore," he rasped and lashed down the length of her spine.

"Is that the best you can do," she jeered when, with the next stroke he lashed her rump.

In the heat of the moment he abandoned all pretence and gave her at least twenty strokes delivered in slow measured sweeps of his arm. He knew she was in pain and loving it. Her sex was flowering in front of his very eyes and he dropped the belt over her reddened back and took her immediately, driving his cock in with just one thrust.

"You fuck so well," she sobbed, clutching at the sheets.

"So do you," he replied honestly.

He fucked her until there was no strength left in his loins.

They left the room simultaneously. He lingered in the room below quietly drinking himself into a contented slumber.

She covered her head and set off before dawn, unaware that only just around the corner her young slave was sleeping on the pile of stinking sacks.

CHAPTER TEN

"You exceeded all my expectations in your first combat,"
Quintus complimented Africanus when she arrived back
at the ludus. "My good friend Glaucus has suggested that
you should go to the Colosseum. He will sponsor you there.
So you will be pleased to learn that I have decided to retain
your trainer for a little while longer. Who knows you might
even end up fighting side by side in front of the emperor."

Africanus was beside herself. Fighting in the Colosseum
and in front of the emperor, and so soon! She was unaware
that Glaucus had impressed upon Quintus the urgency of
getting her into the Colosseum as soon as possible before
his rival Polonius grabbed the laurels. And there was the
sobering fact that the ludus was hovering on bankruptcy
and the Colosseum offered the only real chance of filling
the empty coffers.

"We're going to the Colosseum," Africanus told Fortuna
when she joined her that evening. "And my master is
keeping you for a while yet."

"You're not ready for the Colosseum," Fortuna said,
stunned at the news. "Oh, I know you proved yourself in
that flea pit of an arena, but in Rome you will be matched
against your own kind, men and women trained to fight
and with a lot of experience. I just don't want to see you
wiped out so quickly. But if your master is keeping me for
a while I'll have to work on you. Tomorrow we shall be
fully armoured and I will take the part of the Retarius with
the net and trident. You will have the gladius, a real sword.
We won't be hacking each other to pieces. It will be a
mock fight. But you do see my point."

"I understand," she said, unable to hide her
disappointment.

Fortuna lowered her voice to a conspiratorial whisper. "I don't know why, but I just don't trust your mistress. She's up to something, I know it. We shall have to watch our backs. I wonder where my slave has got to. That girl is always to be found when she's not wanted and never when she is. But no matter, I have some bread, cheese, and a fresh bottle of wine, or a flagon of beer, if you prefer."

It was evening and both Nydia and her mistress had stolen away on their respective errands. Africanus and Fortuna were alone with no one to disturb or spy on them. They had taken their baths and felt refreshed. Now they reclined naked in Fortuna's room happy and relaxing in each other's company, knowing that they would not be parted for a while yet. But despite the love that had blossomed between them, Africanus was still missing Circo.

"Have you ever been in love with a man?" Africanus asked, breaking a chunk of bread from the loaf.

"Oh, I've had men, but none that I would say I actually loved. But I think you have."

She told Fortuna all about Circo, their combat together and how magnificent he looked in his leather breeches and the way he'd fought, then how he'd come to her cell and made love to her.

Fortuna opened her cabinet and took out a package. She laid it on the bed and looked Africanus in the eye. "Would it help ease your anxiety if you imagined I was Circo making love to you?"

"Of course, but it's not quite the same is it?"

Fortuna unrolled the package and Africanus stared at its contents.

"It's called a 'dildo'," she informed, picking up a shining male phallus and handing it to her.

It was made of polished wood and wondrously fashioned, even down to the delicate veins on the trunk. The head was of a lighter colour than the shaft and was perfectly carved. The groove under it was deep and sensual. In her hand it felt strangely warm and as real as could be imagined. At the base a long thin leather strap had been fitted to a sort of curved plate which would fit snugly over a woman's pubic mound.

"I shall wear it and make love to you, and you will close your eyes and call me Circo," Fortuna said softly.

"It's very big," Africanus said anxiously, running her fingers along it length.

"It was a gift from the wife of my former master. She had it made to punish her disobedient slaves, men and women. She used to ride the women in their cunts and men up their backsides. It gave her immense pleasure and taught the slaves a lesson they didn't forget in a hurry. But with you I shall be gentle, unless of course you want a long, hard ride. I imagine Circo was a good fuck."

Africanus' eyes misted and looked as if she were in another world. "He rode me 'til I was sore," she whispered.

"Then you need a good, hard fuck. It'll bring back sweet memories, and at the same time get that weight off your mind. Now pass it to me."

Africanus handed her the implement, and Fortuna held it in place over her pubic bush. She adjusted it until the plate covered her sex and fitted tight in her thigh creases. The straps were passed around her hips and another thicker one under her legs and through her buttock crease. At the base of her spine the straps were buckled and fixed tight. It reared up from Fortuna's groin like a tent pole and Africanus couldn't help but admire how beautiful it looked in the lamplight. The surface had assumed a dull, well polished sheen, each vein stood out from the gleaming skin, and the head was large and bulbous.

Without any instructions she knelt before it and closed

her hand around the shaft, lovingly caressing its length. Her fingers gently smoothed the head and followed through the groove. She placed her hand at the middle and guided the head into her mouth. Fortuna watched with a glowing smile. Her protégé was already aroused at the sight and thought of being fucked with suck a splendid weapon. And it had the advantage of staying perpetually erect. No matter for how long she fucked the black gladiatrix, it would never tire or go limp.

Africanus sucked on the phallus, slowly to begin with, getting used to its unnatural hardness and strength. She angled her neck and took in as much as she could, letting the tip nudge her into her cheeks and throat. Her mouth was wide open, stretched all the way around its surface, but still she couldn't go right down to the base. The musky aroma of Fortuna's cunt drifted into her nostrils. At the root of the phallus she could see the outer fringes of the pubic bush, curled and glistening. She was sure she could smell the other woman's arousal. She worked her head up and down the shaft sucking harder with every lift and plunge of her head. She only wished it could come in her mouth. Her fingers stroked the sides of the phallus, going over the gnarled veins and at the base where it joined the plate. She used her free hand to smooth the dimpled skin of Fortuna's hips and buttocks. Fortuna opened her legs wider and Africanus slipped her hand under the hard, wooden plate. Her fingers went under the buttock crease, teasing the sensitive area that had all women panting and gasping. Fortuna caught her breath and placed her hands into Africanus' braids.

"If you keep that up I shall come and I won't have so much strength to fuck you," she whispered hoarsely.

Africanus released the phallus and went to the bed, lying on her back, her long legs thrown wide. She put out her arms welcoming Fortuna's sweating body between her fleshy thighs.

Fortuna placed the tip of the phallus at the dark throbbing lips of the gladiatrix' sex. The labia were already pouted and swollen from the sudden inrush of excited blood. The clitoris was stimulated to arousal even before the sex tunnel was penetrated. The girl was desperate for the phallus to embed itself deep in her sex. But Fortuna hung back, wisely taking her time to arouse the girl still further before she made her plunge. She let her weight fall on the woman beneath her and their breasts squashed into one another, flattening in fat mounds of black and ivory flesh. The nipples, now hard and proud collided and both women breathed a sigh of contentment. Fortuna put her hands on the sides of Africanus' head and held her still while she kissed her full on her voluptuous lips. She buried her fingers in the multitude of tiny, woven braids and raked her finger nails into the scalp. Africanus' hips and belly gave an involuntary heave and the phallus dug deeper against her sex.

"I want it now," she purred, raking Fortuna hard between the shoulder blades.

"Not yet my darling. Not so soon. Let me make love to you." Her voice was low and husky; her eyelids heavy and drooping over her misted green eyes. "There is no hurry. Love should never be hurried. We can fuck all night."

She raised herself on her elbows and let her breasts swing slowly to and fro over Africanus' throbbing nipples. A fine, almost transparent sheen of sweat had broken over the skin of both women as they lay, arms and legs entwined, teasing each other with their nipples and tongues. The air was getting thicker with the heavy, sensuous, sexual lust rising within them.

"I can't last much longer," Africanus breathed. "Please,

167

I want it in me."

"Soon," Fortuna said, prolonging the delicious agony of waiting. The longer she fondled and kissed her companion, the greater the urge stirring in her belly.

Fortuna had neglected to tell Africanus that her former mistress had fallen in love with her, had found her graceful torso, enormous breasts and shapely buttocks irresistible, and had used the phallus on her every night. Fortuna had welcomed it with open legs. After battling in the arena she too was longing for sex. Her whole body cried out for release she was so sexually aroused, and night after night her mistress had fucked her hard, inserting her phallus deep in the soaking tunnel of the gladiatrix, writhing her body on top of her, finally screaming and shaking in her own orgasm. But that was something private between Fortuna and her mistress and she had taken an oath of secrecy, never to betray what had taken place.

Africanus had thrown her legs over Fortuna's back and Fortuna was caressing the thighs with long sweeps of her palm. She loved the feel of her skin so soft and silky and so solid. She reached for the calves and ran her fingers along the splendid undulating contours.

"You have such magnificent legs, my darling. When you are in Rome, be careful who you let between them."

"I only want you and Circo," she whispered. "Now, fuck me before I come and spoil it all."

Fortuna reached under her belly and wiggled the head of the phallus into Africanus' sex. Her legs fell from the woman's back and went as wide as she could throw them. She placed her hands on Fortuna's buttocks and gently squeezed the cheeks, urging her to drive the phallus home.

Fortuna gathered her strength and began a slow gyration of her hips, moving them in magnificent serpentine motions. Her buttocks opened and clenched, each half revolving and colliding with the other. Africanus could just see them reflected in a polished copper mirror and her heart pounded.

"You're so fucking beautiful," she whispered, hardly able to control her emotions.

She was lost, buoyed up on a sea of ecstasy, flushed with her success in the arena and all she wanted now was total and uncompromising sex. And Fortuna was going to give it. Her back and shoulders snaked over Africanus pressing and squashing her breasts against the larger globes of the woman beneath who now writhed and squirmed as the phallus eased its way into her soaking sex. The hard shaft stayed rigid inside her and the momentum gradually increased. Fortuna was jerking her hips and buttocks faster and faster, going from side to side making sure that Africanus felt every inch.

"This is just wonderful," she breathed, trying now to imagine it really was Circo inserting his throbbing cock into her willing sex.

"I knew you'd like it," Fortuna smiled, kissing her again.

She arched her back and gave a final thrust ramming the phallus as far as it would go. Africanus' body broke into a colossal shudder. The phallus might not be a real penis, but the pleasure she was getting from it defied all description.

"Please suck my tits," she begged, and Fortuna's lips were there at once, puckering over the throbbing buds and sucking on them.

Then she drew back and started licking the sweat from Africanus' chest, licking the hot skin with her equally hot tongue, going everywhere, diving into the well of her throat, around and over her breasts, teasing the nipples, then angling her head and licking under Africanus' arms. She reached between her legs and inserted her fingers alongside

169

the phallus, wiggling them fast over the trembling clitoris. Africanus cried out and her bottom lifted from the bed. Her feet slammed into the base board and she reached out grabbing the head rails. Her back arched into a magnificent bridge lifting her buttocks high off the mattress. Fortuna clung to the head rails and rode her lover like a demon, slamming and smacking her pelvis into the apex of Africanus' thighs. The hard phallus moved so fast that Africanus was helpless against the power of her orgasm. It had taken control of her mind and body and there was nothing she could do to stop the hot river of love juice streaming from her quivering sex lips. But Fortuna exercised greater control and held back, riding her lover with slow, powerful thrusts of her hips and thighs. Africanus let out a deep groan and crashed to the bed in a soaking pool of her own juice.

"I've come," she sobbed, throwing her arms around Fortuna's shoulders and hugging her close.

They kissed for what seemed an eternity, their mouths, lips, and tongues searching, searching. Their hair became a confused tangle of dark braids and flowing locks. It tumbled over their faces and they were submerged in darkness. Both women were sweating so much their chests and bellies slithered over one another. The air in the room was hot and close, but still Fortuna had not come.

"I want you to fuck me," she said suddenly.

Africanus looked into her eyes, deep, fathomless pools of emerald, glowing with lust and passion. How could she refuse after giving her selfless and willing body?

Fortuna deftly released the tiny bronze buckles at the base of her spine and the phallus was speedily fitted over African's wet and glistening pubic curls. She stood up and saw her reflection in the polished copper and heaved a lustful sigh.

170

"I look magnificent," she said, amazed at just how devastatingly sexual the phallus looked strapped hard onto her mound.

She was naked and dripping, one hand resting on her hip, the other gripping the phallus and stroking it, running her hand up and down its length, feeling the juice slicked texture of the wood. Dimly, she became aware of the power a hard throbbing cock possessed, and why women would fall on their knees for it.

Fortuna was on her knees and with her arms encircling Africanus' waist she sucked the phallus deep into her throat. The aromatic taste of Africanus' love juice was strong and scented on her lips. Africanus put her hands into Fortuna's wild mane and dug her finger nails into the scalp. Fortuna returned the compliment, raking her talons over Africanus' buttocks, leaving long red scars from spine to thigh. She drew her head away and dragged Africanus to the floor, spreading her legs and easing the gladiatrix between them.

"Now do your stuff," she smiled. "Ride me until I'm sore."

Africanus began slowly and uncertainly at first, accustoming herself to her new found power. Again she realised why women worshipped men with rock hard, massive cocks. It was not unlike wielding a sword, but instead of dealing a killing blow, she was inserting part of her own body into another woman, and she thrust harder, driving her cock, for it seemed as it were now a real part of her flesh and blood, deeper and deeper, experiencing for the first time what it was like to penetrate another woman's sex. Fortuna grunted when the phallus' head touched the base of her womb, and closed her sex walls around the shaft. Her legs went around Africanus' back and they were locked fast.

"Take your time," Fortuna groaned, feeling the wooden

171

shaft hard inside her. "Ride me slowly. I want to feel every inch of you."

More than ever, Africanus felt that the phallus was hers and had been part of her from time immemorial.

"I'm going to ride you like a man," she whispered, and thrust her loins so hard Fortuna jolted from the floor.

But Africanus had learnt to control her ardour and rode her lover with steady heaves of her hips and buttocks. Fortuna could see her buttocks reflected in the mirror and it was her turn to watch how the gleaming black moons revolved and snaked. Africanus legs were wide and stiff, her toes digging into the boards for greater leverage. Her calves and thighs had gone solid and muscular, beautiful in their graceful curves and planes. Fortuna had always admired Africanus' thighs and had been attracted to them from the start. When they had finished making love she was going to lick the sweat from every pore.

Africanus lifted her weight on her fully stretched arms and let her enormous breasts swing over Fortuna's chest. She judged it just right and the erect nipples grazed the paler flesh with a touch of a feather. Fortuna cupped the globes in her hands, lifting and weighing them, marveling at their size. She rolled them tightly together, let them wobble back into place, and then squeezed, softly at first but then increasing the pressure until the dark flesh oozed from between her fingers. She raised her head and bit hard, sinking her teeth into the ample breast flesh. Africanus let out a cry of pain and rode harder, driven on by the pain darting into her like a myriad hot needles. When Fortuna bit hard on her nipples, Africanus' hips slammed into the open groin. Every fresh onslaught of pain from the sharp biting teeth brought forth a harder thrust of her hips and buttocks. It was Fortuna who was controlling the tempo of their love making, inflicting the pain at steady intervals

172

and feeling the reaction between her legs. But there was nothing she could do when her orgasm started to rise in her tingling belly. Africanus sensed she was coming and urged her lover to bite and crush her breasts. The pain was exquisite when fiery darts shot through her belly and breasts. She was still riding Fortuna with long, rhythmic thrusts, but the phallus had gone deeper and she could feel the resistance coming from within Fortuna's sex.

Fortuna stopped biting and slapped the sides of Africanus' ribs.

"Now you can fuck me hard!" she shrieked, and dragged the gladiatrix down onto her chest.

They were all buttocks, breasts, and hips, riding and slamming, grinding their pubic mounds until the skin rubbed raw. Africanus, overwhelmed by the sheer power of her cock rose to another galvanic orgasm and in a welter of thrashing limbs and writhing bodies they both climaxed.

"Oh, Venus, Goddess of all that is sacred, save me," Fortuna wept, feeling the phallus slithering from her soaking slit.

It was all Africanus could do to refrain from having her again, but instead she loosed the buckles and placed the phallus lovingly on the cabinet, then laid herself beside her lover and tenderly stroked her hair.

And she had hardly given Circo a thought.

For a moment, Fortuna thought she was dreaming. Both women had wakened before dawn and Africanus had gone back to her cell to prepare for the next bout with her trainer. Fortuna had summoned her slave, but the wretched girl had not answered the summons so she had gone to look for her, her face red with anger. It wasn't her place to go hunting for her own slave when she ought to have been on hand. Then, as she crossed the training ground she saw her slinking through the arch and wearing a sack, of all things.

"Where the hell have you been?" the trainer raged. "I've been looking all over the place for you. And why are you dressed like that?"

Nydia broke into a flood of tears and fell on her knees. "Oh, mistress, please don't be angry with me. I was sent on an errand by the master's wife and was waylaid. A gang of robbers stripped and raped me and left me naked in the street. A kind drover gave me this sack to cover myself. I was lucky to escape with my life. Look at me."

It was true. The girl had been abused, that was plain to see, and Fortuna's anger quickly abated.

"What have you got in your hand?" she asked, noticing her clenched fist.

The sobbing girl opened her fist and displayed a single sestertius.

"Where did you get this?" she enquired, putting it between her teeth.

"I found it in the street, mistress."

Fortuna bit the coin in half. "You should've saved yourself the trouble. It's a dud and not worth the lead it's made from."

She tossed the worthless coin in the sand and told Nydia to fetch her oils and come to her room at once. Lady Octavia had got home safely and had let herself in through a side door and was sleeping soundly as if she had never left her bed.

It was an hour later after Nydia had finished oiling Fortuna and the two gladiatrices were now locked in combat that she found her master, Quintus watching them battling in the training ground. With only two weeks to go before her first contest in the mighty Colosseum, he wanted to be absolutely sure that Africanus was up to the mark. He had a lot on his mind, what with Glaucus preparing the sponsorship with all the risk that entailed. He had offered to sponsor Africanus independently as a contract gladiatrix and had even hinted he might buy her if she was victorious in the Colosseum. It was a deal well worth considering. Africanus wouldn't come cheap, but the profit would clear his debts. Of course, he had no idea that both Glaucus and his own wife, Octavia had been planning it all along, waiting until Africanus had been trained and armoured at his own expense, watching him get deeper and deeper into debt, then Glaucus would offer to buy both the ludus and her at only half their worth before the creditors came battering at the door and took it all as payment. The only thing that Glaucus didn't know was that Octavia had made other plans and was one step ahead in the great game of treachery.

"Please, master I have some important news," Nydia simpered, bowing her head.

Quintus ignored her. His attention was caught by Fortuna, naked except for a shoulder guard, and armed with a deadly trident and net with which to ensnare Africanus looking resplendent in her wide brimmed helmet, short leather skirt that did little to hide her gorgeous bottom, and wielding a gladius, the short sword now swinging expertly in her hand. She was using her shield well and was parrying every blow of the trident. Her bare breasts were wobbling and swaying beautifully and the nipples were suitably erect. Both women looked splendid thrusting out their inviting buttocks and moving like predatory cats on their long shapely legs.

"What news?" he asked, keeping his eyes on the combatants.

"About the lady Octavia," she said slyly. "I know where she goes at night."

"At night?" he said, becoming interested.

Fortuna advanced quickly, keeping the trident aimed at

175

Africanus' throat and swinging the net in an arc. Africanus was keeping out of range, deftly leaping over the net and catching the trident with her sword. She moved in and the sword bounced off the shoulder guard. Fortuna ducked behind it protecting her face and stepping backwards, tripped and fell. Africanus was there in a flash, falling on top of her, aiming the tip of the blade at her throat. But Fortuna was ready with her trident and knocked the sword from her hand. Africanus rolled off her and snatched it up, ready to begin again.

Nydia waited patiently until the master turned to face her.

"I followed her, master, all the way to the docks."

"The docks!" he said, now staring hard at her. "What on earth was she doing there?"

"I don't know, master, I only saw her go in one of the brothels and she was talking to a man."

"If you're making this up, I'll have you flogged."

"It's true, master. The brothel was called, 'The House of Olives.' And there is something else, master," she said quickly, her tone bordering on panic. "I saw that black gladiatrix and my new mistress fucking with Lacinius. She sent me into the gladiators' quarters to fetch him and they were fucking all night,"

"He had both of them?" he asked, astonished.

"They were at it like goats," she smiled.

But Quintus wasn't smiling. It seemed that there was a lot going on behind his back that he didn't know about.

The combat was drawing to a close and Africanus had acquitted herself admirably. In two weeks she would be more than ready for the Colosseum. It was generous of his good friend, Glaucus offering to field her as a contract gladiatrix and take on all the financial risks. He looked at Nydia convinced that she was telling the truth.

"Soon, you shall have your freedom. In the meantime I want you to keep a close eye on your mistress, and if she goes there again you are to follow her and report everything she says and does."

Nydia bowed low and scurried off, wondering how she was going to get in and out of the brothel without being fucked by half of its horrible inmates.

CHAPTER ELEVEN

Octavia was getting more and more agitated, losing her temper and beating her slaves for the slightest little thing. It was getting closer to the time when the gladiatrix would make her first appearance in the Colosseum. Glaucus had everything in place and had paid to stage her first combat, but Quintus had inconsiderately remained fast in the ludus, watching Africanus improving with every bout. She had no objection to battling in the nude and seemed to enjoy displaying her magnificent naked body. Fortuna seemed equally pleased to show off her finely honed limbs. Quintus didn't consider himself to be much of an expert on women but he was sure that they were lovers. Well, that was no business of his as long as they continued to battle each other and Fortuna was really earning her fee, which reminded him that he had to travel to Cantiacorum, a small town some few miles inland from Marcellum to formalise his latest loan, which he hoped would be the last before Africanus had been fully trained and armoured. The road between the two towns was a lonely one, winding over mountains and through deeply wooded valleys; the ideal place to stage an ambush, if one were a highway robber, or bent on kidnapping attractive young women from isolated farms and selling them in Rome. When he told Octavia of his intended journey, she knew she had to move fast. Plutarc would need time to put his plans into operation, kidnapping her husband and doing whatever it was he did with his victims. She was past caring now the great day at the Colosseum was approaching, and she set off for the House of Olives that very night closely shadowed by Nydia. This time her slave had no intentions of being sexually abused, stripped and left wandering home dressed in a vermin

178

ridden sack, not to mention being fobbed off with a false coin. That really stuck in her gullet. If her mistress could pose as a prostitute and get away with it, well so could she, posing as a brothel servant. All right, she might have to put up with some mild banter and perhaps some groping and fondling, that was to be expected, but it was nothing compared to gaining her freedom. She set off in a plain brown dress, looking like a down at heel servant and her plan was a simple one. Keep out of sight until her mistress went upstairs with the man and eavesdrop on whatever was taking place between them, then bolt back to the ludus and report to her master.

The place was in uproar when her mistress arrived. The Roman battle fleet had docked and sailors crowded the rooms, drinking and brawling and grabbing the nearest whore they could lay their hands on. Her mistress had met the man and they had gone up the rickety staircase and into one of the rooms above. Nydia mingled with the crowd, giving her mistress time to settle, but never reached the first step. The sailor's arm was as thick as her thigh and his body like a tree trunk when it barred her way.

"How much for your cunt?" he said crudely, reaching out to fondle her breasts.

"I'm not a whore," she smiled sweetly. "I'm just a servant, so please let me pass."

If she'd told him to fuck off and get out of her way she might have got away with it. Flashing him a sweet smile was the worst thing she could have done. It was the sweetest smile he'd seen in a long while, and she had that little girl look about her that some whores not yet fucked completely rotten still maintained. He guessed she was pretty new to the game, her cunt not yet totally ravaged.

"I'll give you four sestertii," he offered, which was one more than the going rate, and grabbed her slim waist, steering her to the stairs.

In his strong grip she was like a lamb being led to the slaughter. Up she went, two steps at a time, tumbling, tripping and crashing through the nearest open door. It was a rule of the brothel that if a door was left open the room was free to use and the customer paid the old harridan sitting on her stool for the use of it. He threw a copper coin and she instinctively bit on it and satisfied it was genuine, motioned them into the room and closed the door.

"Phew!" Nydia breathed, "What's that smell?"

The previous occupants had only left the room moments before and it stank to high heaven of cheap perfume and stale sex sweat. The battered mattress sagged in the middle and the sheets were stained and ripped. The sailor shrugged. He'd been in worse places and any room was good enough for a fuck if it had a bed in it, particularly with the delicious morsel he was fortunate to share it with.

"Get your rags off," he said, wrestling his salt caked tunic to the floor.

"I want the money first," she said quickly, remembering the advice she'd been given from the last lot of tramps who'd fucked her.

He counted out four sestertii and slapped them in her hand, and like a professional whore, she bit on each one and then slipped off her clothes.

"You've got a big thing," she said genuinely alarmed, looking at his huge erection, wondering if she should ask for another two sestertii.

He guffawed, pleased with the reaction, and warming more and more to what he assumed was her innocent little girl act.

"Hold it in your hand," he said, taking her wrist and closing her slim fingers around the shaft.

"It's throbbing," she whispered, feeling the veins

180

pulsating in her palm.

He chuckled and put his hairy arm around her tiny waist. His hand went to her buttocks and he smiled a mouth full of yellowing teeth. Her buttocks were small and compact and his hand easily gripped the whole cheek, which made a change, most of the dockside whores had backsides as big as a bullock. Her cunt hair was silky soft and a mass of tight curls, as soft as the texture of the hair on her head. He squeezed her bottom and her body jolted from the shock. Her hand started to move slowly up and down the shaft. She thought that if she just stroked him gently, imitating the feel of her cunt, and he kept fondling her pretty little bum, he might come quickly and she could get on with the more important business of spying on her mistress, wherever she had gone.

In the dim light he closely resembled a satyr, with his goatee beard and very hairy chest and legs. A pair of hooves would not have looked out of place. But he still hadn't come, and reached for her shoulders forcing her knees to the floor.

"I'd like you to wash it first, please," she said, guessing what was coming next.

The water jug was empty, but there was a half bottle of wine on the cabinet. He snatched it by the neck and tipped the whole contents over his erect prick, spilling a good deal of it over her chest and nipples.

"Now suck on that!" he said, laughing at the look of distaste creasing her lips.

She slipped her mouth over the head and lapped at the wine droplets gathered at its base. She sucked slowly at first, hoping he would come quickly, and as soon as she felt his balls tremble she'd let go and let him spatter his filthy intentions all over the equally disgusting mattress. But he put his hands on her slender shoulders, manipulating them under his fingers and thumbs, kneading them like dough. He liked the feel of her bones and tight skin. That made a change too, not a bit of fat on her anywhere. He could just see her aroused nipples and nearly choked at the sight of them. They weren't like most girls' nipples, the buds rising from the usual pimpled discs, but the whole areola rose from her breast in a dark succulent bump, and the teat seemed to twitch, just begging for his lips.

"I want you sitting on my cock," he told her, taking her head away and lifting her in his strong arms.

He carried her to mattress and they both fell in a heap, rolling over and lying in the middle where the bed groaned and the mattress sagged. She was lying on top of him, feeling his cock neatly compressed against her cunt. His hands were swiftly on her buttocks, squeezing and rolling the cheeks.

"How old are you?" he asked, biting her earlobe.

She winced and told him she was twenty.

"You're lyin'" he said abruptly, and shot her a searching grin. "I think you're no more than fourteen. Look at you, thin as a bull rush."

What a cheek, she thought, calling her a fourteen year old, when she was seventeen, well, nearly eighteen. But she thought it unwise to argue. There was no telling what he might do with her alone in this stinking room.

"Yes, I'm fourteen," she smiled, and wriggled her bum over his cock. It seemed to be larger and throbbing a lot more urgently.

"And this is your first time with a man, isn't it?"

"Yes, it's my first time with a man," she agreed.

The Gods knew that wasn't true either!

He lifted her hips effortlessly over his middle. She was up on her knees with his cock nudging into her sex. Both of them knew it was all a game but harmless and she went

182

along with it, thinking that as soon as this frustrated old man was inside her he'd come in no time.

"Are you going to fuck me hard?" she purred, rolling her eyes in mock terror.

"No, I'm going to fuck you slow and gentle," he assured, moving her hips into position.

Her hand went under her legs and held his erection. Then she did roll her eyes. No need to put on an act now. He was huge and as hard as a rock.

"Please go in slowly," she said, her lips quivering at the thought of that thing inside her.

"It's all right, little one," he consoled. "This is your first time and I promise not to hurt you."

"Thank you," she whispered, keeping up the charade, and smiling now.

She lowered herself slowly and gently over his thing, pausing to catch her breath as its girth forced open her sex lips. Her nipples enlarged like raspberries, and just as inviting, as he sucked on them, not gently but almost biting them clean from her breasts.

Then he lost control and slammed her arse hard on the root of his cock.

"There, there," he said tenderly, looking at the shock in her wide and watering eyes. "Did that hurt my darling little girl?"

"Yes, it fucking well did," she blurted, and the spell was broken in an instant.

"That's your hard shit," he growled. "Now ride me, you little whore, or I'll you'll have my belt on your bare arse."

She put her hands on his chest and rocked her arse so fast the bed board beat the wall like a drum. Someone in the room next door laughed and thumped the wall in return. He thought that was funny and returned it with a crash of his fist on the partition. A layer of fine dust descended

183

from the ceiling, settling on her hair and shoulders and stuck to the sweat.

It was all good natured fucking from then on, and Nydia wiped the sweat from her brow thinking it wasn't quite so bad after all, fucking and riding a complete stranger with a massive cock punishing her arse. And she was being paid for it. Four sestertii was no mean sum to a slave paid absolutely nothing. She made a quick calculation. If she could manage at least ten, or maybe fifteen men a day, perhaps even twenty when she got really used to it, she could make a small fortune. No wonder there were so many whores fucking like crazy. She leaned right over so he could feel her bum. She was beginning to like his hands on her cheeks, showed what a nice arse she had if her client liked fondling it. After all, he was her client, and there she was fucking her arse off in a back alley brothel, and the thrill of it made her go wet.

His hands were on her hips and bouncing her up and down so fast her head swam.

"I love your cock!" she shrieked, and someone in the next room laughed again.

Now she was really entering into the spirit of it all, bouncing her bottom and shaking her breasts as his teeth nibbled on her teats. Neither of them saw or heard the door creak open and a young sailor creep stealthily into the room. He had finished with his whore but was still erect and wanted another piece of fucking flesh to play with. Without being invited he shamelessly climbed on the bed and knelt behind Nydia, pressing his hard cock against her back. He waved his purse at the sailor she was straddling indicating that he was willing to pay his share. The sailor didn't care a fig either way; he was too busy riding the little mare, screwing her arse over his bursting cock. Nydia looked over her shoulder and blew him a kiss, not realising that

184

was a well acknowledged sign in the brothel inviting a man's cock into a whore's mouth. He stood up on the edge of the bed and turned her face towards him. Now she really was a professional, taking on two men at once, fucking one and sucking the other. When she had been fucked on the sacks it had been painful and dirty, now she was fucking for pleasure and profit. But she still had to find out what was going with her mistress and that man. Until her master granted her freedom she was still his slave and couldn't take up whoring until she was formally freed. That thought made her ride like a rampant mare and the man beneath responded by clutching her hips and holding her still while he pumped his juice deep inside her. Her head bobbed over the cock in her mouth and it didn't take him long to come. He slapped her back and she swallowed his juice, gulping it down her throat in a single heave. The young sailor tossed a coin on the bed and left promising he'd look for her again. The man beneath her eased her off him and dragged her onto her back, throwing her legs open.

Before she could utter a word of protest he was in her again, ramming his cock in her belly and riding her.

"Always ride a whore twice," he told her. "Once for the pleasure of opening her cunt, and twice so you don't forget her face."

He asked her name and she lied and told him it was Satia. It sounded nice and had a ring to it.

Satia the whore. Satia the best fuck in Marcellum. And she couldn't help smiling at his ugly face when he came for the second time that hour. He got off her and shook out his tunic. She noticed the coin on the floor and something else lying under the bed that hadn't been there when she first looked. He slapped her arse and left, promising that he'd have her again too. Nydia crawled under the bed sweeping away cockroaches and spiders that had made their home in the dust and dirt and brought out a leather purse.

She closed the door and tipped out a pile of coins, counted them and went wide eyed. More then twenty sestertii! And that wasn't counting the four she'd already earned, plus the one the young sailor had tossed on the floor. Not bad for an hour's work bouncing on her bum. Well, if the old fool couldn't take better care of his money that was his look out. She got dressed and went along the corridor and met the old sailor coming along the corridor. Unlike her he had been in more brothels than she had ever dreamed of. He had also been robbed in his time and knew a thief when he saw one. Without a word he tore the dress from her shoulders and found his purse hidden in its folds. The slap that landed on her face sent her flying along the corridor.

"You thieving little whore!" he barked.

"I was going to give it back," she shrieked. "Honest I was."

"Don't lie. You lifted that. I can see it written all over your face."

He went downstairs leaving her under the care of the brothel minder who, sensing a reward, grabbed Nydia's arms and held them fast.

"That's her," the old sailor declared to the brothel mistress. "Thieving bitch lifted my purse. I caught her red handed."

The brothel mistress eyed her malevolently. In her establishment whores came and went, but it was taken for granted that they parted with a percentage of their earnings for using the brothel facilities. This one, it seemed had not only tried to bilk her of her rent, but also robbed her clients into the bargain. It wasn't good for business getting a reputation like that.

"You come with me," she grated, hauling Nydia to her

feet and dragging her naked to the cellar.

In no time, Nydia was tied hand and foot while a brothel minder went off to summon one of the town protectors whose job was to take thieves and other undesirables into custody. The prisons were full of thieves and murderesses and runaway slaves, just like the ones that Africanus had battled with in her first public combat. Now with fresh combats about to be staged at the Colosseum this little lot would fetch a tidy price when they were sold to the sponsor as sword fodder, or paraded naked and defenceless for the wild, half starved beasts.

Octavia and Plutarc had a room on the top floor and were oblivious to the commotion going on below. Just another brothel room fight that occurred everyday in a hole like this, and hardly worth a thought. She wasn't interested in animal sex at the moment, but eager to get down to the real reason for being there, although it was hard resisting his superb rippling chest and that blue chinned stubble, not to mention the powerful arms folded across his chest.

She told him exactly when her husband was making the journey to Cantiacorum and the route he would take, the number of guards accompanying him and whether he would be armed or not. Plutarc listened carefully. He knew the road well and had already worked out where, when and how Quintus would simply vanish. Now there was only the matter of his fee, which was considerable, given the risks involved. Quintus owned a gladiatorial training school and might even take along a couple of trained gladiators. It would take at least three men to one to overcome them and of course, they all had to be paid.

"A thousand sestertii!" she exclaimed, going pale.

"I would've thought it a very reasonable price considering what you expect to get in return." She was still gaping at him and he continued talking in a flat emotionless tone. "Oh, don't look so surprised. In my line of business I have to be one step ahead of my customers. I know that after he's gone you'll inherit the whole lot, or why else would you want him out of your life?"

There wasn't much she could say to that. The artful bastard had stolen a lead and she wasn't quite as clever as she thought.

"All right, I agree," she said ruefully. "But where do I get that kind of money?"

"That's your problem," he said dryly. "Bring the money to me at the Temple of Venus the day before he sets out and, by the way, what exactly do you want done?"

She'd thought about that and for once her conscience had got the better of her. He hadn't been a bad husband and she didn't want him killed, and besides if things did go wrong there was always the chance she might be implicated in his murder, then she would be in the arena as sword fodder.

"Can you just make him disappear?" she asked softly.

He thought that might be the case. He told her the galleys needed slaves and it wouldn't be too difficult to get him on board, no questions asked. Once he was at sea it was unlikely he'd ever return, but he could falsify the death by leaving another body in his place dressed in his clothes. After the jackals and wolves had feasted on it no one would be any the wiser.

"You're very thorough," she complimented him, genuinely admiring his professionalism, and thinking the same fate could befall Glaucus when the time arrived.

"Now, are we going to have a little fun, or are you just going to sit there with all that love juice oozing from your cunt?"

"What did you have in mind?" she smirked, aroused at

188

his cool calculated mind and the sight of his bulging cock.

"What do think if I send my belt across your arse, but you have got to try and stop me?"

"What's the penalty if I fail?" she smiled.

"You get a hard fucking and," he hesitated, "I might reduce my price a little."

She was up at once, stripping off her robe and baring her naked bottom. He stripped off his tunic and lashed his belt at her buttocks, but she was too quick and leaped over the boards. The sexual thrill of having to avoid the belt winging into her bare body had her heart racing. She knew he was eager to fuck with her as she with him, but being chased around the room and lashed into the bargain added spice to the banquet. He lashed at her with the end of the belt, catching her painful blows now and then across her naked rump and thighs. Watching her body bending and arching, her breasts bouncing from her chest made him more desperate. Every time the belt whistled against her naked skin he heard her catch her breath and saw a hot flush spread across her face. She was gasping for it, he could see that, but was enjoying being chased and whipped with the certainty she was going to be well fucked afterwards. Her bottom was turning red from the constant lashes he sent smacking against her soft flesh, but still she managed to avoid the blows he was aiming under her legs. If he could land a hard lash on her sex that would be enough to have her begging for it. But she stopped breathless and leaned against the wall, panting and gasping.

"I've had enough," she said, brushing the tumbling hair from her flushed face. "Let's just fuck."

"Not until you get on your knees and beg me," he returned, thrusting an inviting cock at her sweating sex.

"Please fuck me," she trembled. "My cunt's wet for you."

"Do you think I should whip you before you get on your

189

back?"

"I think I need whipping."

"Hard?"

"As hard as you can, on my bottom, my thighs, anywhere you want, but please fuck me afterwards."

"Only if you don't make a sound while I whip you. One peep from your mouth and I'll flog you unconscious and leave you unfucked."

"I won't make a sound," she promised.

"Then bend over and touch your toes. And remember, if you want my cock you don't cry out, no matter how much the belt hurts."

She shook her head and thrust out her willing bottom; waiting. He shuffled behind her and she heard him draw closer. Knowing she was going to be whipped and there was no escaping added to the thrill, but it was not seeing him, or knowing where he was going to strike that had the sex juice trickling down her thigh.

"Keep your legs together," he ordered. "And squeeze your cheeks. They're all the better for being tight. Now, up on your toes, and remember what I've said. One little peep out of you and you won't get my cock."

"Yes, master," she replied, without knowing why she suddenly came out with that.

She went up on her toes and he saw the whole length of her legs stiffen and tense. There was no doubt of it, for an older woman she had a magnificent pair of legs, long, straight and perfectly symmetrical. Her buttocks had clenched tight and he watched the buttock halves harden into the crease. Her back was bent in a splendid arc and under her chest her breasts quivered in anticipation. He could see how much her nipples had sprouted from her areolae. Her whole body was just begging for a lashing that would have her sex craving for his cock.

He stood at one side of her bent body and flicked the end of his belt over her bum cheeks. She caught her breath expecting a lash that would send her tumbling over the floor. When it didn't come she looked behind her to see what had stopped him. He was coiling the belt in his fist and tested its mettle by smacking it where she least thought it would fall. She gritted her teeth and hissed when it cracked over her shoulder blades. She rocked forward but managed to keep up on her toes swaying precariously, her fingertips just touching the floor.

"Hmm, very good," he complimented, surprised she hadn't fallen or screamed. The woman had more resilience than he thought possible.

The next lash winged into her flanks and she fell forward banging her head on the cabinet and uttering a groan of pain.

"I'll let that pass," he said in a conciliatory tone. "A grunt is not a scream."

"Thank you, master," she replied, bracing herself.

He sent the leather strap whistling into her taut arse cheeks and heard her heave. But still no cry of pain came from her lips. She was so desperate for his cock that she would endure any amount of whipping to have him inside her dripping sex. He could see her dark tuft glistening at the apex of her thighs and lashed across the back, not once but six times in quick succession, leaving fearful throbbing red lines. She was sobbing, but whether from pain or sheer sexual longing was difficult to tell.

"Break, you stubborn bitch!" he rasped, winging the belt on the backs of her thighs.

Her knees buckled and she collapsed into the cabinet and, nodding his admiration, he tossed the belt over her belly.

"You deserve your reward," he admitted, and carried her

to the bed.

Her put his arms under her knees and bent her legs over her head until her toes touched the wall. Her sex lay gaping and wet and he plunged right into her, fucking her without pausing for breath.

"You've got guts," he said honestly. "I don't know of any woman who could take a belting like that and not beg for mercy."

"I wanted your cock," she grinned, but not admitting the pain was killing.

"You would've got it anyway. I couldn't let you go without fucking you."

"Who else have you fucked in here?" she inquired curiously.

"Most of them," he said. "Apart from the woman who empties the pots. She's not bad looking but she's not actually a whore. She just works here."

"Would you fuck her given the chance?"

He shrugged. "I suppose so, if she were willing."

"Would you fuck her now?"

She got up and bawled along the passage for the pot woman.

"Are you serious, you really want me to fuck her?"

She said nothing until the pot woman came into the room carrying a large wooden bucket. She was in her early forties with slim sinewy legs and a firm waist. Her skin was tanned a dark brown from so much exposure to the sun when she carried the buckets through the sun baked streets to the fullers. She was quite good looking in a timeless sort of way with long hair tied in a tail. She wore nothing more elaborate than a short woollen shift and an old threadbare tunic, and carried a sort of neglected and wild look that appealed to some men. She also had good breasts, firm and round and tight buttocks.

192

She put down the bucket and reached under the bed for the pot.

"But it's empty," she said confused.

"Look at this man," Octavia said darkly. "Do you think him handsome?"

"Oh, yes, mistress," she replied. "Any woman would want him."

"In that case, would you fuck with him?"

The pot woman looked amazed at the suggestion. No one really bothered her with sex, even though with a bit of face paint she would have looked very pretty.

"That would be nice," she said simply.

"Take off that shift and tunic and straddle his cock."

The pot woman looked first at the high class whore, then at the rugged, handsome man she'd obviously been fucking only minutes before.

"Do as the lady tells you," Plutarc said sternly.

The pot woman wriggled the woollen shift over her hips and took off her tunic. She stood naked revealing a muscular and wiry body, surprisingly athletic and shapely. Plutarc lay on his back, his erection touching his navel. The pot woman swung a shapely thigh over his middle and squatted over his cock.

"You're not taking a piss," the high class whore told her. "I said, 'straddle him', unless you want a beating, or your head in that bucket of urine."

The pot woman looked for sympathy at the man stretched on the floor, but finding none, aimed his cock into her cunt. Her knees bent and Octavia silently admired her thighs and calves and tightly formed buttocks. Her hand wriggled the shaft into her widely gaping sex lips and she dropped onto his middle.

"Now ride him," the high class whore ordered. "Ride him hard. I want to see you come."

The pot woman rested her hands on her slender hips and worked her arse with fast jerks. Her pert breasts quivered on her chest and Plutarc reached up and grabbed them both.

"Squeeze them and make her eyes water."

Plutarc wasn't used to being ordered around by any woman let alone by a whore, but there was something in the timbre of her voice that demanded obedience. He squeezed the pot woman's tits until he saw tears gathering at the corners of her eyes.

"Good. Now slap her."

Plutarc hesitated, unsure whether to go through with this strange ordeal. The pot woman was fully engulfed on his rod and seemed to be enjoying having it inside her, and he had to concede, she fucked well. But he obeyed his high class piece and slapped the pot woman on the flanks. She jolted and let out a muffled grunt, but managed a curious half smile.

"Not hard enough. I want to hear her scream."

He wondered whether it was too much scheming, plotting to get rid of her husband and seize his goods that had driven her off her head. He looked briefly into her fiery eyes and slapped the pot woman's thighs. Then he slapped her face and breasts. He could feel her flesh tingling after the scream that reverberated through the open door. The pot woman's eyelids started to droop and her lips parted in short jerky pants.

"The dirty bitch is coming," Octavia announced.

The pot woman might be a lowly citizen but there was nothing dirty about her. Her long hair had been regularly brushed and was fine and flowing. Her face flushed as her orgasm mounted and for a brief moment in the lamp light she looked beautiful. The string tying her hair loosened and she reached up and tossed it about her shoulders. Then she was really stunning, her hair flying all around her. Not for a long time had any man fucked so hard and long. Octavia saw the admiration in Plutarc's eyes and snatched up the belt, lashing it over her wiry back.

"Ride him faster, you scum!" she raged.

The woman's face turned pale with terror and Plutarc thought that Octavia had gone out of her mind.

"Easy, girl," he chided. "The poor cow's doing her best."

"Her best isn't good enough. So ride faster, you filth," she barked.

The woman squirmed and wriggled like a ferret, shrieking with pain as Octavia's arm rose and fell, her mouth shouting obscenities with every stroke. She whipped until the pot woman climaxed and slumped over Plutarc's broad and perspiring chest.

"Get off him, you miserable wretch," Octavia snapped and sent her foot flying into the woman's belly.

She gurgled and rolled off clutching her stomach. Octavia would have renewed her lashing but Plutarc stopped her and snatched away his belt and sent her headlong over the bed.

"Put on your things and get out," he said softly to the abused woman, and reached into his purse and passed her a silver coin.

"Thank you, master," she sobbed and took up her bucket and left.

"Why did you do that?" he asked. "The wretch did you no harm."

Octavia made no reply but dragged him on top of her, throwing her long legs around him.

"Now fuck me again. And fuck me hard."

It was late before she left the House of Olives, walking home slowly through the darkened streets, her legs slightly bowed at the knees and her cunt throbbing. She made up her mind to sell Nydia and a couple of other girl slaves to raise the money she needed to pay for her husband's removal, but the little vixen was nowhere to be found and, as the dawn broke, the ludus became a frantic hive of activity.

"What's going on?" she asked, when Quintus entered her bed chamber.

He looked at his wife's ravaged face, her bleary eyes and unkempt hair.

"Had a rough night?"

She ignored him and repeated her question, averting her eyes from his searching face. He seemed to be looking right through her, his mind in anguished turmoil when he spoke.

"The emperor has brought forward the date of his inaugural games and the gladiators have to be dispatched immediately. Drucus is making the necessary arrangements, and I'm leaving for Cantiacorum tomorrow. When you see Nydia tell her to report to me at once, and if I were you I'd take a bath, you smell."

"Fuck," Octavia swore, sitting up and summoning her personal slaves.

Her husband was setting out two days earlier than his original plan and all because that confounded emperor had brought forward the games.

She got out of bed where she had pretended to have been all night and ordered the slaves to fetch her carriage. There was no time to take a bath and she contented herself with a liberal sprinkling of perfume and paint, hoping that Glaucus wouldn't ask too many embarrassing questions when she arrived at his villa asking for a private loan of a thousand sestertii, but she knew instinctively that when she sucked his cock she would get what she wanted, then she would have to rush back to find Plutarc and pay his fee and tell him of all the changes.

She was stiff and sore when she arrived at Glaucus' villa. Her cunt still throbbed and her legs ached where Plutarc had bent them over her head and fucked her almost into a coma. Glaucus too was in a frantic state of urgency, making last minute preparations, signing contracts and putting the finishing touches to the sponsorship, buying up the necessary slaves and criminals from the prisons. Her timing was perfect. She managed to get there only minutes before the emperor's envoys arrived demanding his presence at the imperial palace.

"A thousand sestertii!" he balked. "Why on earth should you want all that?"

She had her answer at once, that Quintus was making off to Cantiacorum, hadn't left her a single sestertius, and how was she going to pay for her lodgings in Rome and all the other expenses that she was bound to incur, and if he lent her the money he could take it out of her share of the profits at the end of the games, plus interest if he chose.

There was no time to even think about it except go to his treasury and hand over a bag of silver because the envoys were marching into his villa and he must come at once to Rome and meet the emperor.

Octavia didn't wait for nightfall but went to the House of Olives in broad daylight, and what did it matter anyway, her husband would be gone the next day in more than one meaning of the word.

Plutarc was there as she thought he would be, sitting quietly in the ground floor room drinking and generally taking things easy. He took her news with outward calm and put the money in a leather satchel.

"It'll all be taken care of," he assured her. "Now go home and get some sleep. You look like shit."

And he smiled and walked off to the docks.

CHAPTER TWELVE

"The emperor has commanded you to fight naked," the games' master informed them, as Africanus and Fortuna made their way through the labyrinth of passages and tunnels under the Colosseum.

It was something out of a nightmare. Dim figures moved in the gloom hauling on ropes raising platforms to the arena above. Wild beasts prowled angrily inside their cages, baring their fearsome teeth and roaring their hunger and discontent. Gladiators were buckling on their armour and selecting their various weapons, and inside their cells, dozens of naked slaves huddled together in sheer terror wondering what fresh horrors awaited them.

The two women had arrived the previous night and had gone straightaway to the gladiators' barracks. Too late to join the customary festivities the night before the games, they went to their respective cells and slept. In the morning they made their devotions to Nemesis, praying for victory. Slaves oiled their skin and a guard escorted them below.

They had no idea whom they were matched against or what the sponsor had arranged in the way of entertainment. But one thing they had learned was that later, one of them would be fighting in full armour against a gladiator, which just might result in death, depending on the emperor's whim.

But there was no time to think about that now. Each was given a thong, a mere strip of leather that covered their sex, for all the good it did, they may as well have not troubled themselves to put it on. Africanus' armour consisted of a short handled trident and net and a stout leather whip, well oiled and supple. Fortuna also carried a three tailed whip and a gladius, sharp and deadly.

"You know the drill," the games master said to Fortuna, whom he recognized from previous bouts.

Fortuna nodded and selected a trident from a pile of gleaming weapons. She handed it to Africanus and they made their way to the platform.

"Just do as I do," Fortuna advised. "And may the Gods be with us."

The slaves hauled on the ropes and the platform creaked upwards and into the arena.

Africanus' jaw dropped open. She had not had a chance to see the Colosseum in daylight, now she stared in disbelief. She knew it was vast, but this exceeded her wildest dreams. Fifty thousand Romans were on their feet and cheering madly. The noise was deafening. The arena in Marcellum was village market compared to this multitude. In the front seats sat the senators and beside them the Vestal Virgins resplendent in their white robes. Behind them sat the freemen and wealthy citizens. Slaves and women were relegated to the poorest seats high up at the back. At the centre the emperor was seated on a marble throne surrounded by his slaves and attendants, looking magnificent in his purple robe and crown of golden laurel leaves. She also glimpsed the lady Octavia and Glaucus sitting side by side in seats reserved for the sponsor, but was disappointed not to see Quintus. Looking all around the perimeter she saw wooden crucifixes and huge wooden wheels mounted on triangular frames. Great clouds of incense burned and a sweet fragrance of pine cones wafted across the arena. For a fleeting moment she had the impression that she was the most important woman in the whole empire. Glorious in her nakedness, her black skin shining, and her hair in woven braids she knew just how beautiful she looked and felt that her whole life had been but a preparation for this moment of glory.

"Remember what I told you," Fortuna whispered. "Play up to the emperor. You've got a great body, make full use of it. He'll be watching your every move."

Africanus nodded and turned at the sound of blasting trumpets. The audience fell silent and the master of ceremonies took the stand.

"This is it," Fortuna breathed. "Now we'll hear what the sponsor has arranged."

"Today we re-enact the conquest of Britannia," he announced. "There, on the wild Northern hills stood the Fourteenth Legion commanded by Suetonius, standing alone against the barbaric and savage horde of the barbarian queen, Boudicca, bent on slaughter and revenge. All hail the Legion of Suetonius!"

The audience rose and cheered the two gladiatrices who bowed in return. They had broken into a sweat and their skin glistened magnificently. Already, Africanus felt her nipples harden and a cold chill stirred her belly. She was sure the emperor raised his hand in salute.

"The brutal savages were painted blue and red as was their custom," the master of ceremonies continued. "Their numbers so great the earth shook beneath their feet. But they were defeated and crucified by the victorious legionaries and peace reigned throughout the land. Mighty Caesar is pleased to present the barbarian queen and her savage horde!"

One of the gates in the perimeter walls opened and a crowd of terrified female slaves entered the arena, their bodies naked and painted with Celtic scrolls and circles. The tallest was got up to look like Boudicca and was wearing a long flowing wig of red hair. All the slaves carried whips, lances or bows and arrows.

"Raise your trident," Fortuna whispered. "And salute the emperor."

200

"Mighty Caesar, those about to die salute you!" they both chanted, and bowed low, baring their naked rumps to the crowd.

"What are we supposed to do?" Africanus muttered. "Kill them all, or what?"

"Catch them in your net and drag them to the wheels and the crucifixes. The slaves will bind them. I will fight off the rest. Remember to concentrate. Ignore the mob and let the emperor enjoy seeing your body. Good luck."

"Good luck," Africanus echoed.

And they moved slowly towards the barbarian horde.

"They look splendid in their nakedness," Octavia said triumphantly. "I see the emperor has already taken an interest in our gladiatrix."

Domitian was sitting upright on his marble throne watching intently as the barbarian horde went into a huddle. The tallest with the long red wig seemed to be giving orders. It was a similar situation to the combat at Marcellum, except there were a lot more of them, they were better armed and a lot more organized now that a leader had emerged. The horde split into two groups; the archers at the front and those with lances and whips flanking them.

"Where is Quintus?" Glaucus asked. "He should've been back from Cantiacorum by now."

"Oh, I expect he's been delayed," Octavia tittered, and plopped her hand on his thigh.

She couldn't wait for nightfall, by then her husband's body would have been found, or the one that Plutarc substituted, Fortuna and Africanus would have beaten all their opponents, and the ludus would be legally hers. She slipped her hand into Glaucus' groin, gave his cock an affectionate squeeze, and fixed her eyes on the advancing horde.

Silence fell as the two female fighters responded, getting

closer but keeping tight together, their naked thighs almost touching. A volley of arrows whistled through the air but fell harmlessly all around them. The slaves were not trained archers and clumsily reloaded their bows. Those with lances fanned out and ran towards them. Unlike the lancers at Marcellum they waited until they were in reach before hurling the shafts. Fortuna deflected two lances with her gladius, but a third caught Africanus on her thigh.

"It's only a flesh wound," she assured Fortuna, and advanced quickly on the nearest lancer.

She swung her net in a wide arc and the Celt slipped and was hopeless entangled.

"Drag her to the crucifix," Fortuna bawled, rushing to attack the other three.

She swung her razor sharp gladius and delivered a neat glancing blow across the buttocks of the terrified and disarmed slave. A thin red line appeared and grew wider and more livid. It was just what Fortuna planned. The sight of blood sent the rest into panic.

Africanus ran across the arena, dragging the slave behind her like a sack of garbage. At the foot of the crucifix, male slaves disentangled the shrieking woman and speedily crucified her, stretching out her dust caked wrists and roping then tightly on the cross beam. Africanus was quickly back as Fortuna swiped her gladius into the thighs of another disarmed lancer. The slave leapt back but the gladiatrix kicked her hard in the groin and she heeled over clutching her sex and groaning from the pain.

"Leave her and get the other one," Fortuna yelled.

Now Africanus saw what Fortuna had in mind. She rushed forward and aimed her trident at the slave's belly and simultaneously swung her net into her legs. The painted slave didn't know which to avoid and in her confusion she too tripped and fell. In a second Africanus threw the net over her head and hauled her screaming to one of the wheels. The slaves worked fast and soon had her spreadeagled on the wheel, her legs and arms forming a huge X on the spokes.

Now the slaves armed with swords moved in headed by Queen Boudicca.

"Leave her to me," Fortuna hissed, delighting in a one to one combat.

Boudicca was armed with a whip and wisely kept out of range of her opponent's sword. She was tall and well built, her naked breasts and belly had been painted with blue scrolls and all down her long, shapely legs red and blue serpents entwined, their tongues lashing into her sex. Her pale skinned bottom had been left bare and Fortuna could see the buttocks clenching as she raised her whip. She let out a primitive war cry and brought the lash swiftly across Fortuna's back. The gladiatrix howled and the fifty thousand Romans were on their feet cheering and yelling as she responded by whistling her deadly three tailed whip into the barbarian's buttocks. The emperor applauded the delivery and watched closely as the gladiatrix swung into action. The whip lashed with savage fury into the barbarian queen's back and thighs. She turned to avoid the blows and the whip wrapped around her calf and she tumbled into the dust. Fortuna was taking no chances with this one. She was obviously more used to fighting and had to be dispatched quickly. She kicked her in the ribs, and then hard into her buttocks and, as the barbarian rolled over, she aimed the point of her gladius at the woman's throat. She surrendered at once and, to everyone's surprise, walked dumbly to one of the wheels and held out her arms, knowing it was useless to resist.

Africanus had sustained more lashes from the terrified slaves, but had overcome three of them by stabbing them with the points of her trident, or returning their lashes with her own whip. Now that Boudicca had been removed all resistance crumbled. Time and time again Africanus dragged them in her net, rubbing the skin from their knees and buttocks as they tumbled and rolled over the ground.

Fortuna was swinging her flashing sword in all directions and one by one the slaves capitulated, but she too had sustained several welts from their whips, and a lance had pierced her left buttock which now throbbed painfully.

Africanus moved in with her trident on one of the last remaining slaves, a pretty young girl whose pert breasts and nipples had been painted blue. Her slim legs were covered in twirling scrolls which artfully coiled under her torso and into her naked sex. Her eyes widened with terror when the tall, naked black woman advanced upon her. The black skin was running with sweat and gleaming like burnished ebony. Her huge breasts wobbled and swung on her sweating chest. Her powerful thighs flexed and hardened as she moved in for the kill.

"Please spare me," the young slave wailed, dropping to her knees.

Africanus gathered her net but stopped in mid air.

"You!" she said aghast. "What the fuck are you doing in the Colosseum?"

Octavia leaned forward in her seat. She too had recognized Nydia and wondered what she was doing there.

"A common prostitute caught thieving," Glaucus told her.

"My personal slave, thieving prostitute!" she said, stunned. "But where for heaven's sake?"

He shrugged. "One of the lupanars near the docks, I think. Caught red handed robbing a sailor in the House of Olives or Figs. I don't know."

Octavia's eyes narrowed and she looked swiftly around

her at the reserved seats. Quintus was still nowhere to be seen, but she was convinced that conniving little bitch had been up to something. She looked down into the arena and saw Africanus dragging Nydia by the hair towards the nearest wheel and kicking her pretty little arse all the way there. All of the slaves were now either crucified or spread over the wheels waiting their next punishment.

The slaves lifted Nydia facing the hub of the wheel and spread her arms and legs over the spokes. First they tied her wrists and ankles, spreading her arms and opening her legs as wide as they could. When she was secure they took leather straps and began buckling them around her calves, the backs of her knees and at mid thigh. A broader strap went around her waist and was pulled so tightly she gasped for air. The next strap circled half way up her back and the slave grunted audibly as he pulled the buckle into place. More straps were fixed to her fore and upper arms and as she was held fast. Some of the other slaves were crucified with the same attention to detail. Leather straps or ropes were first tied to their wrists and ankles, then around their calves, knees and thighs, around the pits of their stomachs and under their breasts.

"Let the punishment begin!" the master of ceremonies announced, and both gladiatrices loosed the whips and cracked them through the air.

This was what the audience had really come to see, the prisoner slaves fastened to the crucifix and wheels and flogged mercilessly by the stalwart and magnificent naked gladiatrices.

Africanus looked superb, playing to both audience and emperor. Her limbs, breasts and torso seemed to shimmer in the glare of the sun. She thrust out her buttocks and started snaking her hips. A roar of approval rippled through the assembly. Her whole arse rose and fell and it was as if her hips were acting of their own accord, revolving in great circles, each buttock half separating and clenching, having every man, including the emperor on the edge of his seat. She made a half turn so that her body was in profile. She took a deep breath and flexed both the whip and her stomach and it was possible to see how high and firm her breasts rose from her chest. Those closest the edge of the arena could see her nipples erect and throbbing.

Suddenly the wheel to which Nydia was bound started to groan on its axel. A slave just visible behind the spokes was turning a handle and the wheel went slowly into motion. Nydia let out a gasp of horror as the thousands of people in front of her seemed to tip sideways. Then she realized why the slaves had bound her body and limbs so thoroughly. Her body was going to turn full circle as the whip descended on her back, buttocks and legs.

Now, with their attention caught at the sight of Nydia's slim body going into a spin, Africanus turned on her charm, making sure the emperor saw everything she had to offer, and she accidentally dropped her whip. Her legs opened wide and she bent over to pick it up. It was impossible not to see the thick mound of pubic curls and the dark, inviting, slit gaping and winking. Her buttocks gave a quick sensuous wiggle and she was back up again, standing tall and erect, raising her arm high in the air and then bringing it down with the speed of lightning. To Nydia it sounded like the crack of doom as it sailed at full strength into her back. The wheel had made a quarter turn and already the straps were straining at her arms and legs. The hub pushed harder into her stomach and she couldn't avoid thrusting her hips and buttocks to the descending whip. Suddenly the world went upside down and Nydia was looking at the feet of the slave turning the handle. The straps cut into her flesh and she felt blood rushing to her head. Half in a daze, she screamed in agony as the whip sailed into her open sex. Now her body was inverted and her legs wide spread, Africanus couldn't miss lashing her cunt. She gave her three strokes, then concentrated on her clenching buttocks, aiming the whip directly into her bottom crease, slicing it through the whole cleft. Nydia's body broke into a myriad spasms as the wheel slowly brought her upright again. But there was no respite. Africanus, knowing she had the full attention of the emperor laid on the strokes thick and fast, even the people at the back of the arena could hear Nydia's screams and urged the gladiatrix on to whip her senseless.

At the crucifix, Fortuna was flogging slave after slave, lashing them with all the fury of her strength. She too, was mindful of the emperor's attention and knew that failure to please him could result in immediate execution. The crucified slaves were bound with ropes at their wrists, waists and ankles, but it was unseen agony they suffered most. Each crucifix had been fitted with a huge phallus impaling the bound women. The more they struggled and writhed under the lash, the greater the pain as the phallus imbedded itself deeper into their sexes. Their faces contorted at the pain and sexual torment they were suffering with every renewed stroke of the whip. Even though their flesh scorched from the burning lash they couldn't fight the mounting orgasm it was bringing on. One by one their harsh cries of pain and ecstasy screamed from their open mouths and they slumped forward in their bonds, sexually drained and laid waste.

Nydia had turned ten times on the wheel before she too succumbed to the lash and the sexual arousal tearing at her belly and sex. Never before had she endured such pain or had such a volcanic orgasm. Her love juice flowed through her buttock crease in a torrent and trickled down her back. Uttering one last scream of agony, she hung limply on the wheel in an upright position, her head pressed against the spokes and she passed out.

"Excellent," Domitian applauded. "Have the gladiatrices brought to me at once."

The two women, soaked in sweat approached the emperor's throne and bowed low. An earthy aroma of feminine sweat and sex filled his nostrils; there was nothing he liked more than the delicious smell of a woman on heat.

"You have both fought with great courage and fortitude," he beamed. "There is nothing I enjoy more than witnessing the defeat of Rome's enemies. As a reward one of you shall fight in the arena tomorrow against the undefeated champion of the ludus of Craxus. I think I shall choose you, the black gladiatrix. You shall be fully armoured and it shall be a fight to the death."

"Thank you, your imperial highness," she bowed, and he reached forward and patted her sweating thigh.

"If you are victorious, I shall grant a thousand sestertii."

He touched her on the shoulder and both gladiatrices bowed low, then turned to the cheering audience and held their arms high.

Octavia and Glaucus were on their feet applauding and watching Africanus favoured by the emperor.

"She has made us rich today," Glaucus remarked.

Not as rich as I'm going to be tomorrow, Octavia thought, and both the ludus and Africanus would be her sole property. If the gladiatrix went on displaying such prowess she would earn her weight in gold. She slipped her arm around Glaucus' waist and smiled grimly as Nydia was taken down from the wheel and dragged to the cells below. Even if the artful little bitch had been up to no good Octavia had little to worry about. Another bout in the arena and she would be dead anyway, and she reached for Glaucus' cock; smiling.

208

CHAPTER THIRTEEN

"I can't sleep," Africanus muttered, turning over on her bed. Fortuna padded softly across the room and climbed beside her. "You're worried about tomorrow. Don't be, my love. You will be victorious. The Gods will see to that. Remember to make your devotions to Nemesis and she will favour you."

Africanus rolled over and laid her thigh over Fortuna. "I'd rather you favoured me with your big cock."

Fortuna clicked her tongue and smiled. "It seems you just can't get enough of my weapon."

They both laughed and hugged each other close. "I've fallen in love with you. Can't you understand that?"

"I knew it from the first time we met, and it may surprise you that the feeling was instantly mutual. Do you want us to fuck each other now?"

The silence and a hand squeezing her breast answered her question, and she got up to go to the cabinet where her personal possessions were stored.

"I have a little surprise for you," Fortuna beamed, and held up a different implement than the one they had used before.

It was a male cock, beautifully fashioned, long and thick, but both ends were the same, each possessing the head of a penis as if two huge cocks had been joined together at the middle.

"Now lie on your back and open your legs," Fortuna whispered. "Bend your knees and then prop yourself up on your elbows if you prefer."

Africanus did her bidding, spreading her legs and bending them. Fortuna slipped her legs under Africanus' raised knees and shuffled her bottom between the gleaming black thighs. Gingerly, she eased the dildo into her own sex, then positioned the other end at Africanus' gaping slit. A gentle push of her hips had the dildo going into both sexes at the same time, and Africanus sucked her breath.

"We're both going to fuck each other with the same cock!" she gasped, as it slipped deeper into her hot tunnel.

Fortuna gave a final shove of her loins and rammed home the dildo until they were both fully penetrated. Then she sat up and held out her arms. Africanus grasped her wrists and, using only their hips and buttocks as levers, they began to rock steadily back and forth, forcing the dildo to ride fuck them both as they bent to and fro like rowers in a heavy swell.

Glorious in their nakedness, sweat now forming on their skin, they rocked harder, admiring their splendid swinging breasts and erect, pulsating nipples, the crease across their bellies which came and went with every thrust. Soon the air was thick with heavy breathing and low throaty moans. Their eyelids grew heavy with longing and they rocked faster, eager to bring each other off. Fortuna wriggled her buttocks harder into the fork of Africanus' thighs and now their pubic hair and swollen sex lips rubbed and sucked, mingling their already hot, flowing juices. Suddenly, as if on a prearranged signal, both women slammed their hips and thighs together with all the strength they could muster. Their ample breasts shook and quivered at every thrust and pant.

"I've never been fucked like this!" Africanus moaned, digging her heels hard into the floor.

"I'm going to make you come like a river," Fortuna returned, thrusting her strong pelvis.

"I'm going to fuck you sore," Africanus sobbed, feeling her whole body tingling.

Now riding on a wave of ecstasy, not caring who saw or

heard them, both women gave vent to their long pent up feelings.

"I want to suck your tits," Africanus laughed, looking at Fortuna's wobbling breasts.

"I'm going to get my tongue so far up your cunt you'll think I'm swallowing the whole of you."

"After this, I'm going to beat you 'til you scream for mercy, you beautiful looking bitch."

"And I shall lick every inch of your shining black skin, you wonderful whore."

And so it went on. Loving abuse poured from their mouths as they rode harder and harder, driving each other wild with their manic thrusting and heaving. Under their buttocks a pool of love juice mingled and stuck to their perspiring skin, making their arses slither and slip and their hips more ardent in their massive plunges.

"You smell like a mare in heat," Fortuna laughed, wrenching at Africanus' wrists.

The black gladiatrix responded with a sudden jolt of her hips and Fortuna's lungs inhaled deeply, pushing out her breasts.

Keeping the dildo deep inside them, they bent their backs, leaning so far into each other their lips crushed. They kissed until it hurt, forcing their tongues to the backs of their throats, twisting and turning them until their mouths ached. Then they lost all control; they let go of their wrists and, keeping the dildo lodged tight in their cunts' began slapping and hitting their breasts and nipples, gnashing their teeth as the globes wobbled and swung from side to side. They slapped and punched their bellies, hips and thighs, then, as the stinging blows increased the pain in their tingling skin they came in a torrent, pouring out their hot, creamy juices. Cries of ecstasy echoed through the subterranean passages and the both collapsed on their backs, panting and gasping, their strength drained, but still the dildo remained deep inside their dripping tunnels.

"Phew," Africanus breathed, wiping her forearm across her brow. "That was the greatest fuck of my life."

"It's not over yet," Fortuna grinned wickedly. She slithered from Africanus' thighs and popped the dildo from their sexes. "Now suck," she whispered, placing the bulbous, juice slicked head into her mouth.

They sucked on the ends of the dildo, drawing it into their mouths, getting closer until their lips almost met, and not stopping until the juice was licked dry. Fortuna reached out and fondled her lover's breasts, pinching and rolling the throbbing nipples. Africanus placed her hand under Fortuna's breast and cupped the freckled globe. Their breathing came in frantic gasps as they tumbled into a long, passionate embrace. Their arms and legs went around hips and buttocks, hugging each other close. Desperately their fingers went between their legs, sliding into their soaking tunnels, teasing their clitorises until they both reached their second orgasm. Sweat dripped and ran from their thrashing bodies, writhing and twisting as their arms pumped faster and faster. Africanus' legs kicked out wide but Fortuna grabbed her thigh and held it rigid. She bent her head, her tongue swept up the long black pillar, licking the sweat from the gleaming skin. Africanus seized her head and held it between her legs.

"Suck my cunt," she breathed.

Fortuna eased her body round and her eager tongue went straight into her sex, lapping at the oozing juice, almost suffocating between the crushing thighs.

"I'm coming again," Africanus sobbed, and lifted her bottom high off the bed.

Juice welled from her sex and Fortuna did not stop licking until every drop had been swallowed. They lay exhausted in each other's arms until daybreak when one of the armourers knocked on their cell door.

"I'm to take the black one to the armoury," he said, wrinkling his nose at the sex laden air.

The gladiatrices parted and stood up stretching their aching limbs. "Who am I fighting?" Africanus asked casually.

"His name is Circo," he said flatly.

She looked as if the thunder God had struck her with his own hammer.

"Circo," she whispered, open mouthed.

"Aye, and to the death. The emperor has commanded it. But I'll let you into a secret," he moved into the cell and closed the door, lowering his voice to a harsh whisper. "The emperor has let it be known that after the contest you are to be scrubbed and taken to his palace. Your body will be his to do with as he pleases."

"Assuming she wins," Fortuna interrupted.

The armourer shot her a sly glance. "She can't fail. Circo is to be disabled before the contest. A knife under his right arm will stop him from wielding his sword. Now, after you've washed all that cunt juice from your stinking skin, make your way to the armoury and select your weapons. If I were you, I'd go for the trident. One good thrust and he'll be out of the contest and you'll be romping in the emperor's bed."

And he left slamming the door behind him.

"It's not fair," Africanus sobbed, stunned at the news.

After all this time she was to fight Circo, the only man she had ever respected or loved, but he was to be crippled before he even lifted his sword. She sat on the edge of the bed and buried her face in her hands.

"Never mind," Fortuna consoled. "It's how things are here."

213

Not if I can help it, Africanus thought, and walked slowly to the baths, her mind in turmoil.

"Get up," the slave master grunted, kicking Nydia in the ribs. "You've been bought, and be thankful for it, or you'd be back in the arena as beast bait."

Nydia struggled to her feet from where she had lain all night long, hugging her knees and cursing the day she'd ever set eyes on the House of Olives and its revolting inmates. Naked, her back, bottom and legs still throbbing from Africanus' whip, she padded softly behind the slave master, wondering what fresh terror awaited.

The slave master showed her into a cell and they were alone. "Your new master has commanded you to take this food to the gladiator, Circo, and also to hand him this note. Do you understand that, you thick little tart?"

She nodded dumbly and lifted a plate of porridge. The note she kept clutched in her hand as she made her way to Circo's cell.

"You!" he said, eyeing her with undisguised dislike. "The crawling little lizard I caught snooping around the gladiatrices' cells."

"I am to give you this," she whispered, keeping her head bowed.

He snatched the note and read it, his eyes widening in disbelief. "Your master will meet you at the gate to the gladiator's quarters," he said softly, crumpling the note in his hand. "Tell him I shall be there as he commands. Move fast, you little shit, and if you so much as breathe a word, I'll slit your throat."

She was gone like an arrow from a bow, running along the corridor, hoping her new master would at least give her some clothes to cover her nakedness. Her new master remained in the shadows and told her to go to the gladiatrix and deliver the same command. She hurried off and found Africanus getting out of her bath. No one paid any attention to a naked slave girl sidling up to the black woman and offering to towel her dripping body. She delivered the message in a hushed whisper, keeping her distance in case the gladiatrix flattened her with a smack of her fist. But she just gave her a towel to wrap around her hips.

"You are to come with me," Africanus said seriously, going to her cell and putting on her tunic.

Fortuna was in her own cell fast asleep and there was no time to wake her or bid farewell.

"Forgive me, my darling," she whispered, and kissed her lightly on the cheek.

Quickly, Africanus and the slave girl made their way to the gate where Circo was waiting in the shadows. As arranged with the turnkey, the gate was unlocked, and all three made their way silently through the gladiatrices' barracks and into the street just as the sun rose over the sleeping city. Both Africanus and Circo were itching to hold each other in their arms, but there was no time. They went speedily to the city gate and passed through, going along the Apian Way to a rendezvous far out in the countryside.

While the three fugitives fled the city, Octavia was reclining on a couch mentally calculating how much profit she'd made out of Africanus' successful bout, and how much more there was to be made when she fought again that day. With the patronage of the emperor and now, Octavia was certain; the gladiatrix legally her property, all sorts of possibilities beckoned. For one thing, she was going to be very rich. The emperor would reward her well for the black gladiatrix' sexual favours and she might even start her own gladiatrix training school which could easily double as a brothel. After all, she had a good idea gained from first hand knowledge how such places operated. She clapped her hands summoning her slave, and stretched out her long, splendid legs.

"You summoned me, mistress," the slave said from behind her.

Octavia's blood froze in her veins as the slave's hand lighted on her shoulder.

"Quintus!" she uttered, her throat suddenly dry.

"Your little plan to have me murdered, or sold into slavery hasn't quite come off," he said, moving around the couch. "Before you set out to double cross, always ensure that you yourself are not going to be double crossed into the bargain."

"That bastard, Plutarc," she hissed.

Quintus was facing her now and terrifying in his placidity. "In exchange for a couple of nubile slave girls and a few sestertii, he told me everything; all about your activities as a part time whore in the House of Olives, the time you met, the things you discussed and your partiality for rough sex. Well, you are about to get as much rough sex as you want, but first I have a little score of my own to settle, my beautiful, faithless, murderous wife."

"Please, Quintus, it was all Glaucus' doing," she pleaded, inching away from his approaching body. "He put me up to it because he wanted to sponsor the black gladia...Aaagh!"

"Liar!" he shouted, smacking her across the head. "I know all about you and Glaucus. He squealed like a pig when the gladiator put a sword to his throat."

He grabbed her hair and dragged her across the floor. A slave dutifully arrived with a long length of rope and a whip.

"You like rough sex, well, here's something for starters."

The slave knew exactly what to do and went to work with the proficiency of an expert. He threw her over his shoulder and carried her to the nearest column. It was about the right size for her arms to reach all the way around its circumference. He tied her wrists tightly on the other side of the column and then, with a single tear, ripped the robe from her back.

"Oh, please, Quintus don't flog me," she pleaded.

"You're going to be flogged and fucked," he told her, without any emotion.

The slave parted her ankles and tied them to the base of the pillar. Next, he passed a length of rope around her waist and pulled it so tightly the air gushed from her lungs. Another length of rope went around her thighs and was knotted to her wrists. The final length was passed over her back and when that too was pulled tight her breasts crushed against the marble. Quintus patted her defenceless bottom, teasing and taunting the shapely moons.

"A splendid arse," he complimented, slapping it a little harder.

Octavia tried to wriggle away from his hand smoothing her cheeks, but the ropes were too tight to allow even the barest of movements. Dimly, she became aware of another figure entering the room. A flickering shadow passed behind her, a peculiar shape, unmistakably feminine with large, heaving breasts, magnificent hips and thighs, and a huge cock rearing from its groin; Leda.

"Beat her until I tell you to stop," Quintus said calmly. "Then ride her arse."

Leda picked up the whip and cracked it, her monstrous erection already hard at the prospect of flogging such a beautiful body, and what she could do with it afterwards.

She placed her hand on Octavia's bottom and smoothed the cheeks. At the very touch of the white, unblemished skin her cock throbbed. She put her finger tips into the crease and pulled the buttocks apart revealing a tight brown hole.

"I think someone else has been here already," she said astonished.

"I wouldn't be surprised," Quintus said drily. "My wife, it seems, likes her cock."

Leda wormed her forefinger into Octavia's anus. "It's still wet from its last cock fight, but her buttocks are firm, perhaps they need softening before I ride her."

"Get this creature away from me!" Octavia shrieked, clenching her arse cheeks.

"You were willing enough to have her fuck the slaves for your pleasure. Let's see how you like that thing up your arse," he rasped. "Beat the treacherous bitch!"

Leda swung her arm in a wide arc, lashing the whip across the crown of Octavia's bottom. She gave another swift blow to the left cheek and another on the right, making a perfect X of livid red stripes. Her victim howled like a wolf and writhed her hips against the pillar. Tears were already coursing down her cheeks. It wasn't so much the pain but the humiliation of being flogged by this strange being, half man and half woman that had her twisting and turning.

Quintus had no sympathy, but urged Leda to finish her work; he had more important matters to deal with.

Leda concentrated on Octavia's thighs, lashing each one in turn, sending the whip into the crease of thigh and buttock, cutting the ample under hang of each cheek. She whipped the sides of the cheeks until they wobbled and went slack. Olivia gritted her teeth and waited for what was to come. It was true, she liked rough sex, but that was with the man of her choosing and on her own terms, but not roped to a pillar and fucked by this thing.

Leda patted her bottom lovingly. "I think these moons

218

are soft enough," she observed, dropping the whip.

Her hand encircled her cock, slowly stroking its whole length until it throbbed almost to bursting. Even Quintus gaped at its size. He was in serious doubt as to whether his cheating wife could take a weapon like that, but all the same it would be fun watching. Leda placed the head carefully between the flogged cheeks still twitching from the searing pain. A gentle nudge opened the bottom hole and the head slipped in to the groove.

"Brace yourself," Leda chortled. "Because I'm going to take you with one push of my hips."

"Quintus, make her stop!" Octavia shrieked, looking over her shoulder.

He leaned against a pillar and shrugged as if to say, nothing I can do to make her stop.

Leda gathered her strength and gripped Octavia's hips, took a deep breath and gave her bottom a colossal heave. Her cock rammed in to the hilt and Octavia thought a stallion had penetrated her. Her whole body froze still, and then broke into multiple spasms as Leda began to ride her. Quintus watched fascinated as Leda's hips and buttocks snaked from side to side, rising and falling, going into a spectacular sexual dance. If she had been a whole woman he would have been sorely tempted to ride her himself with an arse that could move like that.

He stood beside Leda and watched closely as her cock went in and out, driving hard into the anal walls, then suddenly spearing the quaking cheeks. Octavia tried to clench her cheeks, anything to stop the rock hard weapon from grinding into her bottom, but Leda sent a clenched fist thumping into the base of her spine.

"Don't think you can get away with doing that," she taunted, and gave another punch into her ribs.

She took her cock right to the very tip, playing it around

the aching bottom hole, then just when Octavia thought the revolting creature had finished, it was rammed back in again so hard she heaved with pain. Leda was getting the measure of the woman she was riding and started slapping her thighs and flanks, and a slap from Leda was no light thing. The flat of her hand left its mark with every slap, and the more she slapped the more she enjoyed the sound of flesh on flesh.

"You like rough sex," she laughed, "then have this!"

Octavia's body jolted under a blow that went winging into her thigh. It wasn't an open handed slap but a clenched fist that pounded into her ribs and hips, and at the same time the cock rode her with greater ferocity, twisting and driving hard into her throbbing and punished bottom. Quintus, sensing that Leda would soon climax, seized the whip and gave his lying wife a fast dozen lashes on the side of her buttocks and Leda, aroused at the sight of the whip delivering fresh red welts, erupted into Octavia's bottom. Her hips shuddered as she pumped her juice into the bottom tunnel, then drew back and breathed a sigh of exhaustion. A slave cut the ropes and Octavia slumped to her knees.

"Use her hair to wipe your cock," he said, and placed a small bag of coins into her hand.

"Thank you, master," Leda beamed, and rubbed her juice-running cock through Octavia's hair.

Quintus couldn't resist the urge to give his wife a final slap before leaving.

"I just thought I should tell you," he said, slapping her face, "the ludus has been taken by the creditors and there isn't a single sestertius left." He summoned two burly male slaves who rushed forward and grabbed Octavia's wrists. "I could have you executed for the attempted murder of your husband, but on this occasion I have shown more mercy than you deserve. You have been sold to a lupanar, the House of Scorpions, you know the one."

Octavia nodded in terror. It was a brothel which catered for the worst sexual perversions imaginable. Only the most desperate whores ventured inside its doors.

"You can work off the price of your bondage," he continued gleefully. "At my reckoning, if you service twenty men a day, you should have cleared the debt in about six or seven years."

And tossing the male slaves a coin, he left without looking back.

"Take off your jewelry," one of the slaves grunted, looking at her disgust.

Even amongst slaves there was a code of honour, particularly to a master who treated them well.

Muttering dark revenge, she handed them her rings and necklace. The slave put them in his tunic as a gift from his master. Leaving her naked, they bundled her into a cart and drove off to the House of Scorpions.

The brothel mistress was there to greet them and ordered her inside.

Men of all shapes and sizes leered at her nakedness, some even dribbling into their wild, unkempt beards at the sight of her swaying breasts.

"Shave the bitch," the brothel mistress said flatly.

The slaves had Octavia on her back in a second, upending her and throwing her onto a table. The men gathered around her in a circle, staring wild eyed into her open sex. A young brothel slave brought a razor and jug of water.

"Now keep still," Quintus' loyal slave warned, "or I might do you a mischief."

He tested the razor blade and satisfied it would do its work, angled it at the top of her pubic triangle and scraped it hard over her skin.

"You're hurting me!" she wailed.

"Not as much as if you don't shut your fat gob," he smirked, and sent the blade slicing through her curls.

He cut carefully around her sex lips, then to the outer fringes of her bush, going expertly into the join of her thighs until her sex mound was clean and smooth.

"On your belly and spread your legs," he ordered, rolling her over.

Two willing helpers gripped her ankles and dragged them to the table's edge. Her head hung over the end and she stared at the grimy floor. But not for long. A hand went under her chin and lifted it, drawing it level with a naked and throbbing cock. The head passed over her lips and she thought she was going to be sick.

"Open your mouth," the owner of the cock laughed and, using his fingers, forced open her jaws.

She heaved and felt his cock rammed into her throat. Only a few hours ago she was on the verge of wealth and power, now she was being abused by the worst men in creation. The slave wielding the razor passed the blade under her bottom and flicked at the curls close to her arse crease. The ones he couldn't safely cut were torn free with a pair of small tongs happily supplied by the brothel mistress.

Octavia kept rigid on the table, froze in terror while the cock rode her throat, not daring to move lest the razor slip and slice her buttocks. She swallowed and spat as he came into her mouth, filling it with spunk that tasted bitter and salty.

Before another could take his place, she was hauled upright and dragged to a chair, her chin dripping with his disgusting juices.

"Oh, no! Not my hair!" she shrieked, looking at the slave bringing over a huge pair of scissors, the sort used to trim the manes of horses.

"All my whores have their 'eads shaved," the brothel mistress informed. "That way, if they tries to escape, they're easier to find."

The slave wasted no time in shearing his former mistress. She'd once had him flogged for fucking one of her girl slaves, now he was going to enjoy humiliating her. He went to work with the fury of a madman, hacking and cutting at the roots, tossing her long tresses over his shoulder, not stopping until only a prickly down covered her scalp.

"Now the razor," he said joyfully.

Octavia watched through tear filled eyes as his wrist turned the razor over her head, shaving her bald. When he'd finished, he ran the palm of his hand over her head and nodded satisfactorily.

"Anything else, madam?" he mocked, bowing low and laughing.

"You haven't shaved her arm pits," the brothel mistress told him sternly.

It was a rule of the house that new and untried slave whores had to be completely shaved. The men gathered around Octavia seized her wrists and held them high above her head. While a pair of hands mauled her breasts, the slave shaved under her arms, cutting in broad sweeps at the fine hair. Then he closely inspected her legs and thighs, but they had been waxed clean. But he did spot a couple of hairs that had escaped the razor just visible between her labia and her thighs and would have shaved them, but changed his mind and bent his head, taking the hairs in his teeth and ripping them free.

"Aaaagh!" she screamed. "That hurt, you clumsy bastard."

But it didn't hurt as much as the slap that nearly knocked

her head off her shoulders.

"You may beat her," the brothel mistress offered, sensing his desire for revenge on a former mistress. "Use this."

Octavia winced at the long, thick leather whip she handed him. "I didn't mean it," she cried.

Her apology had no effect and, at his gesture, the men threw her bottom up over the table.

"No more than twenty," the brothel mistress advised. "She's going to be busy tonight, bouncing on that fine pair of cushions."

"She's going to be busy after you've whipped her," one of the men grinned, already removing his tunic.

With vengeful precision, the slave lashed the whip across her naked bottom, striking both buttocks and instantly leaving a thin red welt. Octavia's hips jolted upwards from the burning pain and a second later another lash whistled into her flanks. Helpless against the continuing onslaught, Octavia writhed and squirmed her bottom and hips, unaware of the splendid sight she was offering her leering audience. One by one their tunics came off and they moved closer, smelling the rising sexual aroma drifting from her parted legs.

"She's all the better for a good whipping," she heard one of them remark, and howled as the whip licked into her now naked sex.

"See her cunt winking," a voice commented.

Octavia blushed red with humiliation and shame. No one had dared treat her like this, shaving her private parts in public, then flogging her bottom in front of a bunch of ne'er do wells. The slave changed direction, lashing the whip savagely along the length of her spine, and again at the tops of her thighs. She kicked out with her feet, but hands gripped her calves and held them rigid. Another pair slapped onto her thighs and pulled them roughly apart, exposing her sex even further. Tears ran down her cheeks as the slave completed the punishment, driving the tail of the whip against her sex lips and around the curve of her hips and buttocks.

Exhausted from her whipping, Octavia allowed the men to drag her off the table.

"Only the collar to fit and she's ready," the brothel mistress announced, tossing the slave a thick iron collar.

"I'm not a dog!" Octavia shrieked, as he passed it around her neck.

"You're lower than a dog," he said, happily clasping it behind her.

"Just another precaution," the brothel mistress told her. "Now everyone will know where you belong."

On the side of the collar was the name of the brothel and the number of the whore wearing it.

"Take her to her room," the mistress said. "I have no further use for her here."

Octavia was taken up a flight of steps and into a small windowless room furnished with a single bed and a pot.

The men followed her, their erections leaving her in no doubt as to what was going to happen next.

"Please, I need the pot," she pleaded.

"No one's stopping you," one of them said, kicking the pot under her legs.

"I can't do it with all of you watching me."

"In that case, you can fuck with a belly full of piss."

And they threw her on the bed, legs open and stomach churning.

There was nothing she could do but grit her teeth and endure the repeated penetrations that were coming her way. They rode her one after the other, taking her in various positions that suited their individual tastes. Some had her lying on her back, others took her from behind, she sat astride them whilst others took it in turns to ride her mouth. Only one wanted to fuck her bottom. Exhausted and covered in grime and sweat, she lay on her bed sobbing. The mistress came in carrying a long length of chain and a brothel bully hauled Octavia upright.

"Your husband warned us that you just might take it into your pretty head to escape, so until you get used to your new profession, I'm taking no chances," the mistress informed her, slipping the chain through a ring at the back of the collar.

She passed the other end of the chain through a ring in the wall and padlocked it. The bully fitted an iron manacle to each of her wrists and chained them behind her back. Then he carefully seated her over the pot.

"Now you can piss all you like," he smirked.

"But don't be too long," the mistress warned darkly. "A new whore is always good for business and I've been advertising you all over the city."

They stood watching intently as Octavia's water drummed into the pot, and then lifted her off, not even freeing her hands so she could wipe herself.

"I'll release you when your customers start arriving," the mistress announced, as her assistant seated her on the edge of the bed.

As soon as they were gone Octavia got up and kicked the pot across the room, spilling its contents over the boards. It would take a lot more than chains and a collar to keep her prisoner. Sooner or later, hopefully sooner, they would dispense with the chains and she would find a way out. She paced the room, wondering where Quintus might have fled. It was only a matter of time before the emperor issued a death warrant and come what may, even if she had to fuck half of Rome, she would witness his execution in the arena. She hoped his death would be a slow one, and then turned as the mistress came into the room and freed her wrists.

"Your first customer," she said, and left, closing the door behind her.

At the rendezvous, Circo took the immediate precaution of binding Nydia's wrists and ankles. Then, as a further precaution, gagged her mouth with his belt and shoved her sobbing into a corner.

She watched through tear streaming eyes as he and the black gladiatrix fucked each other right in front of her. Some people, Nydia thought had no sense of decency, but she had to admire the gladiatrix' long and splendid legs thrashing wildly over his muscle rippling back while he pumped his frenzied hips. They lay exhausted and sweat soaked when Quintus arrived.

"Master!" Africanus exclaimed, untangling her legs and arms from Circo's massive torso.

She stood up and bowed. Circo came forward and embraced him.

"I knew all about the rigged contest," he said, glancing quickly at Nydia, wondering why she was bound and gagged. "I also knew all about the Lady Octavia's plans to have me disposed, which is why I released the ludus into the hands of the creditors and had you both brought here. Nydia was the only one who could deliver the message without attracting suspicion. Now we must flee before the emperor sends the Praetorian Guard to kill us all."

Circo immediately released Nydia and she went straightway to her master, falling at his feet and throwing her arms around him.

"Get up child," he said tenderly. "You have done well in saving both gladiators from death and suffering. From now on you shall be my new wife and will do my bidding."

"But where shall we go?" Africanus asked.

"To the port of Orculanium. There we can get a ship to take us to Egypt or Britannia. But first there is something I must do."

He led Nydia into a room and closed the door.

"You are a grown woman now, and have proved your worth. Now you must learn to fuck like a grown woman. We have a little time before we set off."

Nydia unwrapped the towel and tossed it aside and stood naked before her master.

At his bidding she got onto her hands and knees, thrusting out her pert bottom.

"You must learn to take a flogging from both your husband and master," he said, determined that this one wouldn't be the trouble the last one had been. "To endure the lash without crying out and, more importantly, learn to embrace the sexual arousal it brings."

"Yes, master," she whispered, hearing his tunic fall to the floor.

For a moment, his hands lovingly caressed her bottom. To his experienced eyes it resembled a pale peach at sunrise, glorious in its beauty and softness. He reached beneath her and fondled her hanging breasts, teasing the enormous, succulent nipples as they hardened quickly to the touch. He put his hand between her thighs and gently rubbed her sex, feeling the soft, satin texture of her pubic hair. He was glad that she hadn't been sex shaved.

His hands left off fondling her and reached for his belt. Nydia knew not to cry out, but to endure the lashing he was going to deliver. She must get used to being beaten and fucked by her master, and must learn to love it.

The belt whistled into her buttocks and she gritted her teeth, emitting only a subdued grunt. But as the belt continued to welt her thighs and buttocks a new-found feeling of lust and longing surged through her slim loins. Every stroke brought an increasing desire to be fucked hard. Quintus lashed her thrusting bottom with increased strength, pausing only to hear her lustful gasps and groans. Louder and louder she grunted at the exquisite pain tingling through her soaking sex. She raised her bottom higher, willing him to beat harder. But Quintus slowed his pace and flicked the belt over her slender hips, teasing her now, testing her endurance not to climax so quickly. It was a test of her womanhood to see how long she could resist the lash before begging for his cock.

When he considered she'd had enough of the belt, he ran his fingertips along the welts, pressing hardest where the welts were broader and more livid. He heard her gasp at the increased pain, but so far not a cry had escaped her lips. Her sex was dripping with desire, her nipples itching for his lips. Now she wanted her lord and master more than ever. But still she kept silent, biting her lip and grinding her teeth. Never before had she experienced such acute sexual longing or the need for a hard cock to ride her pulsating sex.

Quintus knew she had suffered and was ready. His erection slipped easily into her soaking tunnel. There was no need to force it in to her with the brutality of a satyr. He rode with long, thrusting strokes delighting in the gasps and lustful pants of satisfaction coming from her parted lips. She looked over her shoulder, her face ablaze with blissful adoration as her master pumped her relentlessly.

While he rode her, the gladiators kept watch on the road, ready to act if anyone approached, but the countryside was empty.

"I could never have killed you, Circo," Africanus said sadly, her hand resting on his cock.

"Nor I you," he replied, giving her large breasts a fond

229

squeeze. "But you have come a long way, my beautiful black gladiatrix. In time you shall be the best."

"Under your tuition," she replied, fondling his balls. "Have we time to fuck again?"

Without waiting for a reply, she threw her arms around his broad shoulders and lifted her weight. His hands were swiftly under her buttocks, raising them level with his hardened cock. Africanus opened her legs and locked them around his back and was penetrated with one eager thrust. He carried her to the door and leaned her back against the jamb.

"I thought you'd fallen in love with Fortuna," he said, bending his powerful thighs and driving his manhood deep into her trembling slit.

"I thought so too," she whispered, clinging like a limpet and bucking her hips, feeling him riding her hard.

"No man could match her dildo. It's legendary amongst the gladiators, so I thought you'd never want another man inside you."

"It's not the same. A dildo never wilts, but a man's cock is real flesh and blood, and it comes."

"Nothing like pumping you full of hot, gladiatorial spunk," he laughed, and bounced her buttocks as fast as his strength allowed.

Her breasts flattened against his chest and he felt the warmth of her against him. Her arse was firm and solid and so smooth to the touch, and he fondled her buttocks marveling at the silky texture.

"You've gone harder," she gasped, her face lighting up.

"And you've gone wetter," he replied, hearing her cunt sucking and squelching.

He kissed her voluptuous lips; kissed her heavy eyelids; and fondled her gorgeous bottom, could feel her enormous erect nipples on his chest. He fucked her hard, crashing her bottom and back against the door frame until the whole flimsy building shook and rattled. Africanus jiggled her calves around his hips and flexed her muscular thighs. Her eyes misted from the sheer joy of having his cock trapped in her belly. As she rose to her climax, she hoped Fortuna would understand and forgive her hasty departure. But perhaps she knew all along that she would flee rather than kill her lost lover in an unfair contest. Circo gave a final quake of his loins and shot his whole load, flooding her sex and keeping her clinging to his body until his cock went limp.

She fell from him and leaned against the door as Quintus and Nydia emerged from the room.

Nydia tied up her hair and Africanus could tell from the satiated look on her face that she had been well fucked. In a way, she owed the girl her life and the future she would share with Circo. It had taken no small amount of courage delivering the note and messages. If she had been caught she would have been crucified or ripped to shreds by the beasts. She moved forward and kissed the girl full on the lips.

"She is no longer a slave," Quintus announced. "I have granted her her freedom. Now we must go. The sun is setting and we must be in Orculanium before dawn."

They set off, Circo leading the way with Nydia following dutifully behind. Africanus and Quintus brought up the rear, keeping a keen eye on the surrounding hills. Soon, the Gods willing, they would all be at sea, on their way to a distant and foreign land.

They walked all night, stopping only briefly to fill their stomachs and quench their thirsts. The wharves of Orculanium were busy even at that early hour of the morning. Cargo ships were unloading their holds, lead and tin mostly imported from Britannia, along with animal skins

231

and iron ore. Quintus made for one of the ships at the embarkation dock and waited at the foot of the gang plank whilst a horde of young women were taken aboard. They were heavily chained; each fitted with a collar and chained to the woman in front and behind. He watched them herded below in frightened groups and then boarded the vessel.

The ship was destined for Britannia, taking girl slaves to the newly Romanised Britons who wanted females trained in the more refined household arts, rather than the unruly Celts. They would also be useful plying the oars on the voyage. The vessel was fitted with cabins and could carry passengers in reasonable comfort. Quintus motioned his followers aboard and told them to keep out of sight until the ship was at sea. Even now, with Rome far behind, he was still uneasy. Octavia was capable of anything and he was beginning to regret not having her killed. He had an uncanny feeling that he hadn't quite seen the last of her, but dismissed the thought from his mind and went into his cabin.

Circo lay on the bed, arms folded behind his head and staring idly at the roof. Africanus sat stride him letting his cock rest erect against her belly.

"Where are we going?" she asked, sweeping her braids over her shoulder.

A shaft of sunlight came through the cabin window and lighted on her breasts. How magnificent they looked, so large and perfectly shaped, full and firm, the nipples hard and excited now that they were all embarking on new adventures.

Circo reached out and gave each shining globe a gentle squeeze. "I think we're heading for Britannia, my homeland. If Quintus intends to set up in business there, we shall do well my black Goddess. The arena at Londoninium is well favoured and girl gladiators are highly

232

prized."

Her bottom lifted from his thighs and she reached underneath, guiding his cock into her sex. Circo gave a sigh of satisfaction as she lowered her buttocks and began rocking steadily to and fro. There was no need to hurry now. They could take their time and enjoy each other without fear.

"I wish we were going to my homeland," she said softly, wriggling her hips and embedding his cock hard into her belly.

Circo pinched her nipples and she winced at the sharp pain shooting through her breasts.

"Just be thankful we've escaped," he said seriously. "The emperor is probably searching for us right now, and you know what would happen if he caught us."

She nodded and bent forward, swinging her breasts over his hairy chest, letting the erect nipples tease his skin. He gripped her hips and started bouncing her over his middle. Africanus flexed her vaginal muscles, closing the walls around his cock and holding the throbbing shaft tight. He lay still while her cunt petals moved softly around him, caressing his entire length. She was the only woman he had ever fucked who could bring him off using her sex lips while he lay still. He closed his eyes and felt nothing except her lips and sex enveloping his shaft, slowly milking his juice from the tip. It oozed from her sex and ran hot over his thighs. Then she reached her climax, opening her mouth and breathing fast. He liked to watch her face when she came; the eyelids growing heavier, her parted voluptuous lips panting faster, her shoulders and breasts trembling and shaking as she poured out her flowing essence. Her pelvis shuddered and she slumped over his body raking his back with her fingernails.

Then the bed pitched gently from side to side. The ship's

timbers groaned and the sound of running feet bounded across the deck above them. From somewhere below a whip cracked and the oars dipped gracefully into the sea.

Africanus looked out of the window and saw the wharves pass by. Then the vessel turned sharply to port and the whole of the ocean came into view.

Circo ran his hands over her silky buttocks and gave them a playful slap.

"It's been a long while since I whipped these splendid moons," he grinned.

Africanus smiled a broad sexy smile and reached for his belt. She let it dangle from her hand, the buckle resting on his chest.

"No time like the present," she purred, and bared her bottom, the look on her face one of pure ecstasy.

The belt whistled into her buttocks and she jolted forward, her face level with the window. She looked at the endless horizon and smiled again at the pain and pleasure tingling her sex.

"Harder," she whispered. "Much, much harder."

ARICANUS 2. RITUAL OF PAIN.

The second volume of Africanus' adventures is released later this year. Here's a sample of what's in store.

A hard slap landed on her rump and she was spun roughly round, her back pressing on the tree. Without warning the older man bent his bearded face to her breasts and sucked on the erect nipples, drawing each teat into his mouth, sucking as if she were a wet nurse suckling a thirsty babe. She bucked when his teeth bit on the nipple, her hands flying to his head to pull it away. But his son moved fast and unsheathed his sword, aiming the point at her throat. Even though she was a woman and naked, they were taking no chances. Secretly she admired the speed at which he moved and his accuracy in delivery. Gradually she was forming the opinion that they were not so stupid after all. It took a good deal of skilful training to handle a sword like that.

The older man lifted his head and slapped her breast, bringing his hand down in a fast swoop, landing the flat of his hand directly on the bouncing globe. The nipple rose with pain, but inwardly she felt a sensation of pleasure, a cold stirring in her belly and hoped they wouldn't notice it. It wouldn't do, letting them know that pain, particularly sexual pain, brought on an overwhelming desire to have a stiff cock pounding inside her soaking cunt. But they didn't seem to notice the fleeting look of desire in her moistened eyes. The older man hit her again, slapping each breast in turn while his son went wide eyed at the way her breasts swung and wobbled to and fro, each enormous mound colliding with the other, and the nipples! Now they were as hard and stiff as young acorns and he couldn't resist taking them in his fingers and rolling each teat so hard her eyes watered. But still she did not cry out. All those many months of hard, arduous training as a gladiatrix had instilled marvellous self discipline and it would take a lot more than a couple of groping savages to make her scream.

The son started slapping her thighs, delighting in beating the hard, solid fleshy pillars that quivered with every blow.

"The girl shows strength," his father acknowledged, standing back to get a better look at her tight lipped face.

"Let's see how strong she rides," his son leered, taking a fistful of hair and twisting her head.

Mother Superior

By Marie Clair

'Only the sheer little briefs did she remove, retaining her garter-top stockings and high-heels as she eased herself into the chair. 'On your knees!' she ordered, pointing down to the space before her.

Blake hesitated but her expression told him that to disobey would not bode well. Her intention was perfect-ly obvious as he lowered himself to the carpet, for she parted her legs in anticipation of his approach. At the same time, Blake felt his own passions rekindled and saw no reason why he should not do for her what he had done for so many women and for Mother Superior herself.'

When Blake begins work on the mysterious 'Manrose' file in the course of his duties as a lawyer, he little suspects into what dark regions it will lead him.

From the club 'Le Chateau' the trail takes him into wild and dark landscapes of submission that few men dare dream of.......

Mother Superior marks the debut of another new star in the Silver Moon firmament.

Property of a Gentleman

By Toby Abbott.

When a 'talent scout' turns up backstage at a small suburban theatre and offers actress Mary Bowdler a most unusual engagement, she has no idea at all what she is letting herself in for.

She is engaged for a cruise aboard the good ship 'Bonaventure' but what befalls her there is truly life-changing! The ship is well equipped with slaves for the passengers – who are all masters - to play with, and the performances she finds herself giving are more demanding than anything she has ever experienced. As Mary struggles to come to terms with her reaction to all that is done to her, plans are afoot to raid the ship for its valuable cargo. Mary and her sister slaves are fought over by the two groups of dominants and the penalties for those who dare oppose the masters are erotically inventive – in the extreme!

THE WHIPMASTER.

By Francine Whittaker

'He had never held a real cat-o-nine-tails before or any other kind of whip and, as he approached the girl and positioned himself for action, he weighed it as if assessing its force. The handle, around thirteen inches in length, with a loop at the end, was covered in animal hide, though he was not inclined to guess from which animal.'

Tyler Morrison sets out to become a true master of the whip and aided by a fortuitous accident of birth he is able to devote himself to his art.

This spells big trouble for Chelsi; a girl who spurned him in his youth. He is determined that she will pay for his humiliation and he has all the means to accomplish his aim.

This is one of the most erotic books we have been privileged to publish for a long time; Francine is on top form.

There are over 100 stunningly erotic novels of domination and submission in the Silver Moon catalogue. You can see the full range, including Club and Illustrated editions by writing to:

Silver Moon Reader Services
Shadowline Publishing Ltd,
No 2 Granary House
Ropery Road,
Gainsborough,
Lincs. DH21 2NS

You will receive a copy of the latest issue of the Readers' Club magazine, with articles, features, reviews, adverts and news plus a full list of our publications and an order form.